Praise for Mich‹

Sylver and Gold

"I loved Larkin's first two books, *Mercy* and *Unexpected Partners*. *Mercy* was a paranormal thriller and *Unexpected Partners* was more of a police procedural thriller with two women on the run from a psychopath. *Sylver and Gold* is a police procedural with a paranormal twist, and it's a lot of fun trying to solve the crime along with the detectives and Sylver's trusty sidekick Mugshot the dog. My overall take from this book? Fun, romantic, crime without too much violence for squeamish romance readers, paranormal lite for those of us who get annoyed with the woowoo. A pleasure to read."—*Late Night Lesbian Reads*

"*Sylver and Gold* is a paranormal crime/mystery that kept me on the edge throughout the entire reading. It is intense with great leading characters…If you're looking for a riveting suspense, this is your choice."—*Hsinju's Lit Log*

Secret Agent

"I loved everything about this book. Michelle Larkin has a knack for writing romantic intrigue novels. She adds humanity to her characters by giving them enough wit, charm and deep-seated goodness that you can't help but fall in love with them and cheer on their successes."—*LezReview Books*

Endangered

"What a unique and interesting story. Good for fans of urban fantasy and shapeshifters. This was fun, and funny, with a great cast of characters. Plenty of action and great chemistry between the main characters. Loved the world building and can't wait to read more."—*Kat Adams, Bookseller (QBD Books, Australia)*

"When X-Men meets Twilight, the outcome is this wholly enjoyable paranormal fantasy. Grab this book, suspend disbelief and cosy in for feel-good impossibilities."—*reviewer@large*

"This was a very impressive novel. It was a skillfully crafted story, and one does not have to look too far to see parallels in today's America."—*Kitty Kat's Book Review Blog*

"*Endangered* by Michelle Larkin is a delightful novel with some heavy moments but enough lightheartedness to keep you thoroughly entertained."—*Romantic Reader Blog*

"What I liked most about this novel was its tone, mostly linked to Aspen's sense of humor and the banter between the characters in times of danger…[T]he rhythm, the humor, the interesting and endearing characters were enough to keep me hooked…"
—*Jude in the Stars*

Unexpected Partners

"There is a lot of action in this story that will keep you interested and sometimes on the edge of your seat as you read…I liked the main characters and could see the chemistry between the two, and enjoyed the way the romance was treated throughout the story. The secondary characters were also well-developed and made the tale better."—*Rainbow Reflections*

"I loved the fast pace and nonstop action in this crime thriller/ romantic intrigue novel…*Unexpected Partners* finds a nice balance between action and the reality of two strong women facing down their enemy."—*Late Night Lesbian Reads*

Mercy

"The author did a great job creating the characters. The leads have chemistry and share some entertaining dialog. There are no boring or aggravating characters, and they all work well together to advance and enrich the story line. There is even a handsome chocolate Labrador that becomes integral to the tale! Mercy was released last year and was Ms Larkin's debut novel. I can't wait to read more of her work. Overall, an interesting concept that will appeal to readers who enjoy action, law enforcement and the metaphysical. 4.5 stars."—*LezReview Books*

By the Author

Romantic Intrigue

Mercy

Unexpected Partners

Endangered

Secret Agent

Sylver and Gold series

Sylver and Gold

The Value of Sylver and Gold

Visit us at www.boldstrokesbooks.com

THE VALUE OF
SYLVER AND GOLD

by
Michelle Larkin

2023

ISBN 13: 978-1-63679-093-0

This Trade Paperback Original Is Published By
Bold Strokes Books, Inc.
P.O. Box 249
Valley Falls, NY 12185

First Edition: April 2023

CREDITS
Editor: Ruth Sternglantz
Production Design: Stacia Seaman
Cover Design by Tammy Seidick

Acknowledgments

Endless thanks to my editor, Ruth Sternglantz, for her ability to see the big picture AND all the important little details.

Thunderous applause to Cindy Cresap for everything she did behind the scenes to help this book cross the finish line in one piece.

A warm hug to Tammy Seidick for designing another amazing book cover.

Heartfelt gratitude to my BFF, Deb Roberts-Arthur, for reading this story before it all came together…and still loving me anyway.

Jazz hands to Della for being the fastest reader I know and my wonderfully funny friend.

A sincere thank you to Mandi for accepting the fact that my brain functions at just seventy-five percent (okay, fine…maybe fifty) whenever I'm in the throes of writing a book.

I'm also deeply appreciative of Levi, Jett, and Declan for making my heart swell with love, pride, and admiration.

This book is dedicated to Patches...

It's been a long journey. Your wings are strong and glorious. They provide shade when the sun beats down and warmth when the temperature drops. You never fly ahead. You've walked beside me every step of the way. I look forward to the day when we can fly together and hear the joyous music that beckons me at night, when all is still and quiet.

CHAPTER ONE

Detective London Gold sat in the chair across from Reid Sylver's desk and set an oatmeal muffin beside her beat-up travel mug. Reid had left in a hurry this morning. London was certain she hadn't taken the time to eat.

"Give me a sec," Reid said without looking up from her computer screen. Despite all the typing tutorials London had given her, Reid still used only her index fingers. London forced herself to look away. It was just too painful to watch.

"Piece of shit computer." Reid smacked the keyboard and flipped the bird at the computer screen. "Fucking—"

"*That's* what I came here to talk about." London uncrossed her legs and leaned forward in her chair seductively, finally managing to capture Reid's bright green gaze.

Reid slid her cheaters atop her head. Her gaze instantly dropped to London's scoop-neck silk blouse.

London watched as Reid raised one eyebrow and licked her lips. Exactly the reaction she was hoping for.

Her professional attire was almost always ultraconservative because she worked in a precinct full of men. But a sprinkling of cleavage every now and again served to remind her colleagues—the one before her, in particular—that she was, in fact, a woman.

London wasn't on Reid's schedule for a consult today. She'd swapped timeslots with O'Leary. Reid was the only in-house homicide consultant for the Boston Police Department, and she was in high demand. As far as London knew, Reid was the only retired homicide detective in the world who could talk to the dead and solve cases in the time it took to brew a cup of coffee.

The BPD had so far managed to keep Reid's gift under wraps. Every detective with whom she met was required to sign a nondisclosure. Reid would tell them everything they needed to know—who, what, where, when, why, and how—but it was up to each detective to gather the evidence and build a case that would stand up in a court of law.

"You came here to talk about my piece-of-shit computer?" Reid asked, snapping out of the cleavage stare-down and frowning in evident confusion.

"No." London felt her cheeks grow warm. "The other thing."

"Ahh." Reid leaned back in her chair. An amused grin highjacked her face and made her green eyes sparkle. "You came here to talk about fucking."

London didn't curse. At all. Reid, on the other hand, peppered her language with expletives on a regular basis. "I prefer the term *making love*. But considering the circumstances we find ourselves in now..." She trailed off and met Reid's gaze, feeling her cheeks burn hotter.

They were approaching the one-year anniversary of their relationship. Sex with Reid had always been incredible. Their physical chemistry was palpable. They'd never missed a single day of intimacy... until three weeks ago, when everything came to a screeching halt.

London's level of sexual frustration was now at DEFCON 1. It was beginning to affect her focus at work. She wanted—*needed*—Reid to take her. Hard. She couldn't bear the thought of waiting any longer. "Is she here?" She held Reid's gaze, not bothering to look around the room for Reid's dead grandmother.

London had tried desperately, many times over, to see the spirits that Reid saw and communicated with, but she finally had to accept that she'd likely never see them. Or hear them. She obviously didn't possess the same gifts.

"Haven't seen that bitch since last night."

London squeezed her eyes shut. "I wish you wouldn't call her that."

"I've always called her that."

One of the things London loved about Reid was her forthright communication style. None of Reid's social or professional affiliates had to guess where they stood with her. Ever. "But now that she's, well..."

"Dead?"

London nodded.

"Doesn't make her less of a bitch."

"But what if it did?"

"We've been over this. It's like beating a dead horse." Reid crossed her arms. "Except we're beating my dead grandmother, which I don't mind, by the way. After all these years, it feels good to return the favor."

London knew little about the abuse that Reid had endured at the hands of her grandmother. The scars on her body spoke volumes. "What if she's different now? What if she's genuinely sorry and wants to apologize?"

"Then she can do that later, face to face, after I kick the bucket."

Reid had reported that her grandmother was holding the same gift box every time she appeared. It was wrapped in silver paper with gold ribbon. London couldn't help but wonder if the wrapping was symbolic—Sylver and Gold—but she hadn't yet shared her thoughts with Reid. "What about the gift?"

"What about it?" Reid asked defensively.

"Has a spirit ever given you a gift before?"

Reid shrugged. "No."

"Well, aren't you curious?"

"My grandmother never gave me anything, except a good beating."

London bit her lip. "What if she doesn't leave us alone until you let her say her piece?"

"She'll leave. Eventually."

"Okay." She took a breath and met Reid's gaze, undeterred from her decision to practice tough love. "You have one day."

"To do what?" Reid asked absently, pulling her cheaters back down to give her computer screen the stink eye.

"If she's not gone by tomorrow, I'm taking matters into my own hands. And I mean that in the literal sense."

Reid's eyes grew wide. "No way." She slipped the cheaters off and tossed them on the desk. "You wouldn't."

London lifted her cell from her lap, brought up the vibrator she'd been eying on Amazon—it had an average rating of 4.8 stars—and added it to her shopping cart. She held up her phone. "Same-day delivery."

Reid narrowed her eyes. Anger tugged at the corners of her full, pillowy lips. "You're not playing fair."

"It's been three weeks, Reid. *Three.*" She pocketed her phone and stood with a sigh. "Fair is a thing of the past when you're feeling as desperate as I am."

Reid shot up from her chair, stepped around the desk, and reached for her hand with a look of concern. "Why didn't you say something, babe?"

"I'm saying something now."

"But"—Reid slid her fingers between London's and squeezed her hand affectionately—"can't you give me some notice?"

"I just did."

"A day? Shit, London."

"That's the best I can do." London wasn't sure she'd last twelve hours, let alone twenty-four. She squinted and gave Reid a once-over. "How are you so composed?"

"The bitchy grandmother who instantly materializes as I'm about to get it on with my girlfriend can have that effect. It's like throwing a bucket of ice water over my head. Every night. For twenty-one nights in a row." Reid shrugged. "I'm traumatized," she admitted in all seriousness.

London hadn't thought about the situation from Reid's perspective. She'd been too busy throwing herself a pity party to notice how antsy and on-edge Reid had grown over the last three weeks. "I'm sorry." She stepped closer and kissed Reid gently. "I guess this is hard for both of us."

Reid's eyebrows shot up. "Does this mean you'll reconsider the deadline?"

"Nope. One day...or that vibrator's my new BFF."

"Can I at least watch?"

London took a step back. "Seriously?"

"I'm kidding. It was a joke. A bad one." Reid sidled closer, slipped her hands behind London's back, and pulled her in for a slow kiss.

Long seconds ticked by as their tongues danced in a familiar rhythm. "I miss you," London whispered, breathless.

"I miss you more," Reid said, her gaze unwavering. She brought her hand to London's cheek and caressed it with her thumb. "We'll figure this out. I promise."

❖

Reid sat forward and addressed the spirit in the chair beside Detective Garcia. "Your boyfriend?"

My roommate's boyfriend. We were having an affair behind

Brittany's back. I wanted him to break it off with her and be with me. He refused, so I threatened to tell her about us. That just pissed him off.

Reid decided to pose a trick question. She was well aware that she wasn't technically a cop anymore, but she'd always be suspicious of everyone, until they proved otherwise—including spirits who, as far as she could tell, were incapable of telling a lie. "And that's when he stabbed you?"

The spirit regarded her quizzically before shaking her head. *No, he strangled me...with the cord from his laptop.*

Bingo. That was the murder weapon they'd been unable to locate. The boyfriend had made it look like a B and E gone wrong. He'd probably absconded with the murder weapon. Maybe had it tucked away somewhere in his apartment. As if in answer to that thought, the spirit sent her an image of a charging cable folded neatly inside a drawer full of men's underwear.

"Thank you," Reid said sincerely. "You've been very helpful."

Can you tell Brittany how sorry I am for being such a terrible friend?

Reid had never met a spirit who didn't have regrets—some more so than others. She shook her head, adamant. "I don't work like that."

Will you find him so he doesn't hurt anyone else?

Reid answered with confidence. "We will."

The spirit nodded solemnly, stood from the chair beside Garcia, and vanished.

"She gone?" Garcia asked as he let out a thunderous belch.

"Gone," Reid confirmed. She and Garcia and the rest of their unit had tied one on last night in remembrance of their former captain. Hard to believe Cap had been dead a year. Reid got to see him and talk to him because he visited her regularly, but she still missed him. She knew she always would.

"So, it was the boyfriend...with the candlestick...in the study," Garcia guessed, poking fun at her as usual.

"Roommate's boyfriend...with the laptop charging cable...in the kitchen. You'll find the murder weapon in his apartment—middle drawer, under the tighty-whities."

"Always the underwear drawer." Garcia shook his head, clearly disappointed in the killer's lack of ingenuity. "Was he sleeping with our vic?"

"You're getting good at this, Garcia."

He stood and let out another belch. "That's why they pay me the big bucks."

There was a knock at the door. Boyle poked his head inside. "Sylver, you got a sec?"

Boyle's tone tipped her off that something was up. "Who for?"

"Someone important." Boyle exchanged a knowing look with Garcia.

"I saw that," she said, standing. She set her hands on her hips as Garcia ducked out. "What's up?" She made a point of checking the clock on the wall. "I have back-to-back consults today."

"Someone important requested a meeting with you."

"There's no time for important people, Boyle. You booked me with all the unimportant ones."

"Hey!" Garcia shouted from the other side of the door. "I heard that."

"Good!" she shouted back.

"She's an acquaintance of mine. All legs, nice rack. Hot," Boyle said, trying to entice her.

"So is my girlfriend. Maybe you've heard of her?" She raised an eyebrow. "She's a kickass pitcher with a killer arm." London had singlehandedly taken the Toe Tags—the worst softball team since the league's inception—all the way to the championships. They'd faced off against Reid's team, Packin' Heat, who'd ranked number one since the beginning of time. Hell froze over that day when the Toe Tags emerged victorious.

"No need to share this conversational fumble with said girlfriend." Boyle winced. "She'll aim for my nuts next time I'm up to bat."

"Hope you didn't plan on having more kids."

Boyle shook his head. "I'd still like the option, though. If you don't mind."

"You're asking me to give up my lunch break. What's in it for me?"

"What do you want?"

Reid pretended to consider his question. She'd been waiting for an opportunity like this. "Let me captain the team."

"No fucking way." Boyle crossed his arms. "Cap left the team to me."

"If Packin' Heat has any chance of reclaiming the championship title, you and I both know that I need to be the one to take over and run things."

"You'll run us all into an early grave. You're ruthless, Sylver."

"Exactly. And if you want to win, *I'm* who you need."

He paced the small office, clearly agitated.

"C'mon. You know I'm right, Boyle." She'd already devised a kick-your-ass morning workout regimen that players would have to attend if they wanted to stay on the team.

He stopped pacing, set his hands on his hips, and sighed. "Shit."

"We have a deal?"

He reached forward to shake hands but stopped short. "Did Cap approve this?"

"We don't need his approval. He's dead."

"But he left this team to me."

Reid shrugged. "So?"

"What if he thinks I'm shirking my responsibilities?"

"You are," she admitted.

"You're really good at pep talks, Sylver."

"I take pride in the fact that I've never given one. Not about to start now. Besides, a kumbaya pep talk won't be what gets us our title back."

"Teamwork is about more than just winning."

"Said no good team captain *ever*." She extended her hand. "Seal the deal, and my lunch break is yours for the taking."

"The team will have my balls on a platter when they hear about this." Boyle reached across the desk.

CHAPTER TWO

The hair on the back of London's neck stood on end as she felt herself being scrutinized by the lieutenant's visitor. It was a face that looked vaguely familiar but one she hadn't seen around the precinct before today. She'd caught the woman staring at her more than once, and her behavior was now bordering on rude. London turned in her desk chair to meet her gaze head-on from across the room. She was older, in her early fifties. Attractive, fit, refined. But London was sure they'd never met before.

The woman smiled and motioned for London to join her at the coffee bar.

London grabbed her empty *I Like Soft Balls and I Cannot Lie* mug—a gift from her team captain after they took the championship last year—and strode over, curiosity overriding the inner voice advising her to be cautious. She was quiet as she selected a cinnamon coffee K-Cup and set it inside the Keurig. "*Love* the heels," she said finally. The visitor wore black Italian-leather Salvatore Ferragamo stilettos that made London's credit card ache. Her custom-tailored Anne Fontaine pantsuit now held first place in London's rankings of business attire. The midnight-black tuxedo jacket showcased satin lapels and satin-piped pockets with a single button to draw in the waist, accentuating the woman's natural curves with a level of elegance and professionalism too few women grasped, let alone practiced.

"Thanks. I noticed yours, too." The woman glanced down at her boots. "Tory Burch? She's one of my favorite designers."

London nodded, impressed. She added some French vanilla creamer to her coffee, leaned back against the bar, and took a sip from her mug. "You're watching me. Why?"

"Forgive me. You remind me of someone—someone very dear to me." There was a hint of melancholy in her tone.

London sensed that the woman beside her was a force of nature—strong, intelligent, resilient, in-charge. Instinct told her to tread carefully because she was seeing a softer side that few people got to experience. "Where is she now, if you don't mind me asking?"

The woman shrugged, the tears in her eyes rendering her temporarily unable to speak.

London sipped her coffee and thought for a moment. "I lost my parents for ten years. Their decision to withdraw from my life hurt me deeply. In many ways, it felt like they'd died. It actually might've been easier if they had. I really believed they were gone forever," she said honestly, meeting the woman's solemn gaze. "Then, when I least expected it, fate brought us together again."

"They're back in your life?" the woman asked, her tears already under control.

She nodded. "They are."

"And have you forgiven them?" the woman asked candidly.

"As a matter of fact, I have."

The woman frowned. "Why?"

"Because forgiveness is an act of mercy, and it's completely at our discretion. It's never in anyone's best interest to withhold it." She finished the last of her coffee in silence, allowing her mind to wander as she stared out across the squad room. A memory of the woman's face giving a news brief flashed before her. This was the deputy director of the FBI, Katherine Russo. She was sure of it. "I actually considered applying to the FBI."

"Our loss," Russo said. "We would've been lucky to have you." She reached inside her pocket, withdrew a business card, and handed it to London with a wink. "We pay more, and you'd have access to very interesting cases. Call me if you ever decide to switch career paths."

London pocketed the card. She sensed their chat was coming to a close. "I hope the woman I remind you of…I hope she finds her way back to you," she said sincerely.

"Me, too." Russo tossed her cup in the trash, lifted her briefcase from the floor, and strode purposefully to Boyle's office.

London couldn't help but wonder what was going on. Something big. Maybe Reid would fill her in later.

❖

Reid stepped inside Boyle's office, but it was empty. "Well? Where is she?"

"Getting coffee. She'll be back."

Typical power play. The only detail Boyle had shared was that this woman was important. Important people hated to be kept waiting. Waiting, especially inside someone else's office, was disempowering. The way to turn the tables and reclaim your power in a situation like that was to leave and come back later, *after* whoever you were waiting for returned. Then you could reenter the room and introduce yourself with an air of urgent authority, thereby claiming the space as your own. It was a play with which Reid was familiar. She would've done the same.

Boyle left the door ajar, walked around his desk, and gestured to the chair beside her. "Take a load off, Sylver."

"I'm good."

"Why do you do that?"

"Do what?" she asked, glancing over her shoulder to see if the mystery woman was approaching.

"You never sit in the damn chair."

"I've sat in the chair." She crossed her arms, straining to recall a time when she actually sat in the chair.

"I swear on all my wife's shoes, *your* ass has never touched *that* seat." He pointed to the chair in question.

She thought for a moment. "How many shoes does your wife have?"

"Too many." He crossed his arms. "Ever wonder why I worked so much overtime?"

Reid studied Boyle for a moment. Something was up. There were two chairs, but he'd pointed to the one closest to the door. Instinct told her that he wanted her to sit in that particular chair for a reason. Common sense would dictate that she sit in the chair farthest from the door so the mystery guest could saunter in and comfortably join them. Otherwise, his guest would be forced to walk around the chair that was already occupied by Reid's ass to sit in the empty chair on the other side. Boyle's office was small. He and the rest of the squad had essentially cut it in half to make room for her office on the other side of the wall, so the available walking space for two visitors bordered on uncomfortably tight.

Presumably, he'd expected that Reid would be the one to join the party late, which would've landed her in the chair closest to the door. She sidestepped the chair in question and promptly took a seat in the chair on the other side. "There. Happy?"

Boyle's eyes grew wide.

"Something wrong?" she asked, feigning ignorance.

"I just…well…I thought…" he stammered.

"Your chairs are definitely more comfortable than mine." She leaned back and laced her fingers together behind her head. "Five stars. It was money well spent."

The sound of high heels—stilettos, if Reid had to take a stab—clicked purposefully on the laminate floor outside Boyle's office door. Boyle's face reddened as the mystery visitor marched through the doorway and stopped directly in front of Reid.

"Detective Sylver, I'm Katherine Russo, Deputy Director of the FBI." She extended her hand.

Reid didn't budge. She kept her hands behind her head and met the woman's gaze from the comfort of her incredibly comfortable chair.

Russo kept her hand in midair and frowned. "Are you going to stand?"

"Boyle told me to sit."

Russo gave her a once-over and turned to pierce Boyle with an equally unforgiving gaze. "*This* is who you wanted me to meet?"

Reid decided to switch tactics. This woman was a stander, just like her. Sitting in someone else's office was akin to tucking your tail in a wolf pack—something Reid had never done, save for the chair in her former captain's office. "My bad." She stood and extended her hand in truce. "Put in my papers last year, so it's just plain old *Sylver* now." She could feel the deputy director's edges soften as they shook hands.

Reid sat once again, hoping Russo would follow suit. She glanced at Boyle, silent behind his desk. Sweat beaded on his upper lip.

Russo lowered herself to the chair beside Reid's. One long machine-gun fart, worthy of a burrito-loving Boston cop, echoed through the small office. The old whoopee cushion prank. She should've guessed.

Russo remained seated and slowly turned her head to glare at Reid.

Reid shot an accusatory glance at Boyle, who grinned, obviously seeing a way out of the mess he'd made as it instantly materialized before him. Like it or not, Reid was now wedged firmly under the bus. She met the deputy director's gaze. They stared one another down like two Siamese fighting fish.

Boyle cleared his throat. "Kate's heading up an investigation that

I think you'll find interesting. I suggested she consider utilizing you as a resource."

Reid struggled to keep her poker face intact as she felt the sting of betrayal. How could Boyle have shared her secret with the deputy director of the FBI? What the hell was he thinking? If Cap were here to see this...

Out of the corner of her eye, she caught sight of her former captain as he appeared in spirit form. His voice sounded in her mind. *Give her a chance, Sylver.*

Her knee-jerk reaction was to refuse, shut Cap out, keep doing things her own way. But she thought better of it because she trusted Cap. He would never lead her astray. Against her better judgment, she ended the stare-down and met Cap's gaze.

She'd been seeing and communicating with spirits ever since she could remember. She'd always heard their voices in her mind. A spirit's voice sounded very different from a voice produced by human vocal cords. Spirit voices were like thoughts that drifted lazily with the wind and landed, as soft as a feather, in her mind. Prior to the captain, she'd never been able to reciprocate communication in quite the same way. She'd always had to speak aloud for them to hear her until the captain came along. She'd only had to speak aloud for the first few months of his visits. After that, she was able to convey her thoughts in a seamless mind-to-mind stream of communication. It was very efficient. If only she could communicate like this with all spirits and, while she was at it, everyone else in her life, too. It sure as hell would save her a lot of time. *Why?*

She needs your help finding a serial killer. The FBI hit a dead end. Cap shook his head and sighed. *There are a lot of victims left on his to-do list. You can put a stop to that.*

Nothing about a serial killer on the loose had made the news recently. *Why haven't I heard about this?*

FBI's keeping it under wraps. Killer leaves nothing behind—no trace evidence. They have little to go on. Can't warn the public without telling them what to be on the lookout for.

Then bring me some of his victims. Let me talk to them. I'll find out who he is right now.

Sorry. Cap crossed his arms. *No can do.*

Reid studied her former captain. He was holding something back. *What aren't you telling me?*

None of the victims are available for questioning.

She was momentarily confused. For as long as she'd been doing this, she'd never been told that a spirit was unavailable. What did that even mean? *I don't understand. Are the victims dead or alive?*

Dead, he confirmed. But he offered nothing more.

Is it permanent?

From what I understand, it is. Cap frowned. *Unless you're telling me zombies are really a thing.*

Death is obviously permanent. She rolled her eyes. *What I meant was, will the victims ever be available for questioning?*

He shook his head. *'Fraid not, kid.*

Then what the hell does Russo need me for? If she was being denied access to the victims, indefinitely, then she had nothing to offer the FBI that they couldn't figure out themselves.

Cap averted his gaze. *Can't answer that.*

She intuited that he could answer but was choosing not to. *Does this have anything to do with free will?* she asked, alluding to their chat last year when he'd told her that there were limits to what he could share.

He nodded. *By the way, Boyle told Russo nothing. He left that part up to you, so work your magic, kid.* He winked. *Impress the hell out of her.*

Reid took a breath and met the deputy director's gaze once again. "I'll cut to the chase. I don't know how I can help you catch this guy, assuming he's a guy, which—we all know—most serial killers are."

Russo centered her cold, hard gaze on Boyle. "You weren't supposed to talk about this case with anyone. You gave me your word."

"I didn't." Boyle drew an X on his chest with his index finger. "Cross my heart and hope to die. Stick my finger in a pie."

Russo looked at Reid. "Then how'd you find out about it?"

"You wouldn't believe me if I told you."

"Try me."

"My old captain paid me a visit," she said with a shrug. "He gave me a quick rundown."

"I assume you're referring to Captain Konigsbergdormenoffski?"

Reid nodded, impressed. That was the first time she'd heard anyone use Cap's full surname without tripping over a single syllable. Her respect for Russo went up a notch.

"Your former captain died. One year ago yesterday, if I'm not mistaken."

"Do the words *You wouldn't believe me if I told you* sound familiar?"

Russo crossed her arms and studied Reid. "Prove it," she demanded, shaking her high-heeled foot in annoyance.

Boyle slid open his desk drawer, withdrew a sheet of paper, and set it on the desk with a pen. "Sign here first."

Russo glanced at the document and chuckled, clearly amused. "You're asking me to sign a nondisclosure?"

"If you want permission to consult with my detective about your case, yes."

"Firstly, I'm not signing a damn thing." Russo cast a sideways glance at Reid. "Second, she's not your detective. Not anymore."

"Technically, that's true." Boyle leaned back in his chair and met Russo's gaze with his no-nonsense cop face. "But she's part of my team. As such, I have her back." He slid a silver pen across the desk. "Sign, or this meeting is over, Kate. And trust me…leaving now, before you see for yourself how indispensable she is, will be the biggest mistake you've ever made."

Russo stood. "Did you just threaten me, Adam?"

Reid could see where this was going. She understood Russo all too well. Boyle was trying his damnedest to cast his net of protection around Reid—and her gift—by making sure the powers that be at the FBI never gained access to her secret weapon. She cleared her throat and stood, meeting Russo eye to eye. "The killer leaves no trace evidence. He abducts them and tortures them."

"If you expect me to believe that your lieutenant told you nothing about this case—"

"He didn't," she said, unblinking.

Russo turned her attention to Boyle, her disgust palpable. "You two are playing a *very* dangerous game."

A spirit stepped into the room—a woman who strongly resembled the deputy director. Reid intuitively knew it was her sister. "Your sister's here," she said without waiting for confirmation.

"We're done," Russo spat, leaning down to pick up her briefcase.

"Quick." Reid met the spirit's solemn gaze. "Tell me something that only you and your sister knew about."

In first grade, I stole Harold and killed him by mistake.

"Who's Harold?" she asked, curious.

The class hermit crab. I hid him inside my Star Wars *lunch box.*

By the time I got home, Harold was dead—frozen solid by the ice pack. Katie helped me bury him in the backyard.

Reid had to stifle a laugh as she relayed the story aloud.

"Impossible," Russo said. "No one knows about that."

Mention the time we took Dad's car to rescue Stacey from a rave in the middle of the night. Stacey threw up all over the back seat on the way home. We let Tim, our asshead of a brother, take the fall for it.

Reid raised an eyebrow. Sounded like the deputy director had some interesting secrets. "She wants me to mention Stacey throwing up in your dad's car."

The spirit of Russo's sister centered dark, knowing eyes on Reid. *Repeat the words, "Once an asshead…"*

"Always an asshead," Russo finished when Reid was done relaying the message. "Oh my God," she whispered, looking suddenly pale. She reached for the wooden arm of her chair and took a seat unsteadily. "So you…you can…"

"Talk to the dead," Reid said matter-of-factly.

Russo stared at her for long seconds. "How's that even possible?"

She shrugged.

Boyle stood from his chair, stepped around to the front of his desk, and perched on one corner. He held out the silver pen with one hand and pointed to the nondisclosure agreement with the other. "With all due respect, please sign here, Deputy Director."

Russo cast her signature and handed the pen to Boyle.

CHAPTER THREE

Russo returned to her chair. Boyle did the same. She was silent for so long that Reid began to feel impatient, annoyed, and hungry. She should've taken the time to eat the muffin London had brought her. Damn, she'd skipped lunch for this meeting. The least Russo could do was think faster, speed things up. She could hear Boyle's stomach grumble from the other side of the desk. Sounded like he'd forfeited lunch, too. The gesture made her almost respect him. Almost.

"Detective Gold. She's your girlfriend?"

"She's unavailable, if that's what you're asking."

"She's unavailable because the two of you are in a relationship. Is that accurate?"

What the hell? Where was Russo going with this? She threw a glance at Boyle, who frowned and gave her a barely discernible shrug. "Last I checked, that's none of your business," she said, perhaps a little more forcefully than was warranted.

"I had my team look into you."

Reid shrugged. "So?"

"They reported back to me that the two of you are involved."

She wasn't at all concerned that her relationship with London would surprise Boyle. She and London had made the decision together to share the news after she'd put in her papers to retire.

Since cops loved to gossip, news soon spread far and wide that London was off-limits. Reid knew she had earned the respect of her peers because London was, by all accounts, a hot commodity. Her brothers and sisters in blue showed their allegiance by keeping a respectable distance. There was bound to be an asshole cop or two down the road who didn't live by the same code, but the others would pick them off like injured prey. The bottom line was, their relationship was no secret. Reid had no doubt that she'd make an honest woman of London and propose to her someday. She simply couldn't imagine her life without London. They were good together. Really, really good. She had every confidence that their devotion to one another came through loud and clear to everyone around them. "London's my girlfriend. Do you have a problem with that?" she asked point-blank.

Russo met her gaze. "None whatsoever."

She narrowed her eyes, sensing a reason for the inquiry—a reason that extended beyond her realm of knowledge. Russo hadn't shared much about the case yet, but *something* was making her nervous—something big and potentially problematic. Whatever it was, Russo was obviously afraid it would change Reid's mind about getting involved. She bit her tongue, hoping the awkward silence would put a fire under Russo's ass so she could get this meeting over with and finally eat.

Russo studied her, deep in thought. "You strike me as a woman of your word."

"I am," she admitted. "Without exception."

Russo looked from her to Boyle and then back again. "We've been tracking this guy for years. All evidence suggests that he abducted my wife two weeks ago." There was a hint of quiet desperation in her voice. "He keeps his victims for exactly four weeks before he…" She trailed off and stared into the distance.

"Murders them," Reid finished. She could only imagine what Russo was going through. The least she could offer was some reassurance that her wife was still alive. "He hasn't killed her. Not yet."

Russo kept her composure, though Reid could see it was difficult. "How can you be sure?"

"Nicole would be here if he had."

Russo studied her some more and frowned. "I never told you her name."

"Boyle must've mentioned it," she lied.

"I never told him Nicole was abducted. The only people who know are the agents assigned to this case."

The name *Nicole* had just popped into Reid's brain. Things like that had been happening more and more often lately. Thoughts—details about things she couldn't possibly know—formed in her mind before she even realized they were there. She'd come to think of it as the *poof* effect. One second, it wasn't there, and then, like magic…*poof*…all of a sudden, she knew things she shouldn't.

Russo nodded slowly. There was a new respect in her eyes as she studied Reid. "You're psychic."

"I am *not* psychic."

"But you can talk to the dead," Russo said thoughtfully. "Is it really that much of a stretch?"

Russo was FBI, for God's sake. Reid's experience with them had always been that they were by the book. Every special agent with whom she'd worked over the years had consistently proven that they were inside-the-box thinkers. Their box was small and, if Special Agent Barnard had anything to say about it, tidy.

Barnard was obsessed with cleanliness. He carried a bucket of Lysol wipes wherever he went and sanitized the surface of every single object before he actually touched it. He also whistled. Incessantly. His most recent visit included endless renditions of "Baby Shark," inspired by the birth of his son. Reid was ready to punch a wall if she had to look at one more baby photo or watch one more video of that drooling Barnard clone. But London had threatened to sleep in pajamas for a week if Reid didn't acknowledge him with an occasional nod, grunt, or fake smile. The thought of not sleeping naked with London was more painful than Baby Barnard.

And just like that, "Baby Shark" was on repeat in her brain once again. Her next order of business was putting in for vacation ahead of all his future visits. The trick was finding out when his next case would land him here. She returned her attention to Russo. "Since when did the FBI get so open-minded?"

"Would it surprise you to know that we employ several psychics?"

Reid frowned. That didn't sound at all like the FBI she knew. "It would."

"That's because we don't. Yet." Russo pierced her with a knowing gaze. "We've interviewed several worthy candidates. No mediums, though."

Reid knew she was being baited, but she couldn't hold herself back. "And?"

"I'm not at liberty to share anything more."

"Come on. You're telling me that the FBI is actively looking to hire a psychic." She rolled her eyes. "You expect me to believe that?"

"Psychics. Plural."

She couldn't help but feel intrigued as she returned Russo's gaze. "You're pulling my leg."

"I'm not."

"Have you consulted with them about this case?"

"Can't." Russo shook her head. "Not yet. We're still conducting background checks on all applicants."

"Applicants?" She almost laughed out loud. "How'd you advertise for *that* position?"

"We didn't." Russo's expression was stone-cold serious. "We simply sought out the best of the best and reached out to them discreetly."

Reid didn't know if she should be offended or grateful that she hadn't made the cut.

"Had I known about you, I would've tossed your hat in the ring."

"I don't belong in that ring."

"Hands off." Boyle sat up straight. "Sylver's with us. I invited you here as a courtesy, Kate."

"Not to worry." Russo put her hands up in a gesture of surrender. "I didn't come here to poach your star player."

Reid sat back and crossed her arms. She felt tempted to set the record straight—*no one* had dibs on her. She was working as a consultant for the BPD because, well, it was the next best thing to being a cop. Working here post-retirement also let her continue to be around the people she cared about most: London, Boyle, Marino, O'Leary, Boggs, Garcia. They were the only family she'd ever known. She'd put in her twenty with the department and likened herself to her prized 1980 Camaro Z28. She might not have all the bells and whistles of a new car, but the academy didn't churn out cops like her anymore. She came from the good old days when wearing the uniform and walking your beat meant you were accountable to the people in your community. At forty-one, she might have a lot of miles on her engine, but her engine was hardy. She was, simply put, a workhorse. In her mind, there was no other way to be.

"I'm not up for grabs," she said emphatically, as much for her benefit as for Boyle's. She glanced at the lieutenant. Whether she liked it or not, she and Boyle were like family. Just like her former captain, she knew Boyle would always have her back when it counted. And she would always have his.

"Cap told me that the victims of your serial killer are unavailable for questioning."

"You're not being allowed to talk to them?" Russo narrowed her eyes. "Has that ever happened before?"

Reid shook her head. "Never."

"What does it mean?" Boyle asked, looking just as perplexed as Reid felt.

"No clue." Bottom line was, if she couldn't talk to the victims, she had nothing of value to offer. It occurred to her then that something didn't add up. "You really didn't know I can talk to the dead?"

"No." Russo blinked once...twice...as if waiting for Reid to go on.

"Then why'd you come all the way to Boston to consult with *me* about your case?"

Russo looked at her like she was a fool. "Because you solved every case that touched your desk during your thirteen-year career as a homicide detective."

Reid narrowed her eyes. "And how the hell would you know that?"

"Are you seriously that out of touch to think your talent for solving cases has gone unnoticed? Word travels, Sylver. Sooner or later, the FBI hears about these things. We know what's worth knowing."

"If you guys are so good, then why haven't you caught the bastard who took your wife?" She realized it was a low blow—her words probably cut to the bone—but Russo needed to check her ego at the door if she wanted Reid's help. She half expected Boyle to object to her candor from the other side of his desk. He didn't. He knew the FBI wasn't all it cracked itself up to be.

"This guy's meticulous. His attention to detail is, well, not like anything we've seen before. His MO suggests—"

"Stop." Reid put her hand up. "My team should hear this."

"I don't need your team." There was an edge to Russo's voice. "I already have a team in place. It's composed of the most highly trained—"

"I wouldn't give a shit if you had Sherlock Holmes on your team. Boggs, O'Leary, Garcia, Marino, Gold—they work this case with me." She nodded at Boyle. "I want you in on this one, too."

Boyle nodded back.

"No." Russo shook her head, looking back and forth between them. "Absolutely not. Your whole team isn't who I came for."

"You came for me."

Russo nodded.

"But I just told you that I have nothing to bring to the table."

"That could change," Russo argued.

"Not according to Cap."

"And if it does," Russo went on, ignoring her, "I want you with me. Not your whole entourage. Just you."

Reid shot a look at Boyle and grinned. "No one ever called you my entourage before."

He returned her gaze, his expression hard. "I prefer wingman, if it's all the same to you."

"Always thought I was *your* wingman," she said.

"You were. For a minute. Until Cap told me you had superpowers. Since I don't have any superpowers, the rules clearly state that I default to wingman."

Russo sighed. "Which brings us full circle to what I just said. I came here for you, Sylver. No one else."

Boyle centered his gaze on Reid. "Reminds me of my last trip to Home Depot. You go in for one thing—"

"And come out with a shitload of stuff you didn't even realize you needed," Reid finished. "Been there."

"Wallet's never happy," Boyle said, leaning back in his chair, "but it's always a good feeling to know you have everything you need to get a project done the right way."

"Worst thing is getting elbows-deep in something and realizing you don't have the right—"

"Tools," Boyle finished, matching her stride. "Man, I've been there more than once."

Russo interrupted their banter. "I see what you two are doing. The answer's still no. And the *tools*"—she made air quotes—"to which you're both referring are highly skilled, highly trained special agents and behavioral profilers who've been working closely with—"

"My dad's tools aren't new or state-of-the-art," Boyle said, cutting her off. "But they're the tools I grew up with. They're the tools I learned on."

"Tools you can trust," Reid said with just a hint of nostalgia.

"He left them to me when he kicked the bucket." Boyle laced his fingers together behind his head. "I never take on any project, big or small, without them."

"Wouldn't be right to ask for your help with a project in *my* house and expect you to use *my* tools," Reid said.

Boyle shook his head. "But you'd never make such an asinine request."

"Did you just call my request for Sylver's assistance with apprehending a serial killer *asinine*?" Russo asked, incredulous.

"I wouldn't ask because I know better," Reid replied, ignoring the deputy director's protests.

"But mostly because you respect me," Boyle said with a hopeful expression.

"I wouldn't go that far." She stood and held Boyle's gaze as he did the same. "All for one."

He extended a fist across the desk. "And one for all."

She felt Russo roll her eyes as they bumped fists.

"It's subtle," Russo said, climbing to her feet beside Reid, "but I'm getting the message that you need your team to work this case."

"Your powers of intuition are impressive."

"Fine. If that's what it takes—"

"And we work from here." She hated the idea of traveling beyond her home turf. Massachusetts and New Hampshire were the only places she'd frequented for the last forty-one years. Being a creature of habit made her feel safe. It gave her the illusion that she was in control. She had absolutely no control over the frequency with which spirits visited her. In some ways, she felt like she was at their beck and call all day, every day. She'd realized, from a very young age, that there was little she could do to prevent them from seeking her out. She was also intensely aware that she compensated for the intrusion by adopting a rigid and unyielding attitude in all aspects of her life, including, to London's great disappointment, travel.

"A private jet will fly you to headquarters. We'll provide free room and board at any five-star hotel of your choosing and pay all relevant expenses for the duration of your trip."

Reid turned to Boyle. "Is beer relevant?"

He nodded. "Last I checked."

"Gather your team. We'll convene in your conference room, forthwith." Russo lifted her briefcase from the floor, turned in her stilettos, and stormed from the small office, closing the door hard behind her.

Boyle set his hands on his hips and turned to Reid. "Do we even have a conference room?"

"I think so. Somewhere." Reid paused. "Did she just use *forthwith* in a sentence?"

"I heard that on *Blue Bloods* once. Cool word. We should keep it in our back pockets."

She nodded. "For times when we need to look smart."

"Yep."

She took Boyle's advice and committed the word to memory. They were making light of the situation at hand, but she was sure they both knew just how serious this was. There was obviously a lot at stake.

The hairs on the back of her neck stood on end. Reid refused to ask the question that she sensed Boyle was also wondering. What would happen if they couldn't solve the case in time to save Russo's wife?

CHAPTER FOUR

London looked up from her monitor as O'Leary burst from the stairwell, red-faced, sweaty, and out of breath.

"Gold's parents," he wheezed, clutching his side. He looked beseechingly from her to Marino to Boggs. "On their way up now."

"But it's Monday," she said. "Isn't it?"

She, O'Leary, Boggs, and Marino all checked their watches. It was definitely Monday.

"How much time do we have?" Boggs asked, slamming his laptop shut.

"Not much." O'Leary cast a panicked glance at the elevator as the buttons for each floor lit up in quick succession.

Garcia emerged from the restroom. "What's wrong?" he asked, picking up on the tension.

"The Golds," Boggs whispered. "They're coming."

"Shit." Garcia's dark skin turned ashen. "But it's Monday."

Boggs and Marino stood from their desks and gathered around her. "Operation human shield?" Marino offered.

"Been there, done that." London shook her head. "Won't work this time."

O'Leary slid open his desk drawer, grabbed some yellow crime-scene tape, and tossed it to Marino. "Hurry," he said, pointing toward the elevator. "Bar entry. Tape the doors."

Marino made the sign of the cross. "Cover me. I'm going in." He sprinted across the room, deftly leaping over the desks in his path like the track star he used to be. They all watched, frozen in place as the light for the fourth floor blinked on. He couldn't possibly make it. There wasn't enough time. It was a suicide mission.

"Abort mission!" Boggs shouted. "Abort! Abort!"

But Marino refused to back down. He knew what was at stake. An afternoon with her talkative, nosy parents was torture for everyone. Since the guys in her squad were notoriously old school—all of them were raised to respect their elders—they engaged with her parents in polite conversation and patiently fielded their questions, which were both personal and professional in nature. Her parents' interest in the personal lives of her colleagues infuriated her. After their fourth visit, she'd had enough and decided to confront them. But every time she started to protest, someone would run interference and steer her away from the objective at hand.

The guys knew that London's mother and father had been absent from her life—their choice, not hers—for over a decade. That information came to light after her parents were held hostage at knifepoint by the serial killer that London and Reid were hunting in their first case as partners. The entire squad ended up rescuing her parents in the nick of time, which unwittingly created a lifelong bond among all parties involved. No matter how hard she tried, there was absolutely nothing she could do to stop it.

There was another, more pressing reason behind their tolerance for her parents. But no one *ever* spoke of it. All of them—Reid, Boyle, O'Leary, Marino, Garcia, and Boggs—had made a silent pact a year ago never to cross that boundary.

Whenever London's parents visited, they were all trapped. In the fiery depths of hell. For what felt like an eternity.

She held her breath as she watched Marino affix one end of the crime-scene tape to the left wall. He dived to the floor and started army-crawling in front of the elevator when the doors suddenly parted.

London hid behind her desk. Boggs held a folder in front of his face and hurried down the hall to the men's locker room. O'Leary sidestepped to the nearest interrogation room, shut the door, and locked himself inside. Garcia ducked inside the restroom once again. Poor Marino. It was too late to save him. Now it was every man for himself.

She stared at O'Leary's desk. It was the closest. If she stayed low and moved fast, she might make it. She could tuck herself underneath the desk and just wait them out. O'Leary even hid snacks in all his drawers—the gummy ones without the telltale crunching that would give her away. Yes. O'Leary's desk was where she needed to be. Her sanctuary was within reach.

She took a chance and peeked around the corner of her desk. Her mother and father were standing in the elevator, smiling, wearing attire that made her long for the days when they pretended they didn't have a daughter. Her father's matching rainbow hat and T-shirt read: *Proud dad of a gay daughter*. Her mother sported rainbow earrings and a necklace with a diamond-filled rainbow pendant. There was a gigantic, downward-pointing rainbow arrow on her T-shirt. Alongside the arrow were the words: *This proud uterus grew a gay daughter.*

The plethora of rainbows on her mother and father made her eyes hurt. How could she have come from these people? What happened to the prim-and-proper parents who raised her? She realized they were trying desperately to make amends. They were committed to telling everyone who knew them—and every passerby who didn't—that they loved and accepted their gay daughter. But, my God, enough was enough. London shook her head, mortified, embarrassed, and angry all at the same time. Having them visit her place of employment, unannounced, was one thing. Showing up looking like they were the victims of a happy unicorn's drinking binge was quite another.

Marino must've made the mistake of looking up.

She heard her mother's voice. "Detective Marino, what are you doing on the floor?"

It was now or never. She scurried across the tile on her hands and knees and then ducked underneath O'Leary's desk like a hermit crab claiming a new shell. As luck would have it, Boyle's office door opened at that very moment. She watched as the deputy director of the FBI hurried into the squad room, briefcase in hand. Russo stopped abruptly in her tracks as soon as she spotted London.

London pointed behind her and mouthed, *Parents*.

Russo nodded, marched past her, and expertly intercepted them. She had her parents back inside the elevator in under a minute. "All clear," she announced in a no-nonsense tone.

"Really?" London poked her head out.

Marino looked on, agape, the crime-scene tape still in his hand.

Russo peeled the tape off the wall, turned, and continued on down the corridor without another word.

Marino sidled up alongside London and bumped her shoulder playfully. "I think, collectively, we made a stellar first impression on... whoever that was."

She squeezed her eyes shut. "Just kill me now."

❖

Reid looked around the table at Marino, Boggs, O'Leary, Garcia, and Gold. All of them avoided eye contact. They looked like five cats who'd feasted on the proverbial canary. "Okay. What the hell did you five do?"

Boyle peered at them across the table. "I'm wondering the same."

O'Leary was the first to cave, as usual. "It was like watching a train approach a cliff…at full speed…with no brakes."

"Who was the train?" Boyle asked.

"Marino," they all said in unison, turning to stare at him with accusatory eyes.

"What?" Marino shrugged and sank deeper into his chair. "I'm not as fast as I used to be."

London proceeded to fill them in on the Golds' impromptu visit.

"But it's Monday," Boyle protested. "They've never dropped in on a Monday. It's the beginning of the workweek. Who does that?"

"My parents," Gold replied with a guilty sigh. "They've obviously caught on to the fact that we make ourselves scarce on Thursdays."

O'Leary's sigh was more dramatic than London's. "We all scurry like cockroaches when pest control rings the doorbell."

Boggs stared at O'Leary. "Bro, you just compared us to cockroaches."

"Sorry." O'Leary gave it another shot. "Like underage minors at a rave?"

"Yeah." Boggs nodded with enthusiasm. "Better."

"The Golds are switching it up now," Boyle said with authority. "They could drop in at any time, any day of the week. We need a game plan."

Everyone was quiet as they thought.

London piped up, "I could just have a talk with them and ask them not to visit anymore because—"

"No!" they all shouted.

"Be reasonable. It's our best option. They're *my* parents, so they're my responsibility."

Boyle shook his head. "Goes against our code."

Reid couldn't stand it anymore. She took a deep breath. No one—not even London—had acknowledged the truth of what was really happening. "Face it. The *real* reason we put up with the Golds isn't because we saved them from the clutches of a serial killer and created an unbreakable bond." She waited for someone—anyone—to finish her thought and fess up, but the silence was absolute. "We put up with them for the caramels, guys. C'mon."

"Not just any caramels," Marino admitted sheepishly. "For God's sake, we're talking about Fran's Smoked Salt Caramels."

The Golds had them flown in from Washington every four weeks, like clockwork. They each got their own seventy-piece box—a substantial investment. Reid had done the math. London's parents were shelling out close to a thousand dollars every month to keep them fed and happy. She had to hand it to them. It was a smart move. Everyone knew the way to a cop's heart was through food. Doughnuts were a thing of the past. Having those creamy, melt-in-your-mouth salted caramels arrive in a golden box with matching ribbon all but guaranteed a warm reception whenever the Golds decided to visit.

"What on earth were you thinking, pulling a stunt like that?" Boyle pushed his chair out and stood. "You put those caramels on the line today. And not just *your* caramels. Mine and Sylver's, too."

"It's Monday, Lieutenant," O'Leary said defensively. "They caught us off guard."

"Shit," was all Garcia had to offer.

"None of us were mentally prepared," London added.

Marino shrugged. "We panicked."

"Clearly." Boyle shook his head and began pacing the room. "Someone needs to fix this and make things right with the Golds. Ideas?"

Nothing. Not a one. The five compadres were silent.

Reid rolled her eyes. "Invite the Golds for lunch tomorrow. Give them the VIP treatment. Easy-peasy. No harm, no foul."

"Who makes that phone call?" O'Leary asked naively.

London, Marino, Garcia, and Boggs shouted in unison, "Not it!"

Boyle chuckled as he took his seat at the table once again. "Guess the answer to that is *you*, O'Leary."

"But they're Gold's parents," O'Leary whined. He turned his attention to London. "Remember, you said, *My parents, my responsibility?*"

Reid decided now was a good time to change the subject, take the heat off London. "Who knew we had a conference room that looked like *this*?"

"Came as a surprise to me, too," Boyle admitted.

"This is *our* conference room?" Boggs raised his eyebrows. "Wow. Nice."

"When did we get a conference room?" Marino asked.

"Where have all of you been?" London rolled her eyes. "I started using this room my second month as a detective."

"Yeah, but a smarty-pants like you needs a place like this," Garcia chided.

"Right." Boggs jumped on the bandwagon. "For all your charts and graphs and shit."

"Us working stiffs prefer interrogation rooms that smell like urinals," Marino said.

"And vomit. Don't forget the vomit," Garcia added.

Marino nodded. "Clears the sinuses."

They all looked at Reid. "What?" she asked irritably on the heels of an uncomfortable silence.

Marino leaned forward. "Which side are you on?"

"Old-school interrogation-room meetings with tantalizing aromas of urine and barf?" Garcia prodded.

"Or meetings in wicked comfortable ergonomic chairs with a background aroma of"—Marino sniffed at the air and wrinkled his nose—"clean laundry?"

Reid took a swig of her Liquid Death Sparkling Water and let out a loud belch. "Do I really need to answer that?"

"What was the question?" Russo stepped inside the room, marched to the head of the table, and set her briefcase down.

"Whether or not I prefer the smell of vomit and urine to scented Glade PlugIns."

Russo set her hands on her hips. "And?"

"I love my interrogation rooms the way they are. I don't feel the need to try to change them. It's called unconditional love."

"Why?" Russo pressed.

She shrugged, suddenly uncomfortable with being put on the spot. Unless she was up at bat, she hated being the center of attention in a group.

"Answer the question, please." Russo sat casually on one corner of the table and crossed her arms. "The interrogation rooms at the BPD are an assault on a normal person's olfactory sense. Why do you prefer them?"

"I think she just called us abnormal," Boggs murmured.

"Speak for yourself." London gave him the stink eye. "I'd take Glade over bodily fluids any day."

Russo turned her attention to London. "And why is that, Detective Gold?"

"Because I feel more comfortable and think better in a room that doesn't smell like death."

"Exactly." Russo began extracting files from her briefcase. "I'd like all of you to keep that in mind as we review the details of this case."

Reid couldn't help but roll her eyes. Did Russo think she was training a bunch of third graders? Shit, everyone in this room knew serial killers hunted and committed their crimes in territory that was familiar and comfortable. She was preparing to say as much when she felt London's hand on her thigh under the table. London met her gaze and shook her head. Her girlfriend knew her too well.

Reid sat in rapt attention as Russo presented each victim—all women, aged twenty-five to forty-five. While their ethnicities were all over the board—Caucasian, Asian, African American, Hispanic, Latina—their physical traits were strikingly similar: long hair, fresh-faced, beautiful, lean, and fit. Each woman was professionally accomplished in her own right with expensive taste in clothes. Some were single. Some had partners. Some were married. Some had children. There were eighteen, in all.

Russo let her and the rest of the team examine the files, one by one. No one spoke. The photos of each victim's ultimate demise were gruesome. They'd endured weeks of torture and unimaginable agony. The psychological makeup of this particular serial killer was uniquely disturbing in a way that made Reid physically uncomfortable. She couldn't help but wonder how the deputy director was keeping her composure in the face of what the killer might be doing to her wife at that very moment.

When the last file was added to the pile in the center of the table, they all looked around at one another with haunted eyes.

"Set the emotion aside." Russo was the first to break the silence. "Let me hear your thoughts and observations. Keep it short. We'll go around the table, starting with Lieutenant Boyle."

CHAPTER FIVE

Reid watched Boyle as he gathered his thoughts. His habit of twirling his wedding band with his thumb always gave her a heads-up that something had gotten under his skin. This case was gruesome. If there ever came a day when a case like this didn't bother him—or any of them—it would be time to call it quits and find another line of work.

Boyle leaned back in his chair. "Anyone working this would think this guy's pissed off, that he has a beef with women—a certain type of woman, from the looks of it, because he definitely has a type." He laced his fingers together on his chest. "But I don't think he's angry. I think he's curious. He's digging around in these bodies like they're an island with a treasure." Boyle looked up. "Feels to me like he's searching for something."

Deputy Director Russo shot a glance at Marino. "You're up, Detective."

Marino rubbed the unshaven scruff on his chin as he pondered the case and stared at the ceiling. "What stands out to me is how messy it was in the end," he said finally. "Seems like the killer got carried away, lost sight of the big picture, forgot that he was working on a living human being. Bodies have limitations. He obviously exceeded those limitations with eighteen different women. Might sound out of the box"—he looked around at the group—"but I don't think he meant to."

Boggs picked up the torch. "I'm with you, bro. I don't think he meant to kill them. The crime scene pics made me think of when I do a home reno. There's a point in every reno when it feels like I might not ever be able to finish and, you know, make things right again." He shrugged. "Looks to me like he killed these women then, at the moment when he least wanted them to die, and then he went apeshit because his work wasn't finished."

"Your turn, Detective Garcia." Russo wasn't wasting any time.

Reid watched as Garcia withdrew several crime scene photos from the files. She and Garcia went way back. She'd seen him tangle with some tough guys back in the day, and he *always* came out on top. They graduated from the police academy the same year, frequented the same bar, and threw back countless beers together. She swore he had the same baby face from twenty years ago. He was short, stocky, and tough as nails, but he had a poet's heart.

He lined the photos up, side by side, and studied them as he talked. "I agree this guy's looking for something, but it's not something we would see. Nothing that exists in the human body. I think what he's looking for is intangible, like a reaction from the victims. Fear, maybe. Or loathing. Or love." He picked up one of the photos and studied it more closely. "As twisted as it is, maybe he equates love with pain. I guess it could be anything, though—anger, misery, defeat. He's searching for something, and it's clear he hasn't found it yet." He set the photo down and looked around at the group. "If, or when, he does— if it's even possible to find what he's looking for because I don't know if it is—I believe his MO will change. We'll see evidence of this change in the aftermath, in the story he leaves behind at the crime scene." He met Russo's gaze directly. "Every crime scene has an author. And they *always* sign their work, whether they intend to or not."

Russo nodded. "Detective O'Leary, do you have anything to add?"

O'Leary leaned into the killer's profile like Reid had seen him do a thousand times. "He definitely signed his work," he said, casting a glance at Garcia. "But I guarantee he's not proud of it because it's sloppy. Like Marino pointed out, it got messy at the end. I believe that's the opposite of what he's trying to accomplish. We can see evidence that he's meticulous in the beginning—so meticulous that it makes me wonder if he works with his hands. Maybe he's a pianist or a surgeon. He *wants* to be proud of the work he does on his victims. I bet that's all he thinks about. I bet he obsesses about it twenty-four seven. When you want to be great at something, what do you do?" O'Leary looked around the table. "You study hard and learn everything you can from someone who's already mastered the trade. I'd be willing to bet my pension that he's gathered every piece of information available on every known serial killer in history. In fact, he probably ranked them and paid particular attention to his favorites." He gestured to the crime scene photos that Garcia had set out on the table. "I see some Ted Bundy and some David

Parker Ray in his signature. I also see some Jeffrey Dahmer. Maybe even a little Zhang Yongming. He starts out like Bundy—controlled, precise, careful. But he finishes like Dahmer—sloppy, thoughtless, and, frankly, deranged. We need to figure out why that's happening. When we do, we'll be close to identifying him."

Reid loved listening to O'Leary brainstorm. His instincts were always on point. He had a brilliant mind that rarely made an appearance in his personal life, but it was reliably present at work, particularly when he was sifting through a crime scene. She'd always believed O'Leary had a natural talent for profiling. The look of surprise on Russo's face told her she wasn't the only one.

London was now up to bat. Reid suddenly found herself feeling nervous for London, which was ridiculous because she'd proven, time and again, that she could more than hold her own.

London gestured to the files. "There's nothing in there about drugs."

"That's because none of the victims abused them," Russo replied with a frown.

"Then how did he get them to be so compliant?"

Russo said nothing. She narrowed her eyes and sat in the chair at the head of the table. "Go on."

"There's clear evidence that every victim fought back. We all saw the ligature marks on their necks, wrists, and ankles, but it's not enough."

"Not enough," Russo repeated. "For what?"

"He tortured all of those women, in ways…" London brought her hand to her mouth and bowed her head until she was composed enough to keep going. "In ways that make it difficult to talk about without getting emotional. They would've fought back hard, as hard as they could, to stop what he was doing to them. Hard enough to rip holes in their skin, hard enough to break bones, hard enough to leave undeniable proof on their bodies that they fought as hard and as long as was humanly possible. Each of the women he targeted ran cross-country and worked out regularly. They were certainly capable of fighting harder than they did." London looked around the table with tears in her eyes. "Why didn't they?"

Russo cleared her throat. "Do you have something to add to the profile, Detective Gold?"

London nodded. "I think he gave them some kind of medication or a combination of meds—not enough to knock them out but enough to prevent them from overpowering him. Maybe he's small—lean, thin, or shorter than he wants to be. It's also possible that he's using medication to manipulate them."

"Manipulate them, how?" Russo inquired.

"Garcia said the killer could be looking for something intangible, like an emotional reaction from the victims. What if he's right? What if the killer wants these women to feel the pain, forget the pain, and then love him? I don't believe it's a coincidence that O'Leary mentioned David Parker Ray, do you?"

Russo frowned. "You've lost me."

"What if he's torturing them physically and then giving them something to wipe their memories?"

"Why? What would be his core motivation?"

London answered without hesitation. "To prove that someone can love him after he's hurt them."

Russo crossed her stockinged legs and leaned back. "And why would he want to prove that?"

London returned Russo's gaze, the conviction clear in her voice when she said, "Because it happened to him. Someone he loved hurt him. And, if what he did to those women is any indication of how, the abuse he endured was inhumane...and awful...and beyond our comprehension."

"You got all that from *these*?" Boggs asked, flipping the files open for another look.

London slid several photos across the table to Boggs. "Each victim had deep-tissue burns below the clavicle, as well as on the forearm, the back of the hand, and along the antecubital fossa."

"The cubicle who?" Marino asked.

"The forearm, the back of the hand, and the antecubital fossa are the most commonly used sites for an IV. This is the antecubital fossa." London straightened her arm and pointed to the inside of her elbow. "IVs need to be replaced every three to four days to reduce the risk of infection, which is probably why the killer implants a more permanent IV catheter here." She pointed to a spot on her chest, just below her clavicle. "With each victim, the killer experimented with different forms of torture. The deep-tissue burns were the only consistent injury on all eighteen women. Their autopsies confirm that they sustained those burns postmortem, which indicates to me that he was trying to conceal something, something he considers important, something he's afraid would reveal too much."

"Something that would lead us to him." Boggs nodded, following along.

Reid fought the urge to give London a high five right there in the conference room. London had nailed it. The entire team had held their own. She'd never felt as proud of them as she did in that moment. She met Boyle's gaze as he winked at her across the table. He was also beaming with pride. She made the mistake of seeing his wink and raising him a smile, which just made him even happier. He was so damn happy that he looked like he might start farting rainbows at any moment. She rolled her eyes.

Russo turned to Reid. "And we've come full circle to our resident psychic medium."

"I'm *not* a psychic medium." She felt her blood boil. "If you call me that again, I'm out."

"What would you like me to call you?" Russo asked in a patronizing tone.

"Sylver," she answered. "Two syllables. Easy for most people of average intelligence to remember."

"Technically speaking, a medium is someone who communicates with spirits of the deceased. Isn't that what you do?"

"Technically speaking, my title is in-house homicide consultant."

Russo nodded, clearly amused. "What do you have for me, Sylver? Something good, I hope."

"You've given us eighteen files."

"Obviously."

"How can you expect us to build a profile when you're withholding information?"

"Meaning?"

"There are others—others you haven't included here today," she said with a certainty that caught her off guard. It was just one of those things that she suddenly *knew*.

Russo held on to her poker face. "What makes you say that?"

Time to take off her kid gloves and quit playing defense. Russo was a big dog. There was room for only one big dog on this porch. "We didn't agree to this meeting to play games. This is *my* team. These are *my* people. None of us would be here if we didn't roll up our sleeves and kick ass daily, as evidenced by the working profile that this team just pulled out of thin air for you. Withholding information is not only disrespectful to us as seasoned professionals, but it's a giant fucking waste of time—time that, quite frankly, you don't have because the stakes are high." She was, of course, referring to Russo's wife, Nicole.

London piped up. "How many others are there?"

Reid didn't have a number. She just knew there were others.

"Eleven. I didn't withhold them from you," Russo admitted. "They don't belong in that pile because they're—"

"Alive," Reid finished. "He abducted them and returned them, unharmed." The words fell out of her mouth before she even knew they were in her head. "But they didn't remember a single fucking detail, did they?" she pressed.

All eyes were upon Russo now. "No. Even under hypnosis, none of the eleven surviving abductees were able to recall anything. We discovered traces of propranolol in their blood."

O'Leary elbowed London. "He's giving them propranolol to make them forget, just like you said."

Russo gave a begrudging nod. "We also discovered traces of rocuronium."

"Never heard of that one. What is it?" Boggs asked.

"A neuromuscular blocking agent," London answered before Russo had the chance, "that's commonly used to prevent movement during surgery."

Garcia nodded. "A paralytic drug."

"So," London went on, "he's using rocuronium to subdue his victims and propranolol to erase their memories as he works."

Marino sighed. "Are we thinking our killer has a medical background—nurse, doctor, anesthesiologist? Hell, maybe he's a coroner."

"It's possible." Russo thought for a moment. "That hasn't made it into the profile yet."

Boyle crossed his arms. "What has the FBI stumped is why he returned eleven women, alive and unharmed," he said to Russo in a tone Reid knew all too well.

Reid could tell he was as annoyed with the deputy director's games as she was. Russo probably had no idea that she'd just burned a bridge with Boyle—maybe one of the most important bridges of her life. Boyle was notoriously slow to forgive. When he was slighted, he *never* forgot and rarely moved past it.

"That's what we're in the process of teasing out now," Russo said sadly. For the first time since they'd met, Reid saw just how exhausted and frantic with worry she was. She reached inside her briefcase and withdrew a handful of files. "Here are the women he abducted and ultimately returned. The question is: What set them apart? Why did he reject *these* women?"

The team set to work on reviewing the files. This time, they talked openly and compared notes. In the end, no one—including Reid—could identify the quality, characteristic, behavior, or flaw that kept those eleven women alive.

"Maybe we're thinking of this all wrong," Garcia suggested. "Are we sure he rejected them? What if it's the other way around? What if he let them go because he liked them? Maybe they passed some kind of test, so he decided to set them free."

"It's possible," O'Leary said, running his fingers through the few remaining stragglers on his widow's peak. "My gut tells me it's the other way around. He released them because they *weren't* what he was looking for. They didn't measure up in some way. Maybe they didn't behave the way he wanted or expected them to."

The table was silent. O'Leary had proven himself in the field more times than Reid could count. She trusted his instincts and suspected everyone else on the team did, too.

London sat forward and directed her question at Russo. "Did any of the eleven women remember anything?"

Russo shook her head. "No one could recall a single detail."

"I think you're on to something, O'Leary." London met O'Leary's gaze. "Those eleven women didn't make the cut because the medication worked. But it worked too well. They couldn't remember anything."

"That's how they escaped the torture," O'Leary said, nodding. "His core motivation is to prove that someone can love him *after* he's hurt them. It negates his mission if they can't remember what he did to them."

Boyle frowned. "So he tortured and killed the women who *did* remember what he did?"

"Rocuronium can affect people differently," London explained. "Depending largely on the dosage given, some people can have scattered recollections of an event while others can't recall anything at all."

O'Leary looked around the table. "Since he tortured and murdered the other eighteen, I think it's safe to assume that all of them remembered what he did—maybe not everything but enough to make them fear him too much to love him."

Boyle looked to Boggs. "Which is why his work seems unfinished, just like you said. That's why he loses his temper at the end."

Boggs nodded. "He doesn't want them to die. He desperately wants them to love him."

Marino looked around the table. "This should be our working profile. As much as it *kills* me to say this"—he sighed dramatically—"I think O'Leary's right."

O'Leary grinned and sat up straighter. "Can you please repeat that?" He slipped his phone out of his back pocket and held it aloft.

"Sure." Marino smiled back. "Ready?"

O'Leary nodded with enthusiasm.

Marino leaned forward and spoke directly into the microphone. "Eat. Shit."

O'Leary continued recording. "I'm amending my last will and testament in front of all of you today. Scratch cremation. I want to be buried. Marino's quote should be etched on my tombstone: *I think O'Leary's right.*" He thought for a moment before adding, "Minus the *eat shit*, just to be clear."

Reid shook her head, secretly grateful for the break in tension. Her mind wandered as the team continued to banter. It hadn't taken them long to get to the bottom of why Russo was here. *This* was what Russo had come for—if there was any hope of finding her wife alive, she desperately needed to figure out what had set those eleven women apart. Something told Reid that was the key to unlocking the case and identifying the killer. Russo obviously thought the same.

She met Russo's gaze at the head of the table. At least they agreed on something.

CHAPTER SIX

L ondon watched as Reid locked gazes with Deputy Director Russo. The tension between them was palpable. It didn't surprise her that they were butting heads. She wasn't privy to what had transpired between them in Boyle's office, but she imagined their disdain for one another was immediate. Both women were accustomed to being in charge. Both women were also well-endowed when it came to the size of their egos.

Russo had obviously expected Reid to fall in line behind her, no questions asked. And Reid would expect the same. Reid wasn't made to be a follower. She was built to lead and pave the way. Even if someone else's path was less treacherous and well-worn, Reid always preferred to forge her own. Always. That was just one of the things London loved about her.

Reid was fearless, never cared what anyone thought, and would go to the ends of the earth to help someone who had earned her respect. More importantly, she was someone you could count on to do the right thing one hundred percent of the time, even if it was at her own expense. London had been carefully exploring her deepest layers for the last twelve months of their relationship. Reid held nothing back. There wasn't anything they couldn't discuss. Nothing—not a single topic—was taboo. Day by day, month by month, she fell harder for Reid than she'd ever thought possible. There was absolutely nothing London would change about her. Nothing. Even Reid's rough edges were sexy.

Her colleagues' debate about whether or not O'Leary should be cremated or buried finally ebbed. They all watched as Garcia gathered the crime scene photos and returned them to their assigned folders.

"Deputy Director Russo." Reid pushed her chair away from the table and set her right ankle across her left knee.

Reid meant business. London held her breath.

"There's still one file missing. Did you want to fill my team in, or should I?"

Russo plucked the last file from her briefcase and set it on the table. "Everything you need to know is in there. Now, if you'll excuse me."

Boyle raised an eyebrow. "You're leaving?"

"What if we have questions?" Boggs asked.

London flashed back to her chat with Russo at the coffee bar. The staring, the palpable sadness, Russo's words: *You remind me of someone—someone very dear to me.* Everything came together in a flash. She stood from her chair and called out as Russo tried to make a hasty exit. "He abducted your wife, didn't he?"

Russo paused with her back to the room. Long seconds ticked by in silence. She didn't mean to put the deputy director on the spot, but they needed her to stay. "Don't you want us to find her?"

Russo turned to face them, her expression ripe with torment. "Of course."

"Then you should be doing everything you can to help us. Stay," London pleaded.

"I can't." Russo shook her head. "Not for this."

"Don't be the deputy director right now. We don't know you. We don't work for you. Treat us as your equals. Cry. Yell. Do whatever you need to do to get through this. We get it. All of us would be going out of our minds if we were in your shoes."

"Mug was abducted by a serial killer." Boyle shot a glance at Reid. "Remember that, Sylver?"

"He was only gone twenty-four hours, but it was the worst day of my life," Reid admitted, softening up as she looked over and saw how much Russo was struggling.

Russo returned to the table and took a seat in the chair beside London's. "Who's Mug?"

"My dog," Reid answered.

Boyle corrected her, his tone stern. "My dog, too."

"Fine." Reid rolled her eyes. "We share custody." She missed Mug. He was recuperating from hip surgery with Sister Margaret Mary. He was in good hands. The sisters at Saint Mary's in Waltham were showering him with so much love and attention that she wasn't sure he'd ever want to come back to the job.

"My wife is in the hands of a murderous psychopath, and you're comparing her to a *dog*?"

"Mug isn't my wife, but he *is* my best friend. I was out of my mind with worry," Reid said sincerely. "Couldn't eat. Couldn't sleep. And it was only for one day. I don't know how you've survived two weeks."

"Wait." Marino sat up. "How long has he had her?"

Russo's chin started to quiver. "Today is day fifteen."

Everyone fell silent. He'd returned all eleven survivors, without exception, on the fourteenth day. The window for her wife's safe return had effectively passed.

The truth of what was likely happening to Russo's wife at that very moment hit London hard. She reached out and held the deputy director's hand as the group took turns reviewing and discussing Nicole's file.

"He's obviously taunting the FBI," Garcia said, stating the obvious.

Boggs shook his head. "He's got balls. That's for sure."

"He's confident. Maybe too confident." Marino stroked his mustache as he thought out loud. "What would make someone that confident?"

"Believing they'll never be caught," Boyle answered.

O'Leary picked it up from there. "Who would feel like they'd fly under the radar as a potential suspect?"

"Gold mentioned she thinks he's small in stature." Garcia looked around the table. "What if he's a kid?"

"A kid?" Reid looked as shocked as London felt. "No way. Is that even possible? He sexually assaulted these victims, both pre- and postmortem. I'm no expert on male anatomy, but is a kid even capable of that?"

Boyle shrugged. "Maybe he's a teenager."

"No, doesn't feel right." O'Leary spread the crime scene photos across the table. "The psychology behind this type of torture is too developed. It takes years—decades, maybe—to get to *this*."

Another possibility occurred to London. "What if he's just a small guy? A small guy who was always ignored by the type of woman he's targeting."

"His victims are all so diverse." Reid frowned. "Different races, backgrounds, professions."

"And the age range is broad," O'Leary reminded them. "Twenty-five to forty-five is a pretty big window."

Reid met her gaze, her expression circumspect. "But the one thing they all have in common is that they're beautiful—"

"Intelligent," Garcia added.

"Seemingly well put together," Marino chimed in.

"And active, in shape, and health conscious," London finished, still holding Reid's penetrative gaze.

Boyle spoke up next. "He only wants women who are out of his league, but they've always rejected him because *he* doesn't measure up in some way."

Reid pushed her chair from the table and crossed her legs at the ankles. "So he's physically unattractive, and it pisses him off."

"No." O'Leary shook his head. "Many physical things he could change—lose weight, build muscle, have plastic surgery, get hair implants, whatever. He's angry because the one thing he can't fix is being short."

"And having a tiny dick," Marino added, as brash and unapologetic as ever. "Let's face it. Being short *and* having a tiny dick is a dead end with the ladies."

O'Leary stood, spread out all the crime scene photos in the center of the table, and studied them. "He feels cheated. He believes the world owes him because he's worked hard to be the best version of himself that he could possibly be. He thinks women should be flocking to him now—women who are clearly way out of his league." He stuffed his hands in his pockets and gazed around the table. "And when they didn't, he got angry."

"Can't say I blame him," Boggs said with a shrug. "If I'd been cursed with a micro dick, I'd be pissed off, too."

"He's driven, ambitious, intelligent, handsome, and incredibly fit," O'Leary went on. "He'd choose a career that gives him power, prestige, and lots of money. Given his familiarity with the human body—and his knowledge of medication—he's most likely a doctor, maybe a surgeon." He paused and thought for a moment. "He could even be a psychiatrist."

"Psycho Micro," Garcia said with a humorless laugh.

Reid laced her fingers together behind her head and leaned back in her chair. "So we have a psychopath who believes he's flying under the radar because he's a doctor. He's short, smart, handsome, physically fit, and probably makes more money than all of us combined."

Marino frowned. "Don't forget about the micro dick."

"Are we being serious?" London was out of her element when it came to talk about male genitalia. She'd heard that cis men placed an inordinate amount of importance on the size of their penis but had never discussed it at length with anyone to know for sure. "Do we really think he has a micropenis?" she asked, looking to O'Leary.

O'Leary was quiet as he walked the length of the table, scanning the long line of photos. "Yeah," he said finally. "I think Marino's on to something. It could've been caused by the abuse he endured as a child."

"So the solution here is simple," Garcia said. "Round up all the local psychiatrists, bring them in, and—"

"Put them in a dick lineup," Marino finished, nodding. "If the FBI will give us the green light, I'm in."

Everyone cast a hopeful glance at the deputy director.

Russo squeezed her eyes shut in disgust. "I'm not even going to dignify that with a response."

"Remind me again, why aren't we tapping into Sylver's"— Boggs cast a quick glance at the deputy director and caught himself— "incredible intellect?"

London had wondered the same and suspected she already knew the answer. Erasing the victims' memories before they died would render Reid's talent useless.

"Russo already knows about my *incredible intellect*," Reid said, making air quotes.

"Can't you just do what you usually do?" Boggs cleared his throat a little self-consciously. "Summon the victims, ask them questions, find the killer, and be the superhero we all know and love?"

Marino slapped Boggs on the back of the head. "She can't, knucklehead."

"Yeah." Garcia slapped him even harder from the other side. "How's she supposed to do that when the killer wiped their memories?"

"Oh. Right." Boggs massaged the back of his head. "Might make it kind of hard."

Deputy Director Russo addressed the group. "I'll check in with my team and give them an update on what you've added to the profile." She left her now-empty briefcase beside her chair and exited the room without another word.

"There's something we need to discuss." Boyle stood and set

his hands on his hips. "The deputy director brought a concern to my attention just before the start of this meeting. Something we touched on earlier. Something that warrants careful consideration."

London watched Lieutenant Boyle. She suspected it was serious when he started twirling his wedding band as he paced.

"Russo noticed certain similarities between the victims and someone on this team," Boyle went on.

She was aware that all eyes were suddenly upon her.

"Gold's his type," O'Leary said with a look of horror.

Boyle nodded, still pacing. "It's unlikely that the killer knows we're even consulting on this case—"

"Until we fly to DC and meet with the BAU," Reid said, cutting him off. "Or maybe he's monitoring Russo, and he already put two and two together. All he has to do is get one look at London to see that she's—"

"Stop." London put a hand on Reid's arm. "Let's just hear what the lieutenant has to say."

"I asked Russo if it's possible the killer knows she's here. She said she made no effort to cover her tracks."

"So it *is* possible," Reid affirmed, running a hand through her short black hair. "That's it. We're pulling out. The FBI can go it alone."

"That's not your decision to make." This was a different side of Reid—a side London hadn't seen before. She was visibly stressed. Reid usually managed her emotions better than this.

"I'm sure everyone here agrees with me." Reid threw daggers around the table. "We shouldn't be anywhere near this case."

London shook her head. "We can't let fear dictate our behavior."

"We can when it comes to your safety," Reid said, unapologetic.

Reid was obviously overreacting. Everyone at the table looked just as surprised as London felt. "What are the chances he's surveilling Russo? She has a security detail with her round the clock. Don't you think someone would've noticed?"

"Probably not. We're talking about the FBI, London. The Federal Bureau of Inadequacy. If someone was surveilling one of us at this table, I have no doubt we'd figure it out pretty damn fast. But I *know* this team. I *trust* this team. I have no fucking idea who's working this case at the FBI or who's on Russo's security detail. For all we know, they could be a bunch of clowns."

London leaned back in her chair. "All the more reason for us to assist them with this case," she said calmly.

"He abducted Russo's wife right out from under her nose!" Reid shouted, looking around the table at everyone. "No matter how good I think this team is, that's not a risk worth taking. No way."

Reid was treating her like she was already a victim. She'd never needed anyone to protect her. She was more than capable of taking care of herself and felt momentarily offended that Reid, of all people, wasn't giving her more credit.

London felt her back go up. She took a deep breath and kept her composure with little effort—something her parents had taught her growing up. No matter what was happening, neither of her parents ever raised their voices, cursed, or lost their temper. In fact, they rarely gave any indication that they were feeling anything at all. She often wondered if that was part of the draw to Reid. Reid was raw and abrasive and so, so genuine. What you saw was what you got with her. She didn't hold anything back or pretend to be someone she wasn't, just for the sake of appearances. Even when they disagreed—which happened on a fairly regular basis because they were two headstrong women—she loved Reid, through and through.

She felt the eyes of the entire team upon her and decided to employ her go-to strategy for winning any heated debate: logic. "Abducting the deputy director's wife served a dual purpose—the killer found a victim who met his criteria, *and* he got to poke the FBI."

"Exactly," Reid said, tossing her hands up in frustration.

"But he had reason to poke them," London went on. "The FBI has been trying to capture him for three years." She shrugged. "Maybe they were sniffing around a little too close, and he didn't like it."

Reid sighed. "What's your point?"

"We're brand new to this case," she explained. "He doesn't have a reason to want to poke at us."

"Yet," Boggs interjected from the other side of the table. "Honestly, I doubt it matters. I think he sees something he likes—"

"And he takes it," Garcia finished, crossing his arms defiantly as he leaned back in his chair. He met London's gaze with an expression she hadn't seen from him before—the face of a protective big brother when he thought someone was messing with his little sister.

Great. Reid had nearly two decades of history with everyone at this table. She obviously held more clout than London. If Reid had anything to say about it, they'd make a clean break and wipe their hands of this case immediately. Judging from the way the rest of the team was looking at her now, chances were good they'd follow Reid's lead. Who was she kidding? Everyone at this table would follow Reid to hell and back if that's where she said she wanted to go. Reid had earned their loyalty, respect, and trust too many times to count over her twenty-plus-year career at the BPD. London could never compete with that.

Wanting to press on with this case, it appeared, put her in the minority. She decided then that she wouldn't bend to the majority vote. She would never leave Russo in the lurch like that. If push came to shove, she'd offer her services to Russo privately. How could she live with herself if she decided to quit a case simply because she was afraid? She might as well resign today and switch career paths entirely.

Being a cop came with risk. It was part of the job. Always had been. Always would be. She'd come to terms with that before she even applied to the academy. Every cop had to acknowledge that risk at some point in their career. Early on was usually best. It was the cops who didn't that ended up getting hurt or, worse, hurting someone else.

Boyle sat on one corner of the table, laced his fingers together in his lap, and sighed. London could see he was struggling with the dilemma before him. Her experience with Boyle as her lieutenant for the last twelve months was that he was a good man and a solid leader. All in all, he was fair. His knee-jerk reaction would be to follow Reid, but if he was the type of man she believed he was, he'd resist that urge, assume a neutral position, and encourage everyone else to do the same.

He cleared his throat. "The FBI's Behavioral Analysis Unit did an internal sweep to preemptively identify anyone who could be a potential target for the killer."

"Not preemptive enough for Russo's wife," Reid said sarcastically.

Boyle threw Reid a look of warning. "Extra security precautions were immediately put in place for the personnel deemed at risk."

"If we work this case," O'Leary said, "will they do the same for Gold?"

Boyle nodded. "She assured me the FBI will implement all the same security measures for Gold that they did for their own."

"I'd like to know what those are, exactly," Marino said.

"Well, you'll soon have a chance to find out because Russo's insisting they be implemented forthwith."

Boggs wrinkled his brow in confusion. "Forthwith?"

"You've been watching *Blue Bloods*," O'Leary said excitedly. "That's my favorite show." He turned to face Boggs. "It means *immediately*."

"Good word to use on occasion," Garcia said.

"Yeah, bro." Boggs nodded in agreement. "It'd make us look wicked smart."

"Boyle and I already claimed it." Reid sat up and rolled her chair closer to the table. "Find your own."

"You can't claim a word," Boggs protested.

"We can, and we did." Boyle stood. "End of discussion." He gathered the files in the center of the table and held them under his arm. "Sleep on it tonight. We'll reconvene at eight a.m. tomorrow for a vote."

"I assume we'll be voting on what to order the Golds for lunch tomorrow?" Reid said, clearly trying to throw her weight around. "Because we already decided, unanimously, that we're *not* assisting the FBI with this case."

London couldn't help herself. "No, *you* decided that. But you don't speak for everyone here. The team is entitled to a vote. It doesn't just come down to you being afraid that the killer might notice me, take a liking to me, and decide to make me his next victim. This case is bigger than that. It's bigger than all of us. He's tortured and murdered eighteen women. And he'll keep doing it until we identify him, arrest him, and put him behind bars. That's what we do. Everyone at this table took an oath. Being afraid doesn't change that—at least, not for me."

CHAPTER SEVEN

Reid kissed her way down London's body as London writhed beneath her. "I've missed you," she said seductively. They'd pushed today's meeting with Russo aside, along with everything that the team had discussed on the heels of her departure. Save for London's new bodyguard, courtesy of the FBI, they left all work-related issues behind at the precinct. That was their steadfast rule, and they were both really good at observing it.

They were also both really good at making love. Their chemistry was something Reid had never come close to experiencing with anyone else. She and London fit together like they were custom-made for one another. They moved like they were one soul in two bodies. Their passion in bed was just as all-consuming, just as mind-blowing, as it had been during their first night together. London certainly wasn't her first lover, but she would definitely be her last. Reid was simply incapable of giving her body to anyone the way she did with London. There wasn't anything she wouldn't share with this incredible woman. She knew, without a doubt, that she would never desire anyone else as long as she lived. London was, and always would be, her favorite person.

London drew in short, rapid breaths as she gripped Reid's hands and thrust her hips up to meet Reid's tongue. "Please," she begged.

The urgency in London's voice shot straight to her core. She felt herself aching with needs of her own. Still partially clad in boxers and a white tank top, she settled between London's thighs. Long, gentle strokes with her tongue, just the way her lover liked it. London moaned in ecstasy, released Reid's hand, and finally guided Reid's fingers inside.

From the sounds of it, London wouldn't last long. Just another minute or two would give her lover the release she so desperately needed. Shit, when it came right down to it, this was just as much for her as it was for London. Her sexual gratification came as much from giving as receiving.

Keep going. Ignore everything else. This was the perfect moment to embrace her natural aptitude for tunnel vision. It had gotten her into trouble more than once on the job, first as a patrol officer and then, later, as a homicide detective. When she set her mind to something, she obsessed. That's what she needed right now—that predatory, all-consuming focus. Tune everything else out, except London's need for release. Pleasuring her was all that mattered right now.

They fell into a familiar rhythm. She felt London tighten around her fingers—she was on the edge. All Reid had to do was coax her across the finish line. Cakewalk. She had this. Just let London *finish* for Christ's sake, and they'd be home free.

Just then, she heard it—the dreaded sound of her dead grandmother clearing her throat from somewhere behind her. Reid could all but feel the daggers in her back. Thank God she'd kept the boxers on. The thought of her ass hanging over the edge of the bed as her grandmother looked on was unfathomable.

Fuck. If she didn't stop now, her grandmother would start talking. She couldn't bear the thought of having the old hag's voice inside her head. Once there, Reid had a feeling she'd never leave. The last door would unlock, granting her grandmother full access to her mind, where she'd be able to communicate her thoughts, unobstructed.

She couldn't—*wouldn't*—let that happen. Looked like London would have to take one for the team. Again.

She withdrew her fingers and jerked back like she'd touched a hot burner. She sat bolt upright and turned to pierce her grandmother with her pissed-off cop face. "No," she said firmly. "Leave. *Now.*"

Her grandmother mouthed something in response, but thank God, it didn't come through. It appeared that the last door—the *only* door standing between Reid and her deceased grandmother—was still closed.

London sat up and reached for the throw at the end of the bed. "This is torture," she panted, hugging the blanket against her body. "What she's doing...it's inhumane."

"She obviously hasn't changed." Reid's grandmother had been

saddled with raising her after her parents died. She was a shrewd, callous woman, cruel and abusive in ways few could imagine. Reid had filed for emancipation on her sixteenth birthday, cleared out of her grandmother's house without saying good-bye, and never looked back.

Twelve years ago, she realized her grandmother had passed away before anyone even notified her. She remembered feeling the old woman's presence immediately on the other side of the door in her mind—a door that spirits frequently knocked on to get her attention. Thankfully, there was one steadfast rule that all spirits must follow: they could only step across the door's threshold if Reid willingly invited them.

She'd stumbled upon her ability to communicate with spirits when she was five. Her recently deceased mom and dad started visiting with her regularly at her grandmother's house. Since Reid was always excited to see them, she shared news of their visits with the messages they communicated. But hearing story after story about Reid's dead parents incited her grandmother. As a devout Catholic, she was convinced Reid was possessed. Locking her inside a dog crate in the basement, withholding food and water, and beating her were just a few of her grandmother's attempts at exorcism. Burning the demon out of her with lighters and cigarette butts was Father McGee's advice, which her chain-smoking grandmother was all too happy to add to the mix.

She'd had zero contact with the old hag for twenty-five years. Until three weeks ago. At London's urging, she'd made the mistake of opening the door in response to her grandmother's insistent knocking. That's when all hell broke loose.

Reid had been peripherally aware of her grandmother's presence on the other side of the door since her death. It was a quiet but insistent presence. All that changed a few months ago when her grandmother started knocking. The sound was soft and unobtrusive at first, like fingertips drumming against a table in rhythm to a song. The knocking gradually grew in volume and frequency until it started keeping Reid awake at night, driving her to the brink. Out of desperation for sleep, she finally unlocked the door and backed away—something she'd never done before. Her grandmother promptly opened the door and stepped inside, her presence as jolting to Reid as a live wire dangling above her head. Their gazes met. The old woman mouthed something but, just as Reid had hoped, couldn't communicate fully because Reid hadn't invited her.

The good news was that the knocking stopped, and Reid was finally able to sleep. The bad news: her damn grandmother set up shop and refused to leave. Now, she popped up all over the damn place. It seemed her favorite time to make an appearance was when Reid's guard was down and she was at her most vulnerable—when she and London were making love.

Her grandmother was like a tigress lying in wait at a shrinking water hole during a drought. If Reid let her guard down fully, she had no doubt that her grandmother would pounce. Something told her that the only way to get rid of the old woman was to invite her to communicate, which was something Reid absolutely refused to do.

London sighed. "This isn't working. It's time we rethink our strategy."

"How so?"

"She's obviously here to stay." London hesitated. "Everyone knows three's a crowd."

"Don't tell me you're thinking of jumping ship."

"God, no. I'm not going anywhere." London reached for her hand and squeezed it reassuringly. "Promise."

Reid nodded. "Then what are you proposing?"

"Invite her to talk. Hear her out."

Reid stared at London like she'd just suggested they jump from the top of the Prudential to see if they could fly. She released London's hand and shot up from the bed. "We've been over this a thousand times! That's *not* an option."

"We can't keep going like this, babe. You haven't let me touch you in weeks." London hugged the blanket around her body and stood before her. "And I haven't had...I haven't had..." She trailed off and bit her lower lip uncertainly.

"An orgasm?" Reid raised an eyebrow.

"Oh my God. It's been so long, I can't even remember the word," London said sadly. "I have the female equivalent of blue testicles."

Reid tried, unsuccessfully, to stifle her laugh. "I believe the expression you're looking for is blue *balls*."

"Purple, yellow, pink...whatever color they are, I have them. And it's no walk in the park, let me tell you. All I can think about is you. Your lips, your tongue, your fingers. No matter where I am—working a case, interviewing a witness, watching an autopsy—"

"Please tell me I just heard that wrong." Reid grimaced.

"You didn't." London stepped around to Reid's side of the bed and pulled open the nightstand drawer. She withdrew a silver box, lifted the lid, and grasped the strap-on dildo inside. "We haven't even been able to christen this yet. Do you have any idea how hard it's been, knowing this has been sitting here, just waiting for us to take it for a test drive?"

The thought of penetrating her lover with their new toy excited her beyond measure. "Waiting for *you*," Reid corrected, straining to keep her composure. "Your fingers more than meet my needs."

"And yours meet mine." London stepped closer and held the dildo aloft. "You're really not going to let me try this on you?" she asked, her disappointment palpable.

"Not with an audience." Reid glanced nervously around the bedroom. Thankfully, her grandmother was nowhere to be found.

"Is she still here?"

She shook her head, swiftly closed the gap between them, and pulled London in for a long kiss. Their tongues danced seductively.

London broke away and held her at bay with a stern look. "Do *not* do that thing with your tongue."

"Do what?"

"Don't play innocent with me." London traded the blanket for a silk nightie and slipped it over her head. "You know exactly what I mean. You're trying to seduce me. Again."

"It's the way I kiss." She shrugged. "It's the way I've always kissed."

"Then no kissing from this point forward." London crossed her arms. "Until you figure out how to evict your grandmother from your house."

"Not just mine. She follows us to yours, too." The old hag was particularly skilled at interrupting an intimate moment, no matter where they were. London's houseboat proved no different. They'd even tried booking a hotel room for a night. No place was safe.

London returned the dildo to its resting place and retrieved her phone from the nightstand. She tapped the screen and looked up after a few seconds. "Done," she said with a devilish grin. "My new best friend is scheduled for delivery tomorrow."

Reid set her hands on her hips and bowed her head in defeat. Fair was fair. She hadn't held up her end of the bargain, and she couldn't expect London to embrace a life of celibacy—even if it was on a temporary basis.

She needed to figure out exactly how to banish her grandmother's spirit, once and for all. Maybe she just needed to accept the inevitable and get it over with. Maybe inviting the old woman in for a chat would be enough to let her and London move on with their lives. But something told her it wouldn't be that easy. When it came to her grandmother, nothing had ever been easy.

Reid had no idea how long London would be willing to wait for her, and she realized she was too afraid to ask. The thought of losing London because she couldn't face her grandmother made her feel like a coward. She'd do anything for London. Anything. Donate an organ to London if she needed one, or step in front of a bullet for her without a moment's hesitation. But inviting the woman who brutally abused her inside her mind—her thoughts, her private space, her sanctuary—felt counterintuitive and self-destructive. So self-destructive, in fact, that she feared she might not ever recover.

❖

London set the Starbucks to-go cup at the head of the conference room table, walked around to her chair, and took a seat. Her assigned security for the day—a burly special agent who'd introduced himself simply as Agent J—stood behind her against the wall in true bodyguard fashion. His dark shades, black suit and tie, and starched white button-down reminded her of Will Smith in *Men in Black*. He even had Will's ears. Their similarities were so striking that she couldn't help but wonder if that was the look he was going for.

She checked her watch: 7:28 a.m. Their meeting wouldn't start for another thirty-two minutes. She was usually the first to arrive for everything. It was a habit she'd started early in life as a softball player. Being early gave her a competitive edge.

She believed there was a good chance Deputy Director Russo would arrive early, as well. London was hoping for a chance to talk with her, one on one.

She was pondering the killer's profile when Russo stepped inside the conference room a few minutes later. She regarded London with a look of surprise. "This is the first time someone's beat me to the punch." She set a file box down at the head of the table and glanced at the Starbucks cup quizzically. "Is that…?"

"For you." London nodded. "Hazelnut—black, with a pinch of cinnamon. I watched you make it yesterday."

"You didn't have to do that," Russo said, already taking a sip. She removed the lid from the box, set it aside, and took a seat. "Your team's contribution yesterday was impressive. Your ideas, in particular, were intriguing to the BAU."

"About that…" She stood, closed the gap between them, and sat in the chair closest to Russo. "I'd like to assist the FBI with this case, even if my team isn't on board."

"I suspect that would be counterintuitive. The only reason your team would decline to assist with this case is—"

"Because of me. I know."

"They're worried about your safety, and rightfully so. They'd never forgive themselves if something happened to you. Take it from someone who's been there." Russo's gaze was haunted. "Take it from someone who's *still* there."

"If everyone gave in to fear, who would catch this guy?"

"*We* will. Sooner or later, we'll get him. With or without the help of your team."

"Don't you want it to be sooner?" she asked.

"Of course. But not at the expense of your safety."

This was the softer side of Russo that she'd seen yesterday at the coffee bar—the side she sensed few people ever saw. "You really think he'll come after me?"

Russo stared at the far side of the room as she contemplated the question. "You remind me a lot of Nicole," she said finally. "I see what he would see in you. I think you'd be impossible for him to resist."

"You're making this personal," she said frankly. "That's not a good enough reason to pull me from this case."

"I'm not the one making that decision."

Russo obviously knew about Reid's gift. London wondered if she was also aware that she and Reid were romantically involved. "Are you talking about Detective Sylver? She doesn't get to decide—"

"I'm talking about your team as a whole. This is their call. As much as I'd like you to be a part of *my* team, they're the ones you need to consider here."

"And if they decide not to assist the FBI with this case?"

Russo answered without hesitation. "Then I'll respect that decision."

"I'm not a helpless victim," she said, meeting Russo's gaze.

"Neither was my wife."

London couldn't help but notice that Russo had referred to her wife in the past tense. She obviously felt there was little hope in identifying the killer and finding her alive.

What London couldn't figure out was if Russo's resignation was based on grief, or if it was indicative of just how clever and dangerous this killer really was.

CHAPTER EIGHT

London gazed around the table. Everyone was here—Lieutenant Boyle, Marino, Boggs, Garcia, O'Leary, and of course Reid. Russo had spoken with Boyle privately in the corner before hurrying out of the conference room to take a call.

She heard the room fall silent. Each detective's gaze quietly followed the deputy director as she exited. London suspected they were all on the same page, wondering if the call had something to do with the case. If the team collectively decided to pull out, she knew it would be hard on everyone. Whether they liked it or not, whether they wanted to admit it or not, all of them were emotionally invested in this case. After seeing how those victims suffered, how could they not be?

More importantly, something had happened during their meeting yesterday—something magical. They'd worked seamlessly together, constructing the psychological profile of a complex and multifaceted serial killer in less than a day. If she had learned anything over the course of her first year as a homicide detective, it was that profiling wasn't an exact science. It was an art. As it turned out, the detectives at this table were particularly good at it. Until yesterday, none of them knew just how skilled they were at profiling as a team. Being that skilled at what they did meant they had an obligation to help. Something told her there would be fewer victims if they accepted this case and worked hand in hand with the FBI. There was no way she was the only one at this table who thought that.

Boyle took Russo's place at the head of the table, set the lid over the top of the file box, and cleared his throat.

Garcia couldn't help himself. "What's in the box, Lieutenant?"

"Everything the FBI has on this case. There are two more boxes in my office."

"They sent everything over on paper?" O'Leary frowned. "Hasn't anyone told them digital is more efficient? Not to mention, better for the environment?"

Boyle shrugged. "If we lend our assistance on this case—and that's a big *if*—going through all of this with a fine-toothed comb and memorizing every detail is what each of you has to look forward to. We would need to get ourselves up to speed, and fast, so we don't look like a bunch of fools in front of the FBI."

London glanced at Reid, fully expecting her to protest the mere possibility of such a thing happening, but Reid was uncharacteristically quiet. Had she changed her mind?

"So," Boyle went on, "I figured we'd do this the old-fashioned way and take a vote. We'll go around the table, starting with you, Marino."

"I was afraid you'd make me go first. I was up all night, thinking about this case." Marino sighed heavily. "This bastard—he needs to be stopped. I'm not saying I'm anything special, but I think we all kicked ass at this table yesterday. Doing what we do every day for as long as we have means we've seen a lot of shit, which also means we have a lot of valuable shit to add to the FBI's pot." He shot a glance at Reid. "We all know how you feel about this one, Sylver. We get that you're worried about Gold. Hell, we all are." He threw a glance at Boggs, Garcia, and O'Leary.

In that moment, it became clear to London that the four of them had already discussed it. They'd evidently come to some sort of agreement. Sounded like the votes might swing in her favor, but it could go either way. It was still too early to tell.

"Feels like Gold should be making the call here. She's the one who'd be putting everything on the line." Marino shook his head. "I won't lie. This bastard's wicked smart and really fucking scary. Now that we know you're his type, the solution is simple. We do whatever we need to do to make sure he never gets his hands on you."

Boggs jumped in from there. "But the four of us agree—we don't trust the FBI with keeping you safe. If you decide you want to do this, we'll back you. But you have to agree to *our* security parameters."

Garcia gestured to the agent behind London. "You can keep Agent J as your bodyguard, but one of *us* needs to be with you at all times, too. That's the only way we'll agree to move forward."

O'Leary withdrew a small round container from his pocket, popped the lid off, and emptied a tiny object into the palm of his hand.

"What's this?" she asked, plucking it from his outstretched palm. It was the size of a grain of rice.

"A GPS locator." He withdrew a syringe and held it out. "It can be implanted easily with a—"

"No," she said, dropping it back into his hand like it was a tiny hot potato. "I'm not letting you put that thing in my body."

"What every woman O'Leary's ever dated has said," Boggs chided.

Marino and Garcia cracked up. Reid and Boyle followed suit.

O'Leary, as usual, ignored their juvenile antics and stayed focused on the task at hand. "Figured you might feel that way." He withdrew a second round container and poured out five additional microchips. "Which is why I figured we could all get one."

The laughter quickly faded.

"Wait. What?" Boggs frowned. "I never agreed to that, bro."

London crossed her arms. "What's good for the goose…"

"Is good for the gander," O'Leary finished. "Don't worry. I've got your back," he said with a wink.

❖

Reid listened to her colleagues' thoughts on whether or not they should take the case as they went around the table. Nothing anyone said surprised her. Everyone on her team had a solid moral compass. Despite all the atrocities they'd witnessed throughout their careers as homicide detectives, each of them held on to their sense of humanity like it was a solitary life raft on a planet comprised entirely of water. That's what set these men apart from every other man she'd ever known and why she'd give any member of her team whatever they needed, *whenever* they needed it—no questions asked. These were good men. Vulgar at times and totally imperfect, but they were good to the core. Their only flaw was that they were men. As such, they stank to high heaven on long stakeouts in a vehicle with limited ventilation.

She'd already resigned herself to what would likely transpire in today's meeting. Like Marino—and probably everyone else at this table—she hadn't slept much, if at all. She assumed they'd all be on the same page. You couldn't work alongside these guys for the better part of two decades and not get a sense of how they thought, how they worked, and what their next move would be. She was certain everyone in this room felt as she did, obligated to do right by the women whose lives were brutally stolen.

There was no denying that yesterday's brainstorming session high-lighted their strengths as a unit. What she suspected would happen actually did. This team—*her* team—worked together like they were six different, but equally vital, parts of a powerful machine. Reid felt strongly that, if you had a particular skill as an individual or a group, you were honor bound to use it for the greater good, just as she did with her gift.

When Boyle pointed out that London shared many characteristics with the killer's victims, she'd nearly lost her mind with worry. Her knee-jerk reaction was to step away from the case to shield London, but it was too late for that. The proverbial cat was already out of the bag. She'd be doing everyone a disservice if she dug her heels in and refused to budge. Even if they withdrew from the case today, there was still a chance that the killer had already spotted London because he had Russo under surveillance. Refusing to assist the FBI didn't guarantee London's safety. She and London would never be able to let their guard down—not until the killer was in custody.

The bottom line was, they were obligated to catch this psycho and get him off the streets. Reid had every confidence that her team could pull it off. Knowing that the FBI was at a standstill with the case because they'd hit a dead end didn't change that at all.

It was clear that Boyle was just as uncomfortable as she was with the notion that London could become the killer's next target. She knew him well enough to see that he was struggling to remain neutral. He listened with rapt attention as each of the guys took turns explaining why this should ultimately be London's call.

When O'Leary's time at the pulpit concluded, all eyes turned to London. Reid swore she could hear the room grow quiet as everyone held their breath.

London looked from Marino to Boggs to Garcia and, finally, to O'Leary. Reid knew that O'Leary had been London's favorite from the outset. During London's first week in homicide, they'd bonded over a shared passion for board games. It was obvious that O'Leary had a soft spot for London, as well. It made Reid secretly happy because she and the guys picked on O'Leary every chance they got. They couldn't help it. O'Leary brought it on himself.

London took a breath. "I think this is a great opportunity for us to—"

"Blah, blah, blah," Reid said, cutting her off.

London met her gaze and raised an eyebrow.

"Cut to the chase," she said. "Are you in, or are you out?"

"I'm in," London said without hesitation. "You?"

"I don't like it, but I don't think I have much of a choice. I won't be the asshole who holds everyone back from doing what they believe is the right thing." She sighed and met Boyle's inquisitive gaze. "We haven't even told them about the perks yet."

"Perks?" Marino asked. "What perks?"

"Russo's flying us to DC in a private jet," Boyle answered. "FBI's also footing the bill for a five-star hotel of our choosing—"

"And as much beer as we can drink," Reid added with a grin.

"Beer, bro." Boggs gave Garcia a high five.

"Private jet." Marino gave Boyle a high five.

"Five-star accommodations," O'Leary said with a dreamy look. He reached over to give Reid a high five.

She refused to put her hand up.

"Shit, O'Leary. You're the very definition of uncool." Marino made a face of disgust. "You *would* focus on that."

O'Leary went on, unfazed. "Hope they have Belgian waffles."

"It's okay, O'Leary." London patted the back of his hand like a mother hen. "I'm excited about the accommodations, too."

"Not to toot my own horn, but I was pretty set on taking this case because it was the right thing to do," Marino admitted.

"Bro, you and me both," Boggs agreed.

"Me, too. I'm proud of us." Garcia puffed out his chest a little. "Feels like we should get a trophy."

"Or a superhero cape," O'Leary added.

"A cape would work." When everyone looked over at Marino, he shrugged. "What? A cape would be cool."

"Ooh." O'Leary grew visibly excited. "Maybe we can get capes made and have them embroidered with superhero names. We can all wear them while we're working this case together."

Reid did an internal eye roll. There seriously had never been an easier mark in the entire history of humans. O'Leary did it to himself. Never failed. Marino, Boggs, and Garcia met her gaze. She nodded, giving them the green light.

"Like a team jersey," Marino said.

O'Leary nodded enthusiastically.

"We should get black capes," Boggs added. "They'd make us look badass."

"I like it!" O'Leary withdrew his phone from his pocket, opened his notes, and started typing. He studied the ceiling in thought. "Now, we just need some good superhero names."

"I already know mine," Boyle said, jumping in. "Megalodon. The Meg, for short."

"Nice one. And mine could be Shadow Man," Boggs offered, referencing the color of his skin.

"The Fist," Garcia said, bringing his down with a reverberating *thump* on the conference room table.

Reid had to think on her feet. "Bulletproof." It was the best she could come up with on short notice.

"Those are all great, guys." O'Leary was typing on his phone as everyone spoke. "What about mine? I've never tried to come up with a superhero name for myself before."

It was just too damn easy. Reid almost felt guilty for enjoying a good laugh at O'Leary's expense as often as they did. It'd take a level of willpower she didn't possess to resist such perfect setups.

"Let's see." Boyle leaned back in his chair. He was having a difficult time keeping a straight face. They all were. "A fitting superhero name for you would be…"

"Inspector Clueless!"

"Board Game Boy!"

"Captain Gummy Bear!"

"Crochet Guy!"

"Salad Man!"

O'Leary continued taking dubious notes for several seconds before he finally paused long enough to look up. "Wait a minute." He met London's gaze with a frown. "They're making fun of me again, aren't they?"

"I'm afraid so," she replied with another motherly hand pat.

CHAPTER NINE

Reid watched as everyone gathered their belongings and stood from the conference room table. Boyle met her gaze. "Anything you need to add?" he asked, pushing away from the table with a sigh.

Boyle was taking point. It was an unspoken arrangement between them that he would be the face of the team while Reid ran things from behind the scenes. He didn't mind the spotlight. She did. "I think that about covers it." She stood, effectively adjourning their meeting. "Go home, everyone. Pack a bag."

Boyle checked his watch. "Meet back here at eleven hundred hours."

"Business casual?" London inquired.

Everyone turned to look at her like she'd just suggested they wear their birthday suits to FBI headquarters.

"What?" she asked. "Did I miss the memo on suggested attire?"

"Business casual for you is fine, Gold," Boyle said.

"I've only been here a year," she admitted, crossing her arms. "What aren't you guys telling me?"

Reid sat on the table's edge. "Traditionally, when we travel for training or assist another branch of law enforcement with a case, we keep to the uniform." She tried not to laugh as London wrinkled her forehead in confusion.

"You want us to wear our patrol uniform in DC?" London asked.

"Not *that* uniform," Marino clarified. "We wear something a little…"

"Less formal," Boggs finished with a grin.

"It's a cult," O'Leary warned. "You should resist. They've been trying to get me to join them for years."

Garcia confirmed this with a nod. "He's been the only stick-in-the-mud so far. Feel free to join him in said mud, if you want."

"We wear navy-blue polos with the BPD logo on them," Reid said.

London thought for a moment. "Well, that doesn't sound so bad."

"Beware." O'Leary ruined any chance of inducting London as the newest member of their cult. "The words *Proud Boston Dick* are embroidered under the logo."

London threw Reid the stink eye. "Business casual, it is."

Deputy Director Russo poked her head inside the conference room. She addressed Boyle in a no-nonsense tone. "What's the consensus?"

He refrained from giving her an answer and looked to Reid, instead—his way of suggesting that she clarify their roles on this team.

She consented with a nod.

Boyle nodded back. "We just wrapped up, Deputy Director. Please, take a seat, and Sylver will fill you in." He stepped to the door and held it open the rest of the way for Russo as everyone else filed out.

Reid moved to the head of the table and took a seat. She waited in silence as Russo did the same at the opposite end. The table was long—it seated fourteen people comfortably—so having a conversational chat without needing to shout was pretty much impossible. If she'd had a bullhorn handy, she would've used it. "You should've addressed your security concern with me, not Boyle. What gives?"

"Gold's his detective, not yours."

"Nope." Reid shook her head, adamant. "Doesn't work like that. You can't have it both ways."

"Meaning?"

"When we met yesterday, you said you came only for me. You wanted nothing to do with my team. *I'm* the one who insisted we're a package deal. I invited Boyle in on this case, not the other way around."

Russo narrowed her eyes. "And?"

"They're my team, my responsibility. From this point forward, everything goes through me, not Boyle."

"You're telling me you're in charge."

She nodded. "Damn right I am."

"Then why does it look as though he's heading up this team?"

She shrugged. "That's the way we do things."

Russo narrowed her eyes. "That's the way you do things because you prefer to stay in the background."

"If you already knew the answer, why'd you ask the question?"

"So, everything goes through you, not Lieutenant Boyle."

Was Russo patronizing her now? "Isn't that what I just said?"

Russo studied her. The intensity in her gaze told Reid something was on her mind. "Who tipped you off about the eleven survivors?"

Reid stood her ground. "That's none of your business."

"It's very much my business. It would mean that a member of my team is leaking sensitive information."

She pushed her chair abruptly from the table and stood. "If you plan to micromanage me while we assist the FBI with a case you haven't been able to solve on your own—"

"No one but the BAU knows about those survivors."

"And?" Reid set her hands on her hips. She was being cornered, and she didn't like it. Nobody cornered her. Nobody.

"I made a few calls." Russo stood, walked the length of the table, and met her eye to eye. In all fairness, though, she would've been shorter without the heels. "You have no ties whatsoever to anyone at the BAU."

Russo was heading down a road that Reid had no intention of traveling.

"You're psychic," Russo said, taking a step closer. "What I can't understand is why you're trying to hide it. Your team doesn't even know about the full extent of your gifts. Everyone here thinks all you do is solve cases by talking to dead people."

This was one of the few times in her life when she wasn't able to pull an insult out of her ass. She'd learned early in life that insulting someone always got her out from under the microscope when questions grew too personal. But she was drawing a blank. "I don't know where you come from," she said, deciding on a different tack. "But where I'm from, homicide detectives who can talk to the dead aren't exactly commonplace."

"You can do so much more than that."

She held Russo's gaze, but she couldn't bring herself to deny it. She'd never intended to have this conversation with anyone. Hell, she hadn't even had it with herself yet. "What the hell do you want from me, Russo?"

"It's either Deputy Director Russo or just Deputy Director. Addressing me by my title is a sign of respect, so pick one. Either works."

There was an awkward silence as they stared each other down. It was clear that Russo expected Reid to correct her mistake, which she had zero intention of doing. If Russo thought for one second that Reid would kiss her ass because she was used to everyone else kissing it, then she had another think coming. "Nice chat." She turned to leave. "Good luck with your case. Hope you find the prick."

Russo called out, "What I want is for you to utilize your team *and* your skills, jointly." She stepped in front of Reid and met her gaze with a sincerity that was disarming. "Grant yourself the freedom to explore what you can do. Embrace who you are. There's nothing to be ashamed of, Detective Sylver. You have a gift."

"I told you. I'm retired. You don't need to call me—"

"I know. But *Detective* is a sign of respect."

Shit. Russo was being nice? "I'm good with where I'm at," she said, ignoring Russo's attempt to connect with her. "I talk to the dead. The end."

"But we both know that's not the end. You can—and should—do more."

She crossed her arms, seeing her own body language for exactly what it was: defensive. This was the first time anyone had noticed she knew things she shouldn't. Russo was on top of her game. She was obviously the deputy director of the FBI for a reason.

Russo tipped her head slightly to one side as she spoke. "When you get to DC, I'll introduce you to the people I mentioned yesterday—"

"The psychics?" She laughed. "No thanks."

Russo studied her for so long that she began to feel uncomfortable. "Why?"

"Why what?" Reid asked.

"Why don't you want to meet them?"

"Because I'm sure they're a bunch of weirdos. I don't do weirdos."

"It might interest you to know that these psychics are some of the most grounded, down-to-earth people I've ever met."

Grounded, *down-to-earth*, and *psychic* didn't belong in the same sentence. "Are they...like me?" She hated herself for asking, but she couldn't help it. "Can they talk to spirits?"

"Good. I've piqued your interest." Russo checked her watch. "That's my cue to leave." She walked briskly to the door and set her hand on the handle.

"Wait."

Russo paused and turned to look at her.

"Can they talk to the dead or not?"

"If you really want to know, you can ask them yourself." Russo pushed the door open and slipped out before Reid had a chance to say anything more.

As much as she hated to admit it, Russo was right. Her interest *was* piqued. When it came down to it, what was the harm in meeting people who shared her abilities? Unless Russo introduced her as a psychic medium—if she knew what was good for her, she wouldn't dream of it—Reid was confident no one would ever guess. She looked like a cop, walked like a cop, and talked like a cop—an identity that, in her opinion, was as far from a psychic medium as someone could get. The average joe would never guess that she talked to spirits on a daily basis. She'd been flying under the radar her whole life, and she preferred to keep it that way. Assisting the FBI with this case better not screw that up.

Coming out as a gay cop was one thing, but she'd never had much of a choice there. She was pretty sure everyone just assumed she was gay from the outset. Coming out as a psychic medium, without her identity as a cop to shield her—her days as a homicide detective were officially behind her—was an entirely different world. It was a world she knew nothing about and wasn't sure she ever wanted to be part of. And if she ever did decide to take it and run with it, which was impossible to imagine, it was a world she definitely wasn't ready to embrace at this point in her life.

Reid had never been one to jump into something headfirst. She'd always needed time to let things simmer, time to wrap her mind around something and figure out how she felt about it. Forging into a relationship with London on the heels of meeting her was the only time she remembered being reckless in her forty-one years of living. And she blamed that one entirely on London. If London hadn't been so damn amazing, Reid would still be single.

But London had single-handedly wriggled her way into Reid's private world. When she revealed that she not only communicated with spirits but used this ability regularly to solve the homicide cases that came across her desk, London didn't flinch. In fact, she did just the opposite. She readily embraced her gift and encouraged Reid to do the same.

Reid knew there must be other mediums in the world. She had no real proof that anyone like her existed, but she'd never bothered to look. She couldn't be the only person alive who could see and communicate with spirits. It stood to reason that there *had* to be others, right?

She realized then that she had distanced herself from her gift—from learning more about it, from seeking out and connecting with others who shared it—out of shame. For most of her life, she wasn't even capable of seeing her ability as a gift. London was the very first person to introduce the concept, and it had sent her mind reeling. It was hard to see something as a gift when it felt so much like a curse.

Her grandmother had done a number on her as a kid. She'd never felt proud of what she could do. She still felt like it was something that needed to stay hidden, away from the light, pushed down deep because it was a part of herself that even she didn't fully understand. If she had to name one thing she'd learned from her grandmother, it was that people feared what they didn't understand. Fear, above all else, made people do ridiculous things.

Reid had tried to stop seeing spirits when she was little. She remembered believing that if she couldn't see them, she wouldn't be able to hear them. But that turned out not to be the case. They always found her. Always. The best she could do was ignore them and pretend they weren't there. Her only choice was to act as though she was normal, which was exactly what her grandmother demanded. So, for many years, that's exactly what she did. *Fake it until you make it.* That had been her motto until she grew old enough and big enough to defend herself. But by that point, the damage had already been done. She was physically and mentally scarred.

The fact was, her scars wouldn't exist if it wasn't for the damn spirits. There was a time in her life when she would've given anything not to see or hear them. When all was said and done, she'd come full circle back to her original belief. No matter how many people in her life tried to put a positive spin on it—Cap, London, Deputy Director Russo—her gift was not a gift at all. It was a curse.

Even so, Reid couldn't help but wonder what it would be like to talk to someone like her. She realized then that a part of her had always longed to connect with someone who shared her ability. Maybe, if she met others who could do what she did, she wouldn't feel like such a freak.

Damn Russo for planting this seed.

Despite her better judgment, she found herself looking forward to meeting the psychics Russo had mentioned—the same psychics who were in the process of applying to the FBI. How weird could they be if the FBI was considering hiring them? She flashed back to something

Russo had said during their meeting in Boyle's office yesterday... *We simply sought out the best of the best and reached out to them discreetly.*

Pondering *the best of the best* begged the question: How the hell did the FBI find out about them? They obviously weren't living in secret or hiding what they could do. If they had been, the FBI wouldn't have heard about them or known enough to seek them out.

Another more pressing question gnawed at her. Were they better at it than she was? And if the answer was *yes*, where would that leave her?

Reid was suddenly unsure of herself in a way she'd never felt before.

CHAPTER TEN

L ondon looked around at the disappointed faces of her colleagues. Reid was the only one who wasn't visibly affected by the news. Boyle had just informed them that Joint Base Andrews was restricting the airfield to military-only operations.

They'd all gone home to pack and returned with duffel bags and carry-ons. Now, they were gathered around O'Leary's desk in the squad room.

"So no private jet?" Marino asked sadly.

Boggs gave him a reassuring pat on the back. "Not this time, bro."

"We'll be flying Southwest out of Logan." Boyle checked his watch. "Our flight leaves at two twelve p.m. We have a brief layover in Chicago."

"Southwest?" Garcia repeated, clearly miffed. "Who the hell booked our flights?"

Boyle shrugged. "The deputy director's assistant, I think. Why?"

"We can't fly first class. Southwest doesn't have it." Garcia sighed. "FBI promised us a private jet. The least they could've done was fly us first class."

"Next thing, they'll be putting us up in Motel 6," Boggs said.

Marino frowned. "And sending cases of Coors Light to our rooms."

Reid shook her head. "Good thing we're all doing this for the right reasons and not for the perks," she said sarcastically. She pierced Marino, Garcia, and Boggs with her quit-whining-or-else look.

They all fell instantly quiet.

London didn't care about the private jet, the hotel, or the beer. All she wanted was a chance to collaborate with the FBI and start working the case so they could find this killer and get him off the streets before he hurt anyone else. She realized the guys were disappointed, but she knew, deep down, they all felt the same.

Her thoughts went to Russo's wife, Nicole, as they made their way to Logan airport. Having so much in common with the killer's chosen victims made her feel a kinship with them that surprised and saddened her. Everything she'd read in their files indicated they were good people—honest, hardworking, responsible, and loyal to those they cared about. It hadn't taken her long to realize that each of the eighteen women he'd brutally murdered could've been good friends of hers if they'd crossed paths. She wasn't sure if her sexual orientation would make her more or less appealing to the killer. Based on the intel they'd received, all the killer's previous abductees were cis gender heterosexual women—except Nicole, who was queer. It might work in her favor, which she'd obviously prefer. If that turned out to be the case, then she wouldn't need Agent J shadowing her every move. She'd only had a bodyguard for a day, and it was already wearing on her nerves.

Reid hadn't protested against Agent J's presence, but London knew it was only because she was a big *Men in Black* fan.

She met Reid's gaze beside her as the plane jetted down the runway. Reid had confessed that flying made her nervous as they were packing for their trip to DC. They'd agreed on a hands-off policy during working hours. She and Reid were both comfortable with showing affection in public, as long as it was tasteful—holding hands, rubbing a thigh or a shoulder, giving a quick kiss here and there. None of the guys seemed to notice or give it a second thought when everyone met up for happy hour. But they were both very careful not to cross any lines when they were on the clock. Keeping their professional and personal relationships separate was important, but maybe today was an exception. She reached over the armrest, laced their fingers together, and squeezed Reid's hand.

Reid squeezed back. The tension in her face relaxed. She leaned close and whispered, "Pilot's mother died recently. Nothing nefarious," she said, when London raised an eyebrow. "But she's asking me to tell her son that he needs to see a cardiologist."

"Are you saying there's a chance our pilot could have a heart attack during this flight?" Now it was London's turn to be nervous.

"Shit, London. I hadn't thought of that." Reid's hand in hers grew instantly clammy. "Great. Thanks for those reassuring words."

"Are you going to tell him?" she asked, suddenly curious as to how Reid would choose to handle this particular dilemma. Reid's rules were strict—she never passed messages from spirits to their loved ones. As far as London knew, the only exception to that was her former captain, whom London had never met. She and Reid invited his wife to the house for dinner once a week while Reid conveyed messages back and forth between them. In many ways, London felt as though she *did* know Cap. She'd just gotten to know him in a very unconventional way.

"I don't see that I have much of a choice." Reid sighed. "But this better not become a thing."

"Become a thing, how?"

"Like, what if word travels in the spirit world?" Reid shrugged. "I don't know."

She nodded as it dawned on her what Reid might mean. "So, spirits could start showing up, claiming it isn't fair because you do it for some but not all?"

"Exactly," Reid confirmed. "I have my hands full as it is. I don't want to do anything that increases the number of spirits in my life."

"Maybe you could make a new rule." Reid pierced her with a bright green gaze. Being the recipient of Reid's laser-beam focus still sent shivers through her body.

"Like what?" Reid asked, looking genuinely stumped and more than a little curious.

"You won't pass along a message unless it's a life-or-death warning of some kind."

"Feels like an invitation for disaster." Reid checked her watch as the pilot announced they'd reached their cruising altitude of thirty-five thousand feet.

"You could always try it. If it doesn't work, then go back to the drawing board and try something different. It doesn't have to be—"

"All or nothing, I know." Reid smiled and gave her hand a gentle squeeze.

Good. It was *finally* starting to sink in. It had taken the better part of a year for Reid to stop thinking in such black-and-white terms. At least, Reid was *beginning* to acknowledge the gray. London took every opportunity to point out that life didn't have to be so binary all the time. Little by little, Reid was opening up to the idea.

Reid met her gaze and frowned. London could tell something was on her mind, but instinct told her not to push. Reid would share if and when she was ready.

"Russo mentioned something." Reid spoke in a hushed tone.

London nodded, silently consenting to keep whatever they

discussed confidential. The aisle seat in their row was unoccupied, lending them the privacy they needed.

"The FBI's actively recruiting reputable psychics. Sounds like they're in the final stages of the hiring process."

She waited as Reid gathered her thoughts. London could see that she was weighing what she should and should not share. She had a feeling it had something to do with her abilities—something that she hadn't shared before now.

Reid thought she hadn't noticed that her abilities were growing beyond just talking to the dead. There were countless occasions where Reid simply knew things she had no way of knowing—like when London was getting ready to ask something that Reid would answer out of the clear blue. It had happened too many times to count.

London had never brought attention to it because Reid wasn't ready to talk about it. When Reid was ready, London was confident she'd discuss it with her. If she chose not to, or if she chose to discuss it with someone other than her, then she had to trust it was the right decision. Reid knew herself, and she knew what she needed. She trusted Reid.

"Russo wants me to meet them. She thinks I might be like them." Reid gazed into her eyes with a rawness and vulnerability that made her want to cry. "She thinks I can do more than just talk to the dead."

"What do you think?" London asked, treading carefully. She'd been waiting for this conversation for months, but she wanted to let Reid dictate the pace of whatever she chose to reveal.

Reid was quiet for long seconds, her gaze unwavering. "I'm afraid," she admitted.

London held her hand. "Of what?"

"Of losing you," she answered truthfully.

"Okay. Hear me when I say this." She squeezed Reid's hand. "I am not going anywhere. Ever."

"What if I came down with a bad case of leprosy?"

London shook her head. "Nope."

"It's wicked contagious."

She shrugged. "Then I guess we'd have leprosy together."

"And then a year from now, my nose fell off."

"I'd buy you a pair of glasses—the ones with the nose and eyebrows attached."

"And then a year after that, both my ears fell off, so I couldn't wear the glasses disguise with the fake nose."

She smiled. This game was fun. "Duct tape fixes everything."

"And then six months later, all my fingers fell off."

London shook her head. *"That's* where I'd draw the line. No fingers is a deal breaker."

Reid pretended to look offended. "But we'd still have the toy."

"Not the same." She released Reid's hand and crossed her arms. "Not even close."

"Okay," Reid said, sighing. She found London's hand once again and laced their fingers together. "Good to know you have your limits."

London glanced down at their entwined fingers. Even their hands fit together perfectly. Reid was custom-made for her.

Their conversation hadn't gotten far, but it was a step in the right direction. Reid was trusting her enough in this moment—and perhaps trusting *herself* enough—to reveal the possibility that she was, in fact, psychic. This was huge progress.

It was also noteworthy that it had taken Russo all of one day to recognize this about Reid. She couldn't help but wonder if their colleagues had also noticed but, like London, had chosen not to draw attention to it because Reid obviously wasn't ready. The fact was, they'd known Reid far longer. If their roundtable profiling session yesterday was any indication of just how perceptive the guys in their squad were, then the revelation that Reid was psychic wouldn't come as a surprise to any of them. Which was good because Reid needed their acceptance. She needed that in order to feel okay and accept her own gifts, whatever they were.

Her next order of business was figuring out what to do with Reid's dead grandmother. For the first time in her life, London desperately wished that she could talk to spirits. If she could, she would've already scheduled a sit-down with Reid's grandmother to find out what she wanted and why she wasn't leaving Reid alone.

Granted, she knew next to nothing about how things worked when it came to communicating with spirits. But her cop instincts insisted that the only way Reid would ever be free of her grandmother was if she allowed her to say her piece. London wanted to believe that her grandmother was sorry. Perhaps all she needed was a chance to apologize. Maybe she longed to give Reid the closure she never had.

Reid admitted that she'd never had a bad encounter with a spirit. She wasn't even sure it was possible to have a bad encounter because, she explained, there were certain rules that spirits had to follow in order to be allowed to communicate with her. But she just wasn't willing to give her grandmother any leeway at all to make amends. Understandable, given the circumstances.

London knew Reid was afraid of her grandmother. Reid would never admit it, but she didn't have to. More than anything, she wanted to help Reid and her grandmother find closure. She was committed to helping her work through this, even if it meant they had to abstain from sex for an extended period of time. Yes, it was torture, inhumane, nearly unbearable. But there was nothing in the world that would make her want to leave Reid. Nothing.

The way she saw it, this was just the first of many obstacles they'd likely face in their relationship. Nothing so far had proven to be much of a challenge. There was a twelve-year age difference between them—it had bothered Reid in the beginning, but they'd quickly moved past it. They worked together every day in a high-stress environment—that hadn't bothered either of them because they both loved their jobs and had an abundance of respect for one another, personally and professionally. And, last but not least, Reid could see, hear, and communicate with spirits. It was a world that was totally foreign to London, but it was one that she found endlessly intriguing.

At first, Reid had been reticent to share stories of her encounters with spirits. London was able to draw her out, little by little, with some gentle prodding. As soon as it became apparent to Reid that she couldn't be scared off, Reid started to relax and share more. With Reid, it was a marathon, not a sprint. She'd been conditioned to be ashamed of her gift. London saw it as her job to undo all that. Reid was beautiful, inside and out. She had an amazing gift that she used every day for the greater good.

If London had it her way, they'd spend their lives together, and she'd have years to undo the damage Reid's grandmother had done. Her greatest hope was that Reid would someday learn to accept her gift and feel proud of who she was and what she'd accomplished—and was still accomplishing—in her career. More than anyone she'd ever known, Reid deserved to feel free to do and be whatever she wanted. She had a feeling, if that happened—if Reid broke free from her grandmother's chains—she could finally come into her own and be who she was meant to be. The sky truly was the limit for Reid.

CHAPTER ELEVEN

R eid grabbed her carry-on from the overhead compartment and turned to London with a questioning look. London shook her head, denying her nonverbal request to retrieve London's carry-on, as well. Maintaining autonomy while at work and in the company of their colleagues was important to both of them. London had no problem allowing Reid to open the door for her at happy hour with the guys, but that was only allowed to happen when they were off the clock. London wanted to be sure the squad saw her as capable of doing things for herself. That included retrieving her own carry-on.

Reid glanced at her watch as they deboarded the plane. It was coming up on seven o'clock. Her day had started early, as usual, and she was wiped out. The day was pretty much shot. They'd spent most of it traveling, which, in her opinion, had been a giant waste of time. If the FBI had sent digital files over, they could've spent the last six hours reviewing the case.

She felt a sense of urgency to get the case underway. She wasn't sure if that was because she was going stir-crazy and needed something to do while sitting on an airplane or because her intuition told her that the clock was ticking for Russo's wife. Either way, it would've increased their overall productivity as a group if they'd been allowed to work during their flight. It was yet another example of inefficiency within the confines of the Federal Bureau of Inadequacy. Inefficiency—wasting time, in particular—irked her no end. Especially when there was a killer on the loose, and there were lives on the line.

That's when it struck her. Why had the FBI sent all the files over on paper? Russo had taken a private jet from DC to Boston with three boxes of case-related documents. The FBI had embraced digital technology ages ago. What the hell accounted for the sudden need to revert to paper? Three plausible explanations came to mind.

First, the FBI had a systemwide database failure, which she figured was possible but unlikely. If that was the case, Boyle would've already mentioned it. She thought back to when O'Leary asked why the FBI had sent the files on paper, and Boyle had shrugged. Maybe he didn't know, either.

Second, the FBI didn't trust the BPD with digital files, which also seemed unlikely because they'd been passing files back and forth for as long as Reid had been working homicide.

There was a third possibility—it also happened to be the one she was the least fond of—and it sent shivers down her spine. The FBI was intentionally keeping all case-related information *out* of their database. They would only take such drastic measures if they believed the killer somehow had access to their system. And if that was the case, he would have to be either an employee or a hacker. Both possibilities were disturbing. Both made her blood run cold.

She and London made their way down the terminal with the rest of their group following closely behind them. London nodded toward the bathroom up ahead. "I need to make a quick pit stop."

Reid nodded as London handed off her suitcase and jogged ahead.

Boyle came up alongside her. "Bathroom trip?"

Reid nodded. "Not sure how she lasted as long as she did. She drank, like, eighty-six bottles of water on that flight."

Marino, Garcia, O'Leary, and Boggs quickly followed London's lead. She and Boyle reached the bathroom entrance and leaned against the wall. They were the only two out of the group who could hold their fluids like camels. She'd always respected that about Boyle.

Boyle was saying something about their hotel when she flashed to a vision of a man's fingers typing furiously on a laptop keyboard. The sound was cadent, as if he was tapping to the rhythm of a song. She closed her eyes as a combination of letters, numbers, and symbols scrolled across a black screen. It was a language she didn't understand. He was coding—he was scripting. She heard the man's excited inhalations and exhalations. Slowly, the song he was keeping time with swam up from the depths of her mind, like a leviathan rising to the water's surface to take a breath. "Bad" by Royal Deluxe.

This was the killer. She was in his mind, living one of his memories. Without warning, everything hit her at once. All of her senses were suddenly enmeshed with his. She felt her legs give out as she fell to the floor. She was vaguely aware of Boyle at her side, calling her name, asking if she was okay. But she couldn't bring herself to answer. Couldn't even open her eyes. Her eyelids were too heavy. Her entire body stopped cooperating, like the synapses in her brain had abruptly stopped sending messages to the muscles in her body. She felt pinned down, unable to move, and realized she was no longer in the driver's seat of her own body. Boyle's voice was soon joined by Garcia's, O'Leary's, Marino's, and Boggs's. But their voices soon receded into the background until they were barely a whisper.

She watched as the killer drank from a stainless steel mug. A warm liquid was suddenly inside her mouth. The taste of blood made her want to throw up. She knew then, without a doubt, that he was drinking Nicole's blood.

It was pure sensory overload. The feel of a keyboard under her fingertips. Code scrawled across a black screen in a dark-as-night room. The taste of blood in her mouth. The sound of bone-jarring music blasting at full volume on nearby subwoofers. The not-so-subtle aroma of death. A decomposing body had a distinct smell with which she was well acquainted. All of it assaulted her senses at the same time. It was hard to think through the disgusting metallic taste in her mouth.

Finally, her cop instincts kicked in. *Look around, Sylver. Find something useful.* It was Cap's voice. She wasn't sure if it was really him or if she was just imagining his voice in an effort to calm herself. The smell of rotting meat made her gag involuntarily. The killer didn't seem to notice the putrid stench, but how was that possible? If there were neighbors close by, someone would've reported it to the local authorities. Which probably meant that his hideout was in a remote location. Not a huge surprise, but it was a potentially valuable detail for the FBI to keep in their back pocket.

His arm, Sylver. Look at his arm. Cap's voice again. She pushed everything aside and focused on the killer's arm. His left forearm sported a large tattoo of a green serpent wrapped around a golden staff. She recognized the Rod of Asclepius at once—a commonly used symbol to identify a medical professional. This fell in line with O'Leary's theory that the killer was a doctor.

The tattoo swam out of focus as all of her senses returned to the present moment. She swallowed. The taste of blood was noticeably absent from her mouth, and the air was no longer saturated with the smell of death.

❖

London stepped inside the airport restroom and waited her turn in a short and, thankfully, quickly moving line. As the last woman in front of her finally slipped inside a stall, the janitor slipped out of the last one and removed an out-of-order sign from the door. He glanced in her direction and waved her forward.

She was momentarily conflicted because the stall he'd just cleaned was one of two wheelchair-accessible stalls. She threw a quick glance over her shoulder at the women who were already lining up behind her. No wheelchairs. No one with strollers. She decided to break the rules and use the stall. If she didn't, someone else would. Besides, this was the janitor's domain, and he *did* give her permission, so this probably didn't qualify as rule-breaking behavior.

She listened to the sound of her square-heeled boots on the bathroom tile as she made her way to the last stall. The vast room was a cacophonous orchestra of running water, hand dryers, flushing toilets, and women's voices. She pushed the stall door open to find that someone else had taken the stall while she was waffling—indeed, the woman inside was already sitting on the toilet. London averted her gaze, muttered an apology, and was turning to make a quick exit when it dawned on her that something was amiss.

The woman was wearing slippers and an old-fashioned nightgown. London stepped closer, narrowed her gaze. She looked vaguely familiar. Her mouth was slack, and her eyelids were heavy as she struggled to keep her head upright. Her hair had been pinned to the top of her head in a disheveled bun, and her hands were wrapped in thick white bandages. It looked like some of her fingers were missing.

It hit London like a startling clap of thunder. This was Russo's wife. Nicole was alive but, from the looks of it, just barely. She'd obviously been drugged. Whatever she'd been given was kicking in now. Nicole's eyes fluttered shut, her chin fell to her chest, and she slumped forward. London caught her in time as she tumbled to the floor. "Nicole? Stay with me."

As she was setting Nicole's body on the tile, her mind flashed to the janitor who'd peeled the out-of-order sign from the stall door. A dark realization hit her: the janitor was the killer. Had to be. It was the only plausible explanation. She reached underneath her blazer, unsnapped her holster, and withdrew her weapon.

The janitor slipped inside the bathroom stall. He shut and locked the door behind him, and then turned to face her with a sneer. He pushed his gray hood back to reveal a handsome face with small brown eyes and a neatly trimmed goatee.

Something told her to be cautious—not to call out for help or make any sudden moves. The weight of her weapon felt reassuring in her hands, but she knew from experience that she should never assume she had the upper hand simply because she was armed. Control of a situation could change in the blink of an eye, especially in a confined space. Instinct told her he wouldn't have been so brazen if he didn't have a plan. Training told her to put as much space between them as possible. She slowly rose to her feet and backed away until she was against the wall, her weapon pointed at him.

"I injected her with a combination of pharmaceuticals. She's dying. You have two seconds to decide if you want her to live." He flicked his wrist and checked his watch. "One…"

"I want her to live," she said quickly.

"Then lower your gun and toss it in." He gestured to the toilet.

She did as he asked. If push came to shove, she could take him down without a weapon.

"I'll trade," he said. "You for her."

If she let Nicole die, she could take him into custody now, thereby preventing the abduction and murder of future victims. It came down to sacrificing one for the many.

"I always keep a few of these on back stock," he said, nudging Nicole's limp body with the toe of his shoe. "If you arrest me, the other three die, too. You'll never find them." He met her gaze with soulless eyes. "Ever."

Russo hadn't mentioned anything about the killer abducting victims and keeping them as inventory. More to the point, that information wasn't documented anywhere in the files the FBI had sent to the BPD for review.

"You doubt me." He slipped his phone from his pocket, tapped the screen, and held it up. "Bay one."

London glanced at the screen. A young woman was handcuffed to a hospital bed, an IV in one arm and a blood pressure cuff on the other. There was a monitor that displayed her vital signs at the head of the bed. Her body was still. She appeared to be sleeping.

"Bay two," he said quietly.

London watched as he brought up another live video feed. The room was different, but the setup was identical. She also appeared to be sleeping.

"And bay three." The third bay showcased a woman who was older than the first two. She was calling out for help in a feeble voice that sounded heavily medicated.

"Watch this," he said, tapping on the screen again. "I'm administering a drug cocktail that keeps her effectively sedated. She should calm down in"—he counted on his fingers—"five, four, three, two, one."

Sure enough, the woman in the video ceased all movement. Her breathing slowed, and she appeared to sleep just as hard and just as deeply as the other two.

"Back to my proposed trade," he said. "You for her. What's your answer?"

"What about *them*?" she asked, nodding at the screen on his phone.

He shrugged. "What about them?"

"Save her," she said, bending down to check on Nicole. Nicole's pulse was weak and thready, her respirations shallow. She didn't have much time left. London stood and summoned the courage to meet the killer's predatory gaze. "And release the three women you just showed me, unharmed."

"Done," he said with a curt nod.

The thought of going with this man willingly made her feel sick. Everything was happening too fast. Had she really just made a deal with a serial killer?

"Inject yourself." He withdrew a syringe from his pocket and held it out to her. "In the thigh."

She hesitated, but only briefly, before reaching over to take the syringe. "Nicole first," she demanded. In hostage-negotiations training, she'd been taught to use a victim's name as often as possible to humanize them and make it more difficult for the hostage taker to maim or, worse, kill them. Objectifying a person was always easier if you didn't know their name. But using Nicole's name would do nothing to change the outcome here. The man standing before her was a sociopath.

He knelt down and pulled the neckline of Nicole's nightgown aside to reveal an IV catheter. What if she took him down now, while he was saving Nicole? She'd save Nicole's life, which would just leave the other three women. He claimed no one would ever find them, but maybe he was bluffing. Once they took him into custody and identified him, how hard could it be to retrace his steps and rescue them? If she arrested him now and never located his last three victims, she would have to find a way to live with their deaths, knowing that, in the end, she was the one responsible.

On the other hand, there was no guarantee he'd uphold his end of the deal and release them. She was naive for wanting to believe he would. Not to mention, where would that put her? Drugged, on a table, tortured, and eventually murdered? Reid would never recover.

He grabbed a syringe from his pocket, pulled the cap off with his teeth, and injected the solution into the IV. Nicole's breathing grew noticeably deeper, and she began to stir almost immediately.

London waited until he was finished. She considered calling for help in that moment but decided it wasn't worth it to put anyone else at risk. He was obviously strong. Her team had posited that he worked out to maintain a muscular physique, and they were right. His muscles were clearly defined, even through his bulky sweatshirt.

She was also strong. She ran and worked out every day. She'd taken down bigger guys than him on the job. Subduing a suspect was less about strength and more about agility and rote memory.

She took a breath and felt her heart pick up speed. It was now or never.

CHAPTER TWELVE

Reid opened her eyes. She was sitting on the airport floor, her back against the wall. Boyle, Garcia, Marino, O'Leary, and Boggs flanked her on their knees, their expressions ripe with worry.

"Back up, guys," Boyle said. "Give her some space."

One by one, they all stood and took a step back. Boyle balanced on one knee and looked as though he was getting ready to propose. "Not if you were the last person on earth," she said.

"Come again?" he said with a look of confusion.

"I'm not marrying you. I'd rather put a campfire out with my ass."

He laughed and offered his hand. They both stood. "You okay?" he asked, concerned.

"Fine," she lied, pulling on her ear. "It's an equilibrium thing. Happens to me sometimes when I fly." Had she really just glimpsed the killer's world?

Reid glanced over at Agent J, who was still waiting outside the airport bathroom for London. He wore a black suit, white shirt, black tie, and black sunglasses—yesterday's getup. She couldn't figure out why he was wearing sunglasses inside the airport. He also hadn't removed them at all during their flight. Now that she thought about it, she hadn't seen his eyes since they'd met. It was starting to make her feel uneasy.

Boyle followed her gaze. "Think he tied one on last night and has the mother of all hangovers?" he asked, as if reading her mind.

"We have a bet going." Garcia stepped forward. "I think he burned his eyelashes off at the last family barbecue."

"No, bro." Boggs shook his head. "Shaved his eyebrows on a dare. Has to wear the shades till they grow back."

"Nah." Marino joined them. "Got his ass kicked in a bar fight and ended up with a hell of a shiner."

They all looked at O'Leary and waited.

O'Leary's eyes lit up, and Reid could almost see the light bulb switch on above his head. "He can shoot energy beams from his eyes, like Cyclops from *X-Men*. He keeps the sunglasses on at all times. For our protection," he added on the heels of an awkward silence.

They all stared at him.

"C'mon, you guys." O'Leary frowned. "Mine was the best one. I should get extra points for creativity."

"Dude." Marino slapped O'Leary on the back of the head. "You *lose* points for not being on the same planet as the rest of us."

"Gold would've liked it." O'Leary looked around. "Where is she?"

Reid checked her watch. She wasn't sure how long she'd been down, but it couldn't have been more than a few minutes. What was taking London so long?

❖

London wished she'd worn her sneakers. They would've had better traction on the tile floor. She flashed back to the day she met Reid, when Reid had glared at her square-heeled boots and asked if she could run in them.

London was wearing the same boots today. Was it possible that Reid had experienced some sort of premonition a year ago? Probably not. It was more likely that Reid had just been trying to give her the slip that fateful day—something Reid had actually fessed up to hours later. Thankfully, their relationship had changed quite a bit since then.

Sweetheart, if this goes sideways, I hope you can forgive me. She took a breath and lunged forward, intending to catch the killer off-guard as he was trying to stand.

But she'd underestimated his strength and agility. She felt the needle in her neck and saw the syringe empty out of the corner of her eye. The effects were almost instantaneous. She lost all muscle control and fell to the floor, still fully conscious. He'd obviously injected her with rocuronium—the neuromuscular blocking agent used to prevent movement during surgery. He was staying true to his MO.

As she lay on the tile, she caught sight of the industrial laundry cart parked just outside the stall door. She knew then how he was planning to transport her body out of the bathroom—exactly the same way he'd brought Nicole's body into the bathroom without being detected.

She watched as he hoisted Nicole onto the toilet like a rag doll. Nicole was disoriented, but she stayed in place when he set her down.

Looked like he was holding up his end of the bargain, after all. At least, Nicole would make it out of this alive. With any luck, the three other women would, too. She couldn't say the same for herself.

London realized, too late, that she'd made too many mistakes. She'd let her guard down, believing that she was somehow immune to becoming a serial killer's next victim. Even if she had taken Russo's warning seriously, which she admittedly hadn't, she never could've anticipated that he would act so quickly. Reid would blame herself for this. She knew Reid well—so well that she doubted there was a soul on earth who knew Reid better.

Reid would never forgive herself. She'd never recover from losing London in such a despicable way. Knowing Reid would never recover emotionally scared her more than anything the killer could ever do to her.

The mistakes she'd made now felt larger than life. She watched as they passed before her like a parade of floats. They were hard to miss. How could she have made such obvious errors in judgment? The janitor had waved her into a wheelchair-accessible stall, for God's sake. She should've known better. Just because the janitor gave her permission to use the stall didn't mean she should have. In hindsight, it had boiled down to a test of integrity. And she'd failed, plain and simple.

His short stature and overtly muscular build fell within the parameters of the profile they'd constructed, which should've been her first red flag. Seeing the woman on the toilet, dazed and confused, wearing a nightgown and slippers was clue number two. In hindsight, she never should've stepped inside that stall. She hadn't noticed the woman until she was inside, but she should've been more aware of her surroundings. Seeing a woman already inside a stall that the janitor had just exited should have made her instantly suspicious.

From the moment she'd learned that Russo had assessed her, determined she was the killer's type, and could potentially become his next target, she should've been on high alert. She thought back to the roundtable discussion with the team, remembering Reid's volatile reaction to the news that she shared similar characteristics with the killer's victims. At the time, she believed Reid was overreacting. But she suddenly found herself wondering if Reid had picked up on something psychically that she hadn't shared with the team. It wasn't out of the realm of possibility.

Over the course of the last year, she'd witnessed countless exchanges that made her wonder if Reid possessed psychic gifts—gifts that extended beyond the ability to communicate with spirits. She hadn't wanted to pry. Instead of digging her heels in the sand, she should've trusted Reid, asked questions, and followed her lead on this one. Since assisting the FBI with this case posed a threat to their life together, she should've given Reid the respect of discussing it more in depth. Instead, she'd pushed forward without her. After all was said and done, she'd left Reid behind. Reid never would have done that to her had their roles been reversed. She would've handled things much differently.

Reid also never would have let a dangerous psychopath sneak up on her in close quarters. It seemed Reid was always on high alert. She never let her guard down. A side effect of her childhood, perhaps. Reid was always waiting for the other shoe to drop, which, incidentally, had made her a great cop. More to the point, Reid would've come out on top in a physical confrontation with the killer, no matter the circumstance.

Reid was amazing. London was grateful for the time they'd had together. She prayed that Reid would find a way to let someone else in when she was gone. The thought of Reid returning to a life of solitude made her want to cry.

In that moment, London took accountability for the mistakes she'd likely never be able to correct or have the opportunity to learn from—mistakes that would ultimately cost her life. In the big picture, her suffering would be brief, but Reid's would be lifelong. London said a silent prayer for mercy as the killer lifted her body, set her inside the laundry cart, and covered her with a blanket.

❖

Boyle glanced at the entrance to the women's restroom and locked gazes with Reid. "Go," he said with an urgency that made the hair on the back of her neck stand up.

She hurried to the bathroom, bypassing Agent J altogether—his feet were still spread, arms still folded, sunglasses in place. She had half a mind to rip the sunglasses off his face as she sprinted past him. Was London's bodyguard even awake?

"London, you here?" The bathroom was split down the middle with stalls and sinks on the right and the left. There were seven stalls per side, and each one was occupied. Both sides were bustling with activity—women exiting and entering stalls, washing their hands at stainless steel sinks, drying their hands with wall-mounted dryers. She'd always hated automatic dryers because they were too damn loud, but she loathed them in that moment because they were interfering with her ability to focus. She chose the right-side stalls first and called out, "London?" She quickly scanned the shoes inside each stall as she called out again, louder this time. "London, are you in here?" But there was no response.

She jogged back to the center of the bathroom and paced the length of the left-side stalls. "London, answer me if you're in here." Once again, she scanned the footwear in each stall as she moved, but none of the shoes in any of the stalls matched London's square-heeled leather boots. She was nowhere to be found.

Maybe, just maybe, they'd passed one another as London was exiting and she was entering. If London had used the bathrooms on the left, and Reid was entering on the right, such a thing was definitely possible. She double-checked the shoes in the last stall, looked back over her shoulder, and held her breath, half expecting London to peek around the corner. She'd roll her eyes and shake her head in disapproval because Reid was overreacting.

Her gaze lingered on the entrance. No London. Her blood ran cold.

Boyle rounded the corner with Agent J at his heels. He held out his BPD badge and locked gazes with Reid.

She shook her head. "Gone," she said, shouting to be heard above the noise. Her heart pounded inside her chest as she jogged over to join him.

"Detective Gold isn't in here?" Agent J asked, clearly a step behind.

"Fuck," Boyle said, running a hand through his hair. "You're sure?"

"Not here," she replied with difficulty. The lump in her throat made it difficult to breath. *Keep your head in the game, Sylver.* If there was any hope of finding London, she needed to embrace the all-consuming, laser-beam focus that had always come so naturally to her.

She googled *Reagan National terminal map* to bring up the airport schematics. Boyle peered over her shoulder. They both studied the layout as Agent J conducted his own sweep of the bathroom. "How long was I down?" she asked, referring to her episode outside the restroom entrance.

Boyle shrugged. "Maybe"—his gaze darted around as he scanned passersby suspiciously—"five minutes."

"He can't have gotten far, not with London's body. Shut down all terminal exits before he gets through. I'll call Russo, get some agents to assist in the search."

"Copy that," Boyle shouted, already sprinting down the terminal, badge in hand.

Reid scanned the crowd as she slipped her phone from her pocket, dialed Russo's cell, and briefed her on London's disappearance. Russo wasted no time on emotions. She didn't offer her condolences, an apology, or—worse—false assurances that they'd find London. She also didn't patronize her with questions about how she was coping or threaten to remove her from the scene. Reid was grateful for this small favor, sensing that Russo understood her mental state all too well.

Reid's thoughts raced. She knew the next few minutes were critical. If there was any hope of finding London before the killer made his getaway, they couldn't waste a second. No missteps were allowed. They had to do *everything* right.

"I'm initiating a lockdown at Reagan National as we speak," Russo said in her no-nonsense, take-charge tone. "No one comes or goes." Fingers on a keyboard sounded in the background. "I'm dispatching as many agents as I can to assist you in a search." She paused and sounded momentarily distracted. "I'm also deploying the National Guard. They'll be there momentarily to reinforce the airport perimeter."

"One more thing," Reid added, glancing up at the security camera that faced the entrance to the women's restroom. She requested that someone review the video immediately. They ended the call and agreed to update one another if anything changed.

Reid reluctantly admitted to herself that she couldn't be the one to take the lead on this. She desperately wanted to take point—there was nothing she wouldn't do for London—but she was also experienced enough to know that her own fear and panic could hinder the search. She simply couldn't afford to take that risk. She watched as Boyle rounded the corner at a run. She needed Boyle by her side, now more than ever before.

"All terminal exits are closed," he wheezed. "No one's permitted entry or exit, including airport personnel."

She apprised him of her call with Russo. "I need you to take point," she said resolutely. Tears blurred her vision. It took everything inside her to make the request. "I'll follow your lead."

She and Boyle locked gazes. In that moment, she knew what she was asking of him. From the look on his face, so did he. She was putting everything on his shoulders. If they lost London for good—if her body turned up later, beaten, tortured, and mutilated—he'd be the one to carry it around for the rest of his life.

Boyle nodded. "I'll take point." He extended his hand. "All for one."

"And one for all." She set her hand over his.

CHAPTER THIRTEEN

Agent J looked on from afar as Reid and Boyle shared the news of London's abduction with Marino, Boggs, Garcia, and O'Leary. She watched as their faces tightened with anger and panic. Then, like she'd seen them do a thousand times, they cinched the reins on their emotions to stay in the moment and focus on what needed to be done. Everyone, except Garcia.

Garcia held on to his pissed-off cop face a little longer than the others. He stepped over to Agent J, balled his fist, and clocked him, hard, across the jaw. Agent J's sunglasses sailed through the air, landed on the floor a few feet away, and were subsequently run over by a passing motorized cart.

London's bodyguard rubbed his jaw but didn't retaliate. He obviously knew better. He threw a glance at his crushed sunglasses.

"Trust me." Garcia slapped him roughly on the shoulder. "You'll see better without the shades, man."

Reid knew they were all on edge. Everything they'd seen—the mutilated bodies and autopsy reports, the bloody aftermath of a serial killer's singularly depraved psyche—was still fresh in their minds, like a deep wound that hadn't yet scabbed over. God help this bastard if someone from Reid's team found him. He'd be the one begging for mercy.

Garcia returned to their huddle, his face now calm and in control. "All terminal exits are pinched off?" he confirmed, massaging his knuckles.

Boyle nodded.

"What about those?" Garcia gestured at the airport gates behind him.

O'Leary was quick to point out the obvious. "They all lead to the tarmac."

"If you check your bag at the gate, someone walks it across the bridge and carries it down a flight of stairs to the cargo hold." Garcia glanced around at each of them. "If I needed to escape from an airport with a body, I'd stuff the body inside a suitcase, pose as an employee, and flee from an exit no one expected me to use."

"And go where?" Marino asked. "The tarmac is sealed off from the surrounding terrain with a barbed wire fence."

"Inconvenient." Garcia shrugged. "But not impossible to penetrate."

"Gold's thin," O'Leary added. "Assuming she's unconscious or unable to move, she might fit inside a large suitcase or trunk. It's definitely possible."

Reid cringed at the thought of anyone touching London's body. If the killer stayed true to his MO, he'd found a way to inject her with the paralytic drug. Maybe he'd ambushed her in the bathroom with a prefilled syringe. Imagining that London was conscious but unable to fight back as he stuffed her inside a suitcase was enough to make Reid lose her mind.

"Hang on." Boggs looked to O'Leary. "Can't we zero in on her location with that microchip you showed us?"

O'Leary reached inside his pocket and withdrew the small vial that held the microchip in question. "Haven't put it in yet," he said, holding it up for everyone to see.

"Shit." Marino ran a hand over his face. "We have no idea what this bastard looks like. No idea who the fuck we're looking for."

"Short, muscular, handsome," Reid reminded them. "And he has a tattoo of—" She cut herself off like a bartender with a patron after too many shots.

"A tattoo of what?" Garcia asked.

"I'm not sure." She shrugged.

"You saw him?" Boggs asked.

She shook her head, unable to come up with a way to climb out of the hole she'd just dug. Her mind was too preoccupied with London to think straight. "It's just a hunch."

"We don't care how you got it," Marino said. "Just tell us what to look for."

"He has a tattoo of…this." She unlocked her phone and brought up an image of a green serpent wrapped around a golden staff—the Rod of Asclepius. "Big and hard to miss. Left forearm."

They glanced at the image and looked around at one another, quiet.

Marino bumped shoulders with O'Leary. "O'Leary was right. Looks like Micro Dick's a doctor."

Boggs frowned. "Can we put out an APB for a short, muscular, handsome guy with a tattoo?"

"We can't rule anyone out," Boyle cautioned. "He could be wearing a disguise."

"Okay." O'Leary thought for a moment and said, "Which leaves us with putting out an APB for a man who's wheeling a suitcase through the airport."

"Or transporting luggage on the tarmac," Garcia added. "That's what I'd do. Dress up as an employee and just drive right on out of here with my prey."

They all gawked at the travelers coming and going around them. At least half were men, and nearly everyone in sight was wheeling a suitcase large enough to transport a human body.

Reid's watch vibrated, alerting her to an incoming call. Russo. She accepted the call on her watch so everyone could listen. "Sylver," she answered.

"The National Guard's ETA is twenty-six minutes. We've grounded all outbound aircraft, diverted all incoming aircraft, and deployed several of our drones to keep eyes on the perimeter. We also reviewed video surveillance of the restrooms during the time in question. I'm sending you all relevant images now."

Reid watched as a series of images came through via text. She withdrew her phone and quickly scrolled through the images as her team gathered around.

"He wore a janitor's suit. Wheeled her out in that," Boggs said, pointing to an image of a laundry cart.

"And he's short, muscular, and handsome, just like we thought." O'Leary studied the screen.

"My guy in forensics puts him at five foot four," Russo said, confirming their roundtable speculations. "Keep scrolling. You'll see he left the women's restroom and headed over to the men's. Came out a few minutes later in a baggage handler's uniform with a surfboard travel case."

Reid brought up an image of the killer dressed in blue coveralls with a yellow reflective vest. She zoomed in on the travel case. It was at least six feet tall and dark gray in color with a hard outer shell. No doubt about it, there was ample room inside for a human body.

"Son of a bitch," Boyle whispered, his rage palpable. "He put her inside the damn surfboard case."

"Right under our noses," O'Leary added. "We were in that bathroom." He glanced guiltily at Garcia, Marino, and Boggs.

"Fucker's got balls," Marino spat.

"We sure he's not an employee?" Garcia kept his composure. "He seems comfortable here, like he knows his way around."

"I thought the same," Russo said. "My people are checking on that now."

Reid found herself pondering Garcia's comment. His choice of the word *comfortable* resonated with her. She flashed back to something in the women's bathroom—something that hadn't computed until just now. She prayed she was wrong.

She transferred Russo from her watch to her phone, muted the call, and then handed it off to Boyle. "Keep her talking. Devise a strategy for the search. I think he might've left Nicole's body in the bathroom." She turned to Garcia. "You're with me."

She and Garcia jogged to the women's restroom. He followed her inside as she made a beeline to the last stall on the right. If memory served her right, a woman inside this stall was wearing slippers. It hadn't stood out to her during the search because she was looking for London's black leather boots.

She and Garcia stepped back and peered underneath the stall door. "There," she whispered, pointing. The killer was likely far from here by now, but she wasn't willing to take any chances. He could've rigged the stall door with an explosive device or something equally as destructive. Such a thing was outside the killer's MO, but leaving a body behind wasn't exactly something he'd done before, either. He was evolving. Or, worse, devolving.

A middle-aged Hispanic woman exited the stall beside them and glared at Garcia disapprovingly. He slipped his gold shield from his pocket, clipped it to the collar of his shirt, and held a finger over his lips to keep the woman quiet.

Reid motioned for Garcia to slip inside the stall. She watched as he climbed atop the toilet and peered over the divider.

He shouted to be heard above the sounds of running water, flushing toilets, and hand dryers. "All clear." He hopped down from the toilet and returned to her side with a look of surprised bewilderment. "Nicole," he said simply. "Alive."

"Clear the bathroom. Get everyone out." This was a crime scene now, and they had to treat it as such. She didn't envy the forensics team responsible for gathering evidence in a public restroom.

Garcia promptly herded travelers from the stalls and sinks on both sides of the restroom as she nudged the stall door open with the toe of her sneaker. The woman on the toilet looked up at her. She was dressed in a long, pale blue Victorian-style nightgown with white ruffles along the neckline and cuffs. A big pink bow sat square in the middle of her chest, lending her the appearance of a gift. Both of her hands were wrapped in bandages. The bandage on her left hand was saturated with blood.

"These hurt." Nicole held up her hands and started to cry. "Where am I?"

Reid reached for her phone, momentarily forgetting that she'd left it with Boyle. Garcia would know to call for an ambulance. "You're at Reagan National Airport in Virginia." She squatted down in front of Nicole to examine her more closely. "What's your name?"

"Nicole," she said between tears. "Nicole Russo." Her speech was slurred. Both of her pupils were dilated. She was obviously still heavily medicated. Nicole returned her bandaged hands to her lap and leaned her head back against the wall. "Please, don't leave me."

"You're safe now." She was chomping at the bit to resume the search for London, but she wouldn't leave Nicole's side—not until Russo or someone from her team came to relieve her.

Boyle stepped inside the stall. He was still holding Reid's phone. "I have eyes on her now," he announced. "She's alive, Deputy Director."

She and Boyle listened to the Deputy Director's tears on speakerphone. "I'm on my way," she said on the heels of a sob. "Boyle, don't let her out of your sight. Keep me on the line until I get there."

Reid and Boyle locked gazes. She could see he was conflicted. He obviously wanted to resume the search for London as much as she did, but they also had a responsibility to keep Nicole safe. Right now, neither of them trusted anyone but the members of their own team to do that. She nodded. "You stay here. I'll take point."

Boyle tapped *mute*. "That wasn't our agreement."

"Agreements change. I'm good." She reached over and unmuted the call as Garcia reappeared at the stall door.

"Paramedics are on their way. I'll stay," he said, as if reading their minds.

"What's the extent of her injuries?" Russo asked, the worry in her voice barely disguised.

Boyle passed Reid's phone to Garcia, thereby honoring the Deputy Director's request to remain on the line. Garcia slipped his phone from his pocket, disabled the passcode, and handed it to Reid. "Go. Find her."

Garcia began briefing Russo on Nicole's injuries as Reid followed Boyle out of the bathroom to rejoin the rest of their team.

❖

London listened as the killer wheeled her inside the laundry cart into the adjacent men's bathroom. She couldn't see anything, but the sounds of the men's bathroom were distinct. The killer had taped her eyelids shut, so she couldn't open her eyes even if she wanted. She suspected that she wouldn't have been able to open or close her eyes on her own, not with the paralytic drug in full effect. If he hadn't taped them, they likely would've remained open and eventually ceased to produce the tears necessary for lubrication. But she didn't believe for one second that he was doing that for her. He wanted her to see everything he was going to do to her.

No matter how hard she tried, she couldn't move a single muscle. She could still feel everything, but any movement—no matter how small—was simply beyond her control at the moment. She waited for her lungs to seize up and wondered what it would feel like to suffocate. If she was going to die at the hands of a serial killer, suffocating would be the least of all evils. Suffocating would be merciful. As the minutes ticked by, it became obvious that her lungs were working just fine. But breathing required muscles in the diaphragm, ribcage, and abdomen. The killer had obviously perfected his paralytic drug cocktail so as to prevent the incidence of suffocation. London suddenly found herself longing for suffocation, willing it to happen, to no avail. Had the women before her wished for the same?

She realized then that she was locked in a prison inside her own body, and there was nothing—absolutely nothing—she could do to change it. As blinding panic set in, she willed herself to stay calm and focus on what she could control: her thoughts.

When push came to shove, she'd always been able to hold on to faith. Faith in the greater good. Faith in God. Faith that her prayers would be answered. Faith that a difficult situation would work out for the best in the end.

The women before her had fought and lost. But it was clear from their autopsy reports that all eighteen victims fought back hard—as hard as they could in their medicated states, which, she could now say from firsthand experience, was no easy feat. All eighteen women had wanted desperately to live and would've done or given anything to survive. She was sure of it. Throwing in the towel before the fight had even begun was like a slap in the face. There was no bigger way to dishonor them.

London couldn't give up. Not now. Not ever. As much for her sake as for Reid's. If she abandoned the idea of being rescued, she'd be relinquishing her trust in Reid. If anyone could find her, it was Reid Sylver. She vowed to herself, there in the laundry cart, locked inside her own body with her eyelids taped shut, that she would maintain faith in Reid until her dying breath.

Trusting Reid wasn't anything new. If she was honest with herself, she'd intuitively trusted Reid years before they'd exchanged words— so long ago, in fact, that Reid didn't even recall the encounter.

London had just nine months under her belt as a cop when a domestic violence call came in over her two-way radio. She responded with lights and sirens through the streets of inner-city Boston in rush-hour traffic. By the time she arrived on scene, it was too late. A mother and her teenage son lay on the kitchen floor, each dead from a single gunshot wound to the head. To her rookie eye, it had looked like an open-and-shut case. It had all the markings of a murder-suicide, right down to the note of apology the teen had left for his father. She taped off the scene, called it in, and sat with the distraught father as they waited for forensics.

But Detective Reid Sylver beat forensics to the scene. London remembered watching as Reid brazenly disregarded protocol and ducked under the crime-scene tape only to return minutes later claiming that it wasn't a murder-suicide at all. She arrested the teen's father on the spot and demanded a forensic analysis of the son's handwritten note, insisting it was forged.

London was convinced Reid had it all wrong. She'd sat in the hallway with an inconsolable man—a man who'd just lost his wife and son. There was no way he was callous enough to take their lives and blame it on his own flesh and blood. She would've bet all her worldly possessions on his innocence.

She had followed that case closely, waiting for the day when Reid would be forced to issue an apology to the distraught father on behalf of the department. But such an occasion never arose. Reid presented irrefutable proof in the form of video—the father had climbed down the fire escape after the murders and re-entered the building as if nothing had ever happened. He admitted his guilt and accepted a plea deal soon thereafter.

Looking back, of course, she now surmised that the wife and son had communicated with Reid as spirits and told her who was responsible for their murders. She found Reid just as mesmerizing and mysterious now as she did then. Maybe more so.

That's when it dawned on her. London obviously wasn't a spirit—at least, not yet—but what if she could communicate with Reid telepathically? In ordinary circumstances, the very idea seemed ludicrous. But these weren't ordinary circumstances. And Reid was anything but ordinary.

CHAPTER FOURTEEN

Reid looked on as Boyle pulled up the airport schematics on his phone. He, Marino, O'Leary, and Boggs tried to think like a killer trying to escape from an airport with a body.

"We need to think outside the box," Boyle said. "He'll go somewhere we wouldn't expect."

"Maybe he tunneled underground?" O'Leary proposed.

Boggs shook his head. "Not that far outside the box, bro."

Before today, Reid had never been able to imagine what having a nervous breakdown would feel like—not even when Mug was kidnapped last year. At the time, she'd been consumed with worry. Mug was her best friend, her partner, her rock. He was still—and always would be—all those things, but London was the love of her life. Losing her was simply unfathomable. Reid could hardly breathe. She decided that she couldn't—wouldn't—go on if London didn't make it. She had no idea how Russo had kept it together as well as she had. She felt a sudden kinship with Russo, a new respect, followed quickly by a rage that surprised her. The FBI had brought a violent, deranged sociopath into their lives without properly warning them. Russo predicted that he'd notice London—she'd even gone so far as to assign a bodyguard—but why hadn't she alerted them that an abduction attempt was probable, maybe even imminent? Russo should have been more forthcoming. The FBI had been chasing this bastard for years. Why didn't they have a better grasp on his profile? There were only two possible reasons: the FBI sucked at their jobs, or the killer was just that good.

Reid wanted to believe it was the former. She'd met her fair share of incompetent federal agents over the course of her career. Agent J was just the latest to join the list. But it was foolish to think that *everyone* in the FBI was incompetent. Even with her fiercely competitive nature as a proud member of the Boston Police Department, she had to admit that the FBI's Behavioral Analysis Unit was top-notch. Historically, the BAU left no stone unturned. They utilized a state-of-the-art forensics lab and all the best behavioral analytics software. Which left her with the most likely explanation as to why the killer hadn't yet been captured. He was smart. Maybe smarter than everyone who was trying to find him.

Reid realized then that she wasn't upset with the FBI at all. She was angry with herself for letting London down. She hadn't protected her, hadn't been there when London needed her most. Shit, she couldn't have been more than fifty feet away when the killer abducted her.

Reid flashed back to the moment when she'd dropped to the airport floor. She was in the killer's mind, reliving one of his memories. *That's* when he abducted London. It had to be. Had she inadvertently crossed paths with his thoughts when he was physically close? What other explanation was there?

His adrenaline could've been kicking in at the exact moment Reid had dropped to the floor. She and the killer had been mere feet apart as he was preparing to abduct a member of the team assigned to hunt him down. It was a brazen move—one that only an extreme risk-taker or a supremely confident person would make. She still wasn't sure which category he fell into. Maybe a little of both.

"What do you think, Sylver?" Boyle interrupted her train of thought.

She looked up and realized all eyes were upon her.

"Hang on, Lieutenant. Give her a sec," Marino said.

Boggs nodded. "She's doing…that thing she does, when she comes back knowing stuff the rest of us don't."

They watched her and waited in silence.

The BAU hadn't yet identified how the victims were connected. Instinct told Reid this was the killer's hunting ground. He obviously knew his way around Reagan National. If he was smart, which he obviously was, he wouldn't limit his hunting ground to just one airport. He would hunt at all the airports. All the airports close in proximity to his lair.

His lair would be centrally located, like a spider in the center of its web.

She wasted no time in dialing Russo's cell. "Airports," she said.

"Airports are his hunting ground. Tell the BAU to plug that into his profile. Cross-check local airports with each victim's travel history—"

"And download video surveillance of each victim on the day of travel," Russo finished. "I'm with you."

"If the BAU looks hard enough, I'd bet my pension you'll find him stalking his victims in those videos."

Boyle spoke up beside her. "He preselected them, waited, and then abducted them much later so we wouldn't connect the dots."

Reid suddenly knew what they needed to do. "These are his stomping grounds. He's comfortable here. More comfortable and familiar than we'll ever be." She gestured to the airport schematics on Boyle's phone. "We'll never catch him that way."

"What other way is there?" Boyle asked.

"We talk to people—people who know this airport as well as he does." She thought for a moment. "The four of you need to split up. Talk to security officers and baggage handlers."

"And ask them what, exactly?" Marino asked, looking just as bewildered as Boyle, O'Leary, and Boggs.

It was a good question. She shrugged. "Ask them how they'd get out of the airport if they were trying to evade security. Tell them there's a thousand-dollar reward for whoever comes up with the most creative escape."

Boyle narrowed his eyes. "And where will you be?"

"I'll be on standby, waiting for each of you to report back. Assuming you find someone who comes up with a viable escape plan—I'd advise you to pick someone who's been here awhile—relay it to me so I can try to cut him off at the pass. With any luck, he's still on the grounds here." She also had to accept the possibility that he wasn't. The thought made her feel sick to her stomach.

"Talk to Sylver with these," O'Leary said, pointing to his watch. "Just turn on the walkie-talkie feature."

Everyone hurriedly unlocked their phones and switched the walkie-talkie toggle to *on*. Then, without another word, Marino, O'Leary, and Boggs trotted off in different directions. Boyle hung behind, piercing her with a steady gaze. "What happened outside the bathroom when you collapsed?"

"I already told you. It was—"

"An equilibrium thing, I know." He crossed his arms. "A lie."

"Boyle, we don't have time for this." She started to feel a rising panic and the need to start looking somewhere—anywhere—for London. The clock was ticking. Time was running out.

"We do if it'll help us find her."

"I'm not sure it'll help." She met his gaze and sighed. "I'm not sure of anything right now."

"Then spill it," he said, his expression resolute. "We'll tease it out together."

Instinct had always told her to keep things close to the vest. The biggest mistake she could make was revealing her soft underbelly, which was exactly what Boyle was asking her to do right now. Shutting people out had served her well throughout her personal and professional lives. Protecting what made her vulnerable had let her feel normal— as normal as someone like her could feel. She did her job, kept her head down, and asked for nothing. She'd been ten when she decided to become a cop. All she'd ever wanted to do was solve crimes, find killers, and get justice for the victims who were no longer here to fight for it themselves.

Keeping her ability under wraps had served a purpose. It had allowed her to build a career, first as a cop, and then as a homicide detective. She gave twenty years of her life to the Boston Police Department and had retired with a clean record and no regrets. But, underneath it all, she'd always felt afraid. Afraid of being revealed for who she thought she was—a fraud. A homicide detective who solved all her cases by cheating because she could talk to the dead.

Looking back, she realized she'd gone to work feeling like every day could be her last. Someone was bound to uncover her secret and reveal her for the fraud she was. Not only did she make it through a twenty-year career, but she did it with flying colors. When the killer she was hunting did the very thing she feared most—he shared her secret with the *entire* Boston PD in an email—it turned out to be a blessing in disguise. Her colleagues readily accepted her and her gift. The sky didn't fall. The world didn't end. Everything had worked out for the best.

Maybe it was time to dip a toe in the water with Boyle. Shutting him out to keep the full extent of her gifts a secret was a luxury she couldn't afford right now. London's life was on the line. Reid realized it was time for her to put everything on the line, too. It was time to come clean.

"I saw the killer. I was inside his mind. At first, I thought I was seeing something that was taking place in the present, but it couldn't have been because the killer was abducting London in the bathroom at the same moment I was in his head. Maybe it was a memory? His memory? Could've been something he was thinking about recently. I don't know." She shrugged. "What I do know is that our thoughts crossed."

"Your thoughts crossed," Boyle repeated, looking thoroughly mystified. "Explain that to me."

She was feeling suddenly self-conscious. "I can't."

"Try," he insisted.

She shut her eyes as she tried to recall the process of being inside someone else's mind. Maybe, if she slowed it down, she could untangle how it actually happened. "Thoughts are like trains," she explained, opening her eyes. "They travel in different directions at different speeds."

He nodded. "Okay."

She could see he was doing his best to follow along. "When I'm talking to someone—take you, for instance—all I have to do is slow my train down, wait for yours to pass, and then reach out to grab it."

"I understood that," he said, looking rather pleased with himself. "That actually makes sense to me."

She waited. "Aren't you going to ask me to prove it?"

"Of course not." He frowned. "I trust what you're telling me is the truth."

Reid stared at him. Did he really expect her to believe that? "For Christ's sake, Boyle, I just told you that I can read people's thoughts."

"And?"

It occurred to her then that Boyle might be handling her with kid gloves. Never in the history of their twenty-plus-year relationship had he ever treated her like she was fragile—not even after Cap took his own life and left her to find his body. "Don't you have questions?" she asked, irritated.

"No. Why would I? I might have questions if I was some average joe off the street. But I've been watching you do this for a while, Sylver. It's like coming into work with purple hair for a year and then asking me if I think it's weird." He shrugged. "Guess I'm just used to it now. Hard to remember what you looked like with regular hair."

She shook her head and set her hands on her hips. "If you're handling me with kid gloves right now, so help me God, Boyle, I'll kick your ass from here to—"

"I swear, I'm not." He set his hand over his heart and met her gaze with a sincerity that said he was having a Hallmark moment. "I swear on my custody rights to Mug."

Boyle loved Mug as much as she did. He'd never risk losing their time together.

"So, what's the plan?" he asked, pushing forward. "You obviously have one, or you wouldn't be telling me all this."

"You *made* me share that."

"It was for your own good. Maybe it'll help us find Gold."

Reid was wondering the same. "If my thoughts and the killer's thoughts crossed once..."

"Maybe they'll cross again," Boyle finished. "I see where you're going. You think it's a distance thing?"

She nodded. "I don't know how this works, exactly." In some ways, it felt like a weapon from an alien race had just dropped from the sky into her lap. She had no earthly idea how to use it. "If I get close enough to the killer, maybe our thoughts will cross again."

"Thereby revealing his location." Boyle shrugged. "It's worth a shot." He stared at her. "What now?"

"We need to wait until the guys talk to the airport staff and report back. You and I can rank the escape routes they bring to the table and then tick them off, one by one."

"How?" he asked, looking suddenly lost.

Reid hesitated. What she was about to say sounded ridiculous, even to her. Especially to her. "I'll start heading in that general direction and see if I can pick up on his thoughts. If his thoughts or memories come in, I think it would mean—"

"He's close," Boyle finished. "Interesting. It's like hot or cold."

She squinted at him.

"Didn't you play the hot or cold game as a kid?"

Reid had zero recollection of playing anything with her grandmother, aside from running away as fast as her legs would carry her to avoid a good beating. But she was pretty sure that didn't count as a game per se.

"My daughter and I play it all the time," Boyle went on. "I hide one of her toys, and she walks around the house, trying to find it. When she's far away, she's cold. When she gets a little closer, she's warm. When she's almost right on top of it, she's hot." He shook his head. "No idea how you got through life without knowing how to play hot or cold."

Reid couldn't help but wonder if her abilities—or whatever

psychic gifts she might possess—worked in the same way. She never could've imagined in her wildest dreams that she'd even consider the possibility of exploring anything psychic. And if she had imagined it, she never would've guessed in a million years that Boyle, of all people, would be the one to hold her hand. London, maybe. But Boyle? No way. She reminded herself that these were extenuating circumstances.

"I have an idea," Boyle said enthusiastically. "You've heard of water dowsing, right?"

She flashed back to high school history. "Someone uses a stick to find water."

"Someone uses a stick to find water *underground*."

"You think a stick will help me find the killer?"

"Historically, water dowsers searched for water because it was important to them. Their lives depended on it."

She was still unsure where he was going. Was he telling her to find a stick, or what?

"All I'm saying is, it might be a better idea to look for what's important to you. Forget about finding *him*. Find *her*."

Goose bumps broke out all over her body. Boyle was right. There was a part of her that didn't want to be inside the killer's head ever again. The very thought made her want to gag. What if her psychic abilities wouldn't manifest because, deep down, she didn't want them to? Granted, she knew nothing about how any of this worked. But it would stand to reason that she'd be better at finding someone she really wanted to find as opposed to someone she didn't. And who knew London better than her?

Most days, she knew what London was going to say long before the words fell from her lips, not because she was psychic but because she *knew* her. She was well-acquainted with the way London thought, the way she talked, the way she moved, ate, drank, slept. Familiarizing herself with her favorite person and paying attention to the often-overlooked details had become second nature. Like the way London squeezed the toothpaste from the bottom of the tube to keep it tidy, or the way she made too much coffee every morning because she liked to sip the surplus before she set the lid over the top. If there was such a thing as a psychic bloodhound, who better to search for London than her?

CHAPTER FIFTEEN

Reid shot a glance at Boyle's vibrating pocket. He withdrew his phone, engaged the speakerphone, and answered, "Boyle."

Russo's voice sounded over the speaker. "Our drones found what appears to be a precut hole in the wire fence along the southern perimeter. I dispatched two agents to investigate. There's abandoned luggage in the same location." She paused, and Reid intuited something was wrong. "It appears to be the same surfboard case that the suspect was seen wheeling out of the restroom."

Reid's heart picked up speed. "Is London inside the damn case or not?"

"The case appears to have been set afire. Forensics is on their way now."

She felt her patience wearing thin. "Tell me someone opened the damn case."

"I've instructed them not to touch it until forensics arrives," Russo said with conviction. "The fire burned from inside the case. The body within is visible through small holes in the outer casing. There are no discernible signs of life."

London always wore a simple gold chain with a cross pendant that her parents gifted her for her first communion. "Does the body have any identifying markers?" she pressed, trying with all her might to keep her anger in check. How could the feds not open the damn case?

Russo ignored the question. "I'll have more information soon. I'm sorry, Detective Sylver. Truly."

Sorry didn't cut it. Now that Russo had her wife back, her head clearly wasn't in the game anymore. Reid had half a mind to demand that someone else oversee the search. But she might as well bang her head against the wall because the feds were stubborn as hell. They had their own way of doing things, and it usually made little sense to her.

"We believe the suspect is no longer on airport grounds. It appears he escaped through the hole in the fence."

"On foot?" Boyle asked, frowning.

"A black Ford Explorer was parked a hundred yards away on the other side of the fence. Said vehicle was reported stolen three months ago. We're attempting to locate the owner."

Boyle cleared his throat. Reid could tell from the look on his face that none of this was sitting right with him, either. "So your working theory right now is that he murdered Detective Gold, left her body in a surfboard case, and escaped from the airport through a hole in the fence and a conveniently parked getaway car?"

"Unfortunately, yes," Russo confirmed.

"Don't you find that contradictory to his MO?" Boyle asked, frowning. "Why didn't he just take Gold with him? I mean, he ran the whole race. He was close to the finish line. All he had to do was step across it, literally, to reach his getaway car on the other side."

"There could be any number of reasons for the sudden change in MO. Perhaps the fire was accidental. Or maybe he realized Gold wasn't his type, after all, and he chose to get rid of the body to save himself the trouble of transporting it." Russo sighed. "We may never know."

She met Boyle's gaze as they listened to Russo answer a medical question about her wife on the other end of the line.

"I'm in the ambulance with Nicole," Russo went on. "We're pulling up to the hospital now. I'll reach out as soon as I receive an update on the search. We're expanding our search, tracking the vehicle he used, and actively attempting to identify him. It's only a matter of time before we figure out who he is."

"That's it, then?" Reid asked, incredulous. "You just chew us up and spit us out?" If she didn't know any better, she'd think the deputy director had intentionally used London as bait to lure the killer out of his hidey-hole.

"Your affiliation with us doesn't have to end here. We could obviously still use your help. But I also recognize this is a huge blow. Your team has suffered a tremendous loss. I'm simply trying to be respectful of that fact."

Reid felt her face flush with red-hot anger. It wasn't a fact. At least, not yet. Until a certified medical examiner confirmed that the body inside the case was London's, she would keep working under the assumption that London was still alive. "What about the National Guard?" she asked, but she feared she already knew the answer.

"What about them?" Russo asked absently, her mind obviously preoccupied with her wife.

"Are they coming to secure the perimeter?" she asked through clenched teeth.

"I've canceled the request for deployment. Securing the perimeter after the suspect has fled would be counterintuitive."

"And your agents?"

"Are combing through security videos from every local airport with the best facial recognition software available. They're searching for him as we speak."

"They're searching for him," she repeated, "just not here at the airport."

"No. *Obviously* not." Russo was beginning to lose the calm detachment in her voice.

Reid pressed on. "What if he's still here?"

"That's a big *if*, Detective Sylver. Why on earth would he fake his own escape?"

She didn't have an answer for that just yet. Her mind was still trying to fit the puzzle pieces together. From the look on Boyle's face, so was he.

Russo suggested that they check in to their hotel, get some rest, and reconvene bright and early tomorrow morning at the office.

Boyle ended the call and met her gaze. "Burning her body to get rid of it makes no sense, even if he was cornered, which he wasn't. He had a clear path of escape. If he decided not to keep her, wouldn't he have just let her go, like the others?"

Reid nodded. "An accidental fire seems even less likely. Our guy's too careful for that."

"If something doesn't add up right—"

"Then plug in different numbers." She checked her watch. It was closing in on nine o'clock. She'd wasted too much time standing and waiting. In fact, she'd hardly moved from the restroom where London was taken.

It dawned on her that she was scared to leave the spot from which London disappeared, which was completely irrational. London wasn't a helpless child. She could find her way to safety if she managed to break free from the killer.

"Looks like we're the cavalry," Boyle said, stating the obvious.

Announcements sounded over the intercom system for passengers to begin boarding. The lockdown was over. If the killer was, indeed, still on the grounds, they didn't have much time. The clock was ticking faster now.

"Lockdown's lifted," Boyle said with a disapproving frown. "Why does it feel like the feds did exactly what the killer wanted?"

"Because they did." She and her team were obviously at a disadvantage now. There were only six of them, and the airport was enormous. They'd have to split up and be smart about which areas to target. Federal agents had been sent home, the National Guard had been canceled, and airport security was no longer on high alert. How the hell would they cover an entire airport with just six people? By the time they made a dent in their search and started familiarizing themselves with the lay of the land, the killer would be long gone. If he was even still here to begin with because, right now, she wasn't sure of anything.

Boyle returned his focus to the airport schematics. "We know the killer was here," he said, pointing to the southern perimeter. "What we don't know is where the hell he went after he left this point."

All of Reid's ideas spontaneously combusted inside her mind before they had time to grow wings. Self-doubt loomed over each one like a skyscraper's shadow.

Marino, Garcia, and O'Leary jogged back and rejoined them. The three of them were out of breath as they all huddled together to brainstorm. Boggs was nowhere in sight.

O'Leary huffed and puffed, his face as red as a jalapeño pepper. "Instead of chasing down airport staff—I don't know about you guys, but *nobody* wanted to talk to me—it turned out talking to each other was much more productive."

Marino sighed. "What O'Leary's trying to say is we studied the map and tossed some hypotheticals around. How would *we* smuggle a body out of the airport?"

"A live body," Garcia added. "A dead one's a walk in the park. But a live one's tricky."

"Turns out we're actually pretty good at it," Marino said proudly. "FYI, if you ever need a body smuggled out of an airport, Garcia's your guy."

Boyle raised an eyebrow.

Reid cleared her throat, reticent to share the disturbing news. "A surfboard case was found abandoned near a hole in the fence along the southern perimeter. It looks like it's the same case—"

"We know," Garcia said, cutting her off. "We just came from there."

O'Leary nodded. "We also know about the body inside the case that the feds refused to open. They blamed it on protocol, but we all know the feds are squeamish."

Anyone in law enforcement knew that cops—especially Boston cops—were a hardy breed. No one had a stronger stomach than a Boston homicide detective. The guys could've handled whatever was in that case, even if it turned out to be London. Reid couldn't, however, say the same for herself. She'd always prided herself on being able to hold her own when it came to particularly violent crime scenes or crime scenes with overripe bodies. Unlike some of her colleagues over the years, nothing had ever shaken her to her core. But seeing London's lifeless body would wreck her. Forever.

"We decided we don't need to see the body to know it's not Gold's," O'Leary went on. "Leaving her behind when he was already at the finish line is contrary to his agenda. Our guy wouldn't do that."

"No wonder the feds haven't caught him yet. They're jackasses," Marino spat. "He's leading them around by their balls."

"We saw the hole he cut in the fence, and we heard he had a getaway car parked on the other side. The car's obviously gone, but"—Garcia glanced at his compadres—"we'd bet our pensions he's still the fuck here."

"What'd you come up with?" Reid asked, intrigued.

Garcia's predatory gaze told her they were all lucky—the whole damn world was lucky—that he worked for the good guys. Something told her that he'd probably been tempted to go the other way. More than once, if she had to venture a guess.

"I selected my prey and planned everything out to the smallest detail. I've already abducted her and drugged her, so she's totally still and compliant. There's no way I put in all that time and energy for nothing. I've been hunting here for years, right, so I have a pretty good feel for how this place works. As soon as you guys figure out London's missing, I anticipate there'll be a lockdown. I steal a car ahead of time, cut a hole in the fence, and leave the car on the other side. I know about the security camera that covers the bathroom and use this to my advantage. I change into a baggage handler's uniform, put my vic inside the surfboard case, and wheel her out, knowing the feds will review the video and see me with the case. I pick a gate close by—any gate, doesn't matter—cross the bridge, and head out the exit and down the stairs to the tarmac. I have an identical surfboard case waiting on the tarmac that contains the body of a luggage courier. I killed him, stole his ID, and stuffed his corpse inside a case that looks identical to the original, except one has the victim I want to keep, and the other has the body of the guy I killed. I burned his body to mask his identity and buy me some time. I slap a *misrouted* tag onto the case that has my real victim and pass her off to the baggage handler on the tarmac. His job is to transport all the luggage that missed a connecting flight to designated courier vehicles in the garage. I load the case with the dead guy into a luggage trolley, drive him to the southern perimeter, and leave him near the hole in the fence so it looks like I escaped. I want the feds to think the case contains Gold's body so they'll lift the lockdown and call off the search."

Boyle piped up with, "What about the stolen car on the other side of the fence?"

"Someone's already waiting behind the wheel—someone I paid to drive the car and then dump it in a predetermined spot."

Boyle thought for a moment. "So Gold's still in the original surfboard case. But now she's with the baggage handler on the tarmac?"

Garcia nodded.

"How do you get her back?" Boyle asked.

"I've assumed the identity of the dead luggage courier. My new airport job is to return lost or misrouted luggage to the address on the claim ticket. Gold is inside the surfboard case next on my list, so the baggage handler loads her into my courier vehicle, and away we go."

"You think he's still on the grounds then?"

"Yeah," Garcia said, nodding. "Not sure for how long, though."

"That's where Boggs went." O'Leary met Reid's gaze with confidence. "He's surveilling the courier vehicles to make sure our guy doesn't drive off."

As if on cue, Boggs's voice sounded over Garcia's watch. "Bro, there's a hiccup."

Garcia pressed the button on his watch to activate the walkie-talkie feature. "What's up?"

"There are dozens of identical courier vehicles in this garage. Bring some bodies and get here. Fast."

"Copy. On our way."

They were already on the move, with Marino leading the way at a sprint.

❖

London wasn't sure how much time had passed since the killer had taken her from the bathroom. It was impossible to have any real sense of time in her current condition. Her eyelids were taped, so she had no visual input, which she found extremely disorienting. Fortunately, she still possessed her senses of smell, hearing, and touch—all of which helped to keep her panic at bay.

Since she couldn't see anything, she wasn't sure exactly where she was, but she felt the softness of a faux-fur lining and deduced that the killer had placed her inside a large travel case. She was fully supine, so whatever it was happened to be long enough to accommodate her height. The killer had used three straps—they were cinched around her chest, stomach, and knees—to anchor her body in place. She guessed she was inside a travel case of some kind—one that was made for a surfboard, skis, or, perhaps, a large musical instrument. The occasional voices she heard were muffled, so she guessed the travel case had a hard outer shell.

She couldn't help but wonder how long it would take to run out of air and suffocate. The killer was meticulous, so she figured the chances of suffocation were negligible. But if something went wrong or there was some kind of delay that the killer hadn't anticipated, well, she might be out of luck. If she was going to die anyway, suffocation was preferable to prolonged torture.

The paralytic drug made her very sleepy. She fought hard to stay awake. She couldn't move her body at all to give her muscles the jolt of energy they needed. Her mind longed to drift off, not only to escape the horror of the reality before her, but also because her day had started early and she hadn't gotten much sleep the night before. She and Reid had spent most of the night tossing and turning. Their agreement to leave work at work prohibited them from discussing the case that was keeping them both awake. It was, she decided, a double-edged sword. Part of her regretted making that agreement when they'd started their relationship a year ago, but she also knew it was necessary to be proactive in maintaining a healthy work-life balance. They both loved what they did, and it'd be too easy to make unsolved cases a round-the-clock obsession.

Sleep started tugging at the edges of her thoughts. *No! Stay awake,*

London. Stay awake if you want to live. Dig down deep. She knew she had to stay awake, stay alert, pay attention. Maybe she'd hear something useful—voices, a name, a location. If she managed to communicate telepathically with Reid, she could pass along the information to aid in her own rescue. She decided now was as good a time as any to give it a shot.

London focused her thoughts solely on Reid. She had no idea how to jump-start telepathic communication, or even if such a thing was possible, but she imagined the first step would be visualizing the person with whom you were trying to communicate. Saturating all her senses with the idea of that person seemed like a logical place to start.

She imagined the sound of Reid's voice, the smell of her shampoo, the feel of their fingers entwined, and the taste of her lips. Finally, she imagined gazing into Reid's bright green eyes.

Reid, I'm here. I'm alive, and I love you. She chanted the same words over and over in her mind. She imagined writing those words on a piece of paper, folding it into a paper airplane, and then throwing it from the top of a high building to find Reid somewhere below.

CHAPTER SIXTEEN

Reid ran as fast as her legs would carry her. She and Boyle were neck and neck. Marino, Garcia, and O'Leary were bringing up the rear. She no longer drank like she used to, much to London's approval. Once upon a time, Reid could drink every cop she'd ever met under the table. But she always kept up with her cardio for days like today when endurance and speed mattered.

As a cop, she felt like she had an obligation to stay strong. Her commitment to her runs and workouts post-retirement held true. Sure, she would've loved to sleep past four every morning. Hell, she'd earned it. But even as a homicide consultant, she was still part of a team. Retired or not, they counted on her to toe the line. A lack of endurance, speed, or strength could cost one of her colleagues their life. That was something she just wasn't willing to risk.

Boyle had taken Cap's place as her running partner, so they were accustomed to keeping pace with one another. He'd quit smoking a year ago and could hold his own now. She was giving it her all, and he was keeping up with no problem. He was fast. Maybe faster than her.

She shouted to be heard above the loudspeaker announcements that steadily assaulted her ears. "Go! Get there ahead of me."

Boyle took the lead and disappeared around the corner. Damn, he was fast. Her respect for him climbed a few notches.

No one tried to stop them as they sprinted through the airport. They all had their gold shields prominently displayed on their waistbands, on chains around their necks, or clipped to the collars of their shirts. Each of them ran like their life depended on it. It just so happened that London's life did.

Reid arrived at the elevators for the garage. She glanced at the stairwell and tapped the walkie-talkie icon on her watch. "Boggs, what level are you on?"

"Four," he replied. "From what I can see, courier vehicles are spread out on levels four, five, and six. I've set up a roadblock as a checkpoint, but there's some asshole security guard giving me shit. What's your ETA?"

"Two minutes. Boyle should be there sooner." She held the stairwell door for Garcia, Marino, and O'Leary, tapped the walkie-talkie icon for Boyle, and repeated the information Boggs had just shared.

"Almost there," Boyle replied, out of breath. "I'll head to level five. You take six."

"Copy." She took the stairs two at a time, barking orders as she climbed. "Marino, you're with Boggs on level four. O'Leary, you're with Boyle on five. Garcia, you're with me on six."

Marino exited the stairwell when they reached level four. O'Leary parted ways with them on five. Garcia stayed at her back and kept up with her the whole way. She pushed the door open on six, stepped into the garage, and looked around. Airport courier vehicles filled every parking space as far as the eye could see.

Garcia stood alongside her. "Shit."

Maybe most of the vehicles were empty. She jogged over to one, cupped her hands around her eyes, and peered through the van's tinted rear window. "Boxes in this one. No luggage."

Garcia followed suit, checking the van beside hers. "Suitcases in this one."

"Surfboard case?" she asked.

"No. But what if he removed Gold from the surfboard case and put her inside a suitcase? Or a large box," he added, peeking inside the windows of the van she'd just checked. "She could fit inside one of those heavy-duty wardrobe boxes."

"Shit." They needed to devise a search strategy that was time efficient, but they also needed to be extraordinarily thorough. They couldn't leave a single box, suitcase, or trunk unchecked. The two opposing strategies were the very definition of mutually exclusive. How the fuck could they accomplish both? And not to make the situation worse, but a dangerous psychopath could be lurking inside or around any of these vans. She threw an uneasy glance around the garage.

"We need a game plan," Garcia said, stating the obvious.

"At the rate we're going," Boyle's voice sounded over her watch, "Gold will suffocate long before we find her."

"Same here," Reid replied.

"Another hiccup," Boggs announced. "Airport security is threatening to arrest me if I don't suspend the checkpoint and let cars pass. For the record, I don't mind being arrested, but that would take me out of the search. We need everyone we can get right now."

"Do *not* suspend that checkpoint. I'm sending reinforcements now." She wasted no time in getting Boyle on the line.

Boyle didn't hesitate. "On my way."

"Take O'Leary with you. Do whatever you have to do to keep that checkpoint open."

"If all else fails, money talks," Boyle replied. "Cap's parting words of wisdom."

"Bribery?" she asked, more than a little surprised.

"Yep. But only for emergencies."

Reid made a mental note to ask Cap about that later. She turned to Garcia and opened her mouth to say something, but he cut her off with a look.

"You're about to ask me to leave you here, alone. I don't think that's smart. If he got the drop on Gold, he could get the drop on any of us."

"It's him you should be worried about."

"True dat," he said, shaking his head. "You make a better friend than an enemy. That's for damn sure. Just be careful. Eyes and ears."

"Go to level four," she instructed him, unsnapping her holster. Garcia was right—she wasn't taking any chances. "Help man the checkpoint. Do *not* let any cars through unless—"

"I search every square inch of the vehicle first," he finished. "Gold's here somewhere. I can feel it." He dashed off toward the stairwell and called back over his shoulder, "We'll find her, Sylver. That's a promise."

She watched Garcia disappear inside the stairwell as he hurried down two flights of stairs to join the rest of her team. She knew he'd do everything humanly possible to keep that promise, but she also knew the outcome of this search could go either way. There were no guarantees, and that scared the hell out of her. If there was ever a time to use her psychic abilities, now would be it. But she had no clue how to jump-start them. She didn't even know if she *could* jump-start them.

Information had always just…come to her. Without any effort on her part whatsoever.

Reid imagined the door inside her mind that she used to communicate with spirits. Maybe her psychic abilities worked the same way. Maybe all she had to do was open the door and let them in.

She visualized taking a step forward, turning the knob, and pulling the door open just a few inches—large enough for a paper airplane to sail through above her head. She left the door ajar and turned to watch the airplane as it made a U-turn and quickly descended, coming to rest in her outstretched hands.

The paper airplane beckoned to her. She felt compelled to unfold it and recognized the writing at once. London's. As she read the handwritten message, she heard London's voice, as clear as if she was standing right beside her.

Reid, I'm here. I'm alive, and I love you.

She looked around, but London was nowhere to be seen. Was this really a message from London? It couldn't be. Could it? Her mind was playing tricks on her. She was still contemplating the message when a second paper airplane, identical to the first, sailed through the open door. It contained the same handwritten words. Again, London's voice played in her mind as she reread the message.

Four more paper airplanes landed in her hands, all copies of the original. She suddenly knew that London was behind this. Only London, who was obsessed with covering all her bases—she went to the ends of the earth to dot every last *i* and cross every last *t*—would send the same message over and over again. Reid counted the airplanes that were quickly piling up in her hands: eighteen.

Had to be London.

She called out for London in her mind. *Babe, can you hear me?* When no response came, she tried again. *London, I'm here. Can you hear me?*

She waited, but nothing came back. No voice. No handwritten response in the form of a paper airplane.

She glanced up as another paper airplane sailed through the open door. Was this London's way of revealing that she was in the air? On a plane?

Maybe the only way they could communicate was the way London had imagined. Reid envisioned her own paper airplane—one with racing stripes so London would have no doubt it came from her. She quickly scribbled a reply.

We're looking for you. Are you still inside the airport?

She launched the paper airplane and watched as it disappeared somewhere beyond the door's threshold.

Sending paper airplanes back and forth would likely eat up their time. What would happen if she just stepped outside the door and started walking? She had never attempted such a thing with spirits and wasn't even sure it was possible.

What she and London were doing—despite the absurdness of it all, she thought there was a good chance they were actually communicating telepathically—was very different from the type of communication she experienced with spirits. This felt much more grounded and tangible, like the difference between smoke and water. She and London were both physical beings while spirits were obviously, well, not. Maybe that accounted for the difference.

She opened the door wider and reached her hand out. Nothing ate her hand or tore it off. Besides, this was all in her mind. She reminded herself that she was standing in the garage at Reagan National and still very aware of her surroundings. It was like being in two places at the same time.

She strained to look beyond the door's threshold. There was a warm glow in the distance. Her feet were already moving toward the glow before she had time to process what was happening. The closer she got to the glow, the more convinced she became that London was nearby.

The source of the glow slowly swam into focus. A woman was sitting alone at a bistro table, her back turned to Reid. London? She stepped around the table and felt relief wash over her as London materialized.

London called out, "Reid? Is that you?"

That's when she realized that London couldn't see her. She couldn't see anything because her eyes were taped shut. "It's me, babe. I'm here."

"I'm okay," she said quickly. "He hasn't hurt me."

She swallowed the lump in her throat and blinked back the tears. She wasn't normally a crier. Hearing the courage in London's voice cut her to the bone. "We're searching for you, here at the airport. Tell me everything you can to help us find you."

"He injected me with a paralytic, so I can't move. My eyes are—"

"Taped," she said sadly. "I can see that."

"You can hear me *and* see me?" London asked, sounding surprised.

She nodded as she reached out to hold London's hand. "We're sitting at a small bistro set. The tablecloth is embroidered with roses. There's a rustic lantern in the middle of the table."

London's face lit up. "La Franco's! It was my favorite place when I was a kid."

Reid felt momentarily grateful to be sharing this place, this memory, with London. She waited, not wanting to push London into letting go of the memory before she was ready.

London squeezed her hand. "I'm in some kind of travel case—one that was made for a surfboard or skis or a big instrument. It's tall enough so I don't have to bend. The voices I heard were muffled, so I think this case has a hard outer shell."

"We saw a video of the killer carrying a surfboard case. Are you sure he hasn't moved you into something different?"

"Same case," London confirmed.

If London hadn't been moved from the surfboard case, it probably meant there was a good chance she was still here at the airport. "You mentioned voices. What were they saying?"

"The voices were hard to make out. If I had to guess, the killer was talking to someone—someone who works here. A man. Maybe a luggage handler. I think they were loading me onto a vehicle."

Good. Now they were getting somewhere. "Do you hear anything now?"

"Cars. Honking. Angry shouting somewhere in the distance."

The checkpoint, two levels below her. She nearly leaped for joy, but she refrained from contacting Boyle for fear of breaking their telepathic connection. She had one more question. It was important. "Is the vehicle you're in running?" she asked. "Is the engine on?"

London thought for a moment and finally shook her head. "No. I'm almost certain the vehicle I'm in is parked. The engine is off."

"I know where you are." Even though she knew this place wasn't real, she was reluctant to leave London's side. "Everything will be okay. I'm coming to get you now." She instantly felt London's fear course through her like energy from a Red Bull.

"Wait," London pleaded. "I don't want you to go. Can't you stay until you find me?"

"I wish I could, babe, but I don't think it works that way." She didn't fully understand any of this, but something deep inside told her that they needed to part ways here. "Do you trust me?"

London nodded. "Always."

"Good. I'm coming. I love you." She squeezed London's hand, stood from the table, and took one last look at the woman before her. "I promise, I'll see you soon."

London nodded and managed a small smile as Reid began retracing her steps to the door in her mind. Instinct told her it was important to leave from the place she started and shut the door securely behind her.

CHAPTER SEVENTEEN

Reid made a mad dash to the garage stairwell and reached the fourth-floor landing. She reached out to Boyle on her watch as she stepped out onto level four. "London's here, somewhere on level four. She's in a parked vehicle, inside the same surfboard case. Close enough to hear cars honking and people complaining."

"No shit," Boyle said, sounding amazed. "Where're you at?"

"Coming off the rear stairwell and following the sound of angry voices." She kept talking as she jogged. "Checkpoint's still up and running?"

"Yep, and it cost me a pretty penny."

"I'll cover half," she promised. It was the least she could do. Boyle split the cost of replenishing Mug's tennis ball supply every month.

"Not sure you'll feel the same when I tell you how much we're in for."

"Tell the guys to stay at the checkpoint. Keep searching vehicles as they try to exit."

There was a brief silence. "Done. We'll search parked vehicles together," Boyle said. "I'll watch your six. You watch mine."

She stopped in the middle of the garage and looked around. There were dozens upon dozens of parked courier vehicles on this level. This could take ages.

Boyle's voice sounded on her watch. "Sylver, you copy?"

"Copy," she said quickly to her watch, to put Boyle's mind at ease. He was getting nervous. He always got this way just before the shit hit the fan. The thought of someone getting hurt on his watch made him overly protective. He kept his nerves under wraps for the most part, but she knew all his tells. A voice that was half an octave higher than usual was one of them.

They met near the checkpoint. Reid set her hands on her hips as she thought out loud. "She's in a closed hard-shell case that's locked inside a vehicle. How close would she have to be to hear cars honking?"

As if in answer to her question, an impatient motorist in the long line of cars decided he'd had enough and leaned on his horn for long seconds. The sound was explosive. It bounced off the concrete walls and pillars like a pinball and reverberated through the garage. Reid watched as he leaned out the window and dropped the f-bomb in ways that put her rants to shame.

"Hard to say," Boyle admitted. "Everything echoes. She could be anywhere." He turned in a full circle. "In any of these vehicles."

Reid had promised London that they'd see each other soon. London was waiting, trapped, paralyzed, alone, and scared. She couldn't— wouldn't—break that promise. They would have to search every damn car and van, one by one. She felt the rage build up inside her. She was pissed off at Russo for taking her eye off the ball. If she'd kept her head in the fucking game, they wouldn't be in this position right now.

The spirit of her dead grandmother appeared a few car lengths in front of her. She was holding the same damn gift in her hands.

❖

London listened to Reid's footsteps grow faint as they parted ways. Part of her couldn't help but wonder if the paralytic drug was making her hallucinate. On the other hand, the experience with Reid had felt so *real*.

She had no idea how long she'd been locked inside the travel case. Seconds felt like minutes. Minutes felt like hours. Hours felt like days. She realized then that sensory deprivation was robbing her of her sense of time.

The wait was torturous. Self-doubt made her question her perception of reality. What if she had fallen asleep or lost consciousness and more time had passed than she realized? What if the killer had already transported her from the airport and had cut the engine because she was stuffed in the trunk of a car inside his garage? What if she'd just sent Reid on a wild goose chase?

The thought that she wouldn't be rescued—that rescue was impossible because the killer had somehow managed to smuggle her out of the airport without her knowledge—made her feel like she was about to experience her first panic attack. *Control your emotions. Don't let them control you.*

"Feelings," her dad used to say, "are like taking a dog for a walk on a leash. You take the time to train the dog, or the dog walks you." He'd always peer down at her over his spectacles and end it with, "Golds walk the dog, London, no matter how big and strong that dog is. The leash is loose, and your dog heels beside you the whole way."

She did as she was taught. Her panic was the size of a Great Dane, but she claimed her alpha status and had it heeling beside her in record time. She was surprised to find herself feeling grateful for a skill that had, before now, seemed only to serve her parents' ridiculous agenda—make things look pretty on the outside, and ignore what's really going on. She'd always believed they were encouraging her to ignore her feelings and go against her inner voice. But now, here, alone, she saw it in a very different light. They were teaching her about control. If she could control her feelings, she could use logic to her advantage, thereby eliminating the risk of reacting emotionally. It was a skill she knew not everyone had the capacity to learn in life. It was a skill she wished she could thank them for now.

She promised herself if she ever got out of this mess, she would do just that.

Reid had perfectly described her memory of her favorite restaurant as a kid. As soon as Reid had described the place, she saw it in her mind's eye. Nothing had ever felt so vivid and rich and full of detail. Something told her that Reid had gifted her with the ability to clearly visualize La Franco's, which she was now experiencing for the first time in ages because they'd shut down years ago. Her eyelids were still taped, so she couldn't actually see her surroundings, but she didn't need to. The aromas, the music, even the embroidered tablecloth felt just like she remembered.

She found it amazing that her subconscious had chosen La Franco's as their meeting place. It made sense because she remembered feeling safe and happy there. In fact, she could use a dose of that right about now. As the sound of Reid's footsteps trailed off, she decided to stay at La Franco's. If she really focused, the tight quarters of the travel case, the feel of the faux-fur lining against her skin, and the abysmal darkness that the absence of vision brought melted away. She was free to move as she pleased.

London remained seated at the bistro table Reid had described.

She was just starting to relax when she felt fingers against her eyelids. She desperately wanted to recoil from the touch but was suddenly unable to move.

Someone was trying to peel the tape from her eyes. And instinct told her it wasn't Reid.

❖

Reid set her hands on her hips. "Fuck," she said, under her breath.

"What is it?" Boyle's hand moved to the weapon in his holster.

"My grandmother's here."

He met her gaze. "The dead one?"

She nodded. She'd almost forgotten that her grandmother had been haunting her—figuratively and literally—for the past three weeks. Unbelievable. The old hag knew no boundaries, even at a time like this...*especially* at a time like this, when Reid's heart was in her throat and she was on the precipice of total collapse. Now that she thought about it, that's probably why her grandmother was here. At this very moment. To drive the knife in just a little deeper.

Her grandmother motioned to her and pointed over her shoulder.

"Damn," Reid said angrily.

"What now?" Boyle reflexively reached for his weapon once again.

"I *wish* you could shoot her, but I don't think that'll work." Her grandmother wasn't seriously trying to help, was she? Not after all this time. Not after everything she'd done to make Reid's life a living hell. No. It was a ruse. Had to be. Where the hell did her grandmother want to take her? Straight into the clutches of a serial killer so he could finish the job that her grandmother had started all those years ago? Reid set her hands on her hips, anxious to start the search for London. "I think she wants me to follow her." She had to admit, her curiosity was piqued.

"What's your gut say?" Boyle knew about her abusive history with her grandmother. She'd been forced to divulge some very personal information in an effort to capture a different killer the year before. Boyle had overheard the exchange and asked her about it one morning over coffee and muffins.

"The only instinct I have when it comes to that woman is to stay as far away from her as I can get," she admitted, maintaining eye contact with the old hag, despite her best efforts to look away. "My guess is, she's either trying to lead me to London or into the fiery depths of hell."

"Your call." Boyle unsnapped his holster and set his hand over the butt of his gun. "Look at the bright side. If we end up in hell, at least we'll have each other."

"And the bright side is what, exactly?" Reid withdrew her weapon and started walking toward the old woman. Maybe this encounter—however it turned out—would allow her to face the demons of her past and be done with her grandmother, once and for all. Thankfully, her grandmother remained silent. Reid didn't think she could stomach hearing her voice again. Too many memories. Too much pain. Hearing her grandmother's voice could send her into a tailspin of flashbacks she wasn't sure she'd ever be able to stop.

Boyle kept pace beside her, his weapon drawn. "If we both end up in hell, we get to keep sweating together." He was, of course, referring to their morning workouts at the precinct gym. It was almost funny. Almost. Reid knew that Boyle was too good a man to end up anywhere other than with the Big Guy upstairs. She wasn't positive, but she intuited that hell—at least, the version her grandmother had threatened her with as a kid—didn't even exist. If spirits were sent anywhere other than heaven, she believed it was a temporary placement, where they were given an opportunity to grow and learn from their mistakes.

Her grandmother, of course, was the exception. Reid hoped a fiery, torturous hell had been created just for her.

She stopped in her tracks and turned to meet Boyle's gaze. "Seriously, what the hell are we doing?"

"Following your dead grandmother," he said, looking at her like she'd just sprouted flowers from the top of her head.

"What if she's distracting us, keeping us from finding London? Hell, she could be helping the killer. How do we know she's not?"

Boyle set a reassuring hand on her shoulder. "I don't think we have much of a choice right now."

In ordinary circumstances, she would've removed his hand and maybe broken a finger in the process, but today she welcomed the gesture.

"Give her a chance," he went on. "See where she takes us. At this point, I'm worried Gold will run out of air. I doubt the killer anticipated a checkpoint. Doubt he planned for this delay. This is as good a lead as any right now. In fact"—he looked around at the vehicles surrounding them on both sides—"it's our *only* lead."

"Fine." Reid breathed deeply to steady her nerves. "But if she turns into a demon—I'd be surprised if she isn't already—and takes possession of my body, you'll need to shoot me."

There was an awkward silence as they rounded the corner to reach the next row of cars. "Fuck. Can that really happen?" Boyle's voice cracked with fear.

She watched as her grandmother stopped in front of a white van with tinted windows and looked to Reid beseechingly. "There," Reid whispered, gesturing to the vehicle in question. She and Boyle crouched down and cautiously approached. He took the left side while she flanked the right, ducking below the window line.

She listened, silent, as her grandmother stood nearby and looked on. The engine was off. Everything was quiet. If the killer was hiding inside, he was being just as stealthy as she was. She stood and cupped her free hand around her eyes to peek inside, but the dark window tint obstructed her view of the interior. The windshield was tint free. It wouldn't give her a full view of the interior, but at least it was something. She stayed low and made her way to the front, gun in hand. She heard Boyle jiggle the driver's side door handle. He met her near the grille.

"Doors are locked. I can't see shit," he whispered. "You?"

She shook her head.

"How sure are we Gold's actually in there?"

"On a scale of one to ten?" she whispered back. "Negative nine hundred."

Boyle held her gaze as he considered her answer. "I'll break the driver's side window. Cover me."

CHAPTER EIGHTEEN

London winced as both pieces of tape were slowly peeled from her eyes. She opened them and braced herself, fully expecting to see the killer's face hovering in front of hers. But it wasn't the killer. She couldn't have been more surprised to see the same old woman Reid had described from her childhood. This had to be Reid's grandmother.

Momentarily conflicted, she wasn't sure if she should sit back down or run away.

"Agatha," the old woman said with a sad smile. She took a seat in the chair across from her. "You can call me Aggie if you want."

London was too stunned to respond. She was clearly hallucinating. This *had* to be a hallucination. There was no other logical explanation for what was happening. The paralytic drug that the killer had injected her with was doing weird things to her brain.

An awful thought occurred to her then. Did that mean Reid wasn't coming to rescue her? Had she hallucinated their entire conversation? Of course she had. How could she be so naive? Telepathic communication didn't exist. She felt the edges of her sanity start to crumble. She didn't know what was real anymore.

"No, don't do that," Aggie said sternly. "I'm real. You're real. And Reid *is* coming for you." She scooted her chair closer to London's, set a warm hand over the top of her arm, and squeezed it reassuringly. "Don't lose hope, honey. She's close."

❖

Reid watched as Boyle slammed the butt of his gun against the driver's side window of the van. The glass shattered as he reached in to press the button that unlocked all the doors. They ducked down low, hugged the sides of the van, and hurried to the rear doors. Boyle mouthed, *On three.* With his gun in his right hand, he began counting silently on the fingers of his left hand.

Reid flung the rear door open as quickly and as quietly as she could. She went low as Boyle went high, but the killer was nowhere to be found.

A lone gray surfboard travel case rested on the floor of the van. Tears blurred her vision. Could it be London?

"Got my six?" she asked, hearing her own voice crack with emotion.

"You know it," Boyle replied.

She climbed inside the van, popped open the case's latches, and took a deep breath to steel her nerves as she lifted the lid. Tears coursed down her cheeks. Relief washed over her in great waves of emotion. For the first time in her life, Reid didn't care if anyone saw her crying.

"Babe, it's me. I'm here. You're safe." London's eyelids were taped shut, exactly as they had been during their conversation minutes ago. She carefully peeled the tape from London's eyes and helped her open them.

London stared back at her, expressionless. She was obviously still under the influence of the paralytic drug. "You're safe now," she repeated.

"She alive?" Boyle called out.

"Yeah, but she can't move," Reid answered, crying freely now. She checked her pulse. Strong and steady. London was warm. Breathing. Alive.

"We need to get her to the hospital."

"No ambulance," she shouted. "We take her. All of us." There was no way in hell she'd leave London's side or entrust her transport or care to anyone else. Not after what happened here today.

"Copy that," Boyle said. He tapped his watch and shared the news with the rest of the team, choking back tears of his own.

❖

London felt the whoosh of air glide over her body as the case opened—a welcome reprieve from the case's stuffy interior.

"Babe, it's me. I'm here. You're safe."

No voice had ever sounded sweeter. She felt Reid's gentle touch as she peeled the tape from her eyes. Reid's face was the first thing she saw upon opening them.

In that moment, she wished from the depths of her soul that the victims before her had lived to experience this moment. If only they'd had someone as dedicated, resourceful, and determined as Reid Sylver. She was relentless in her love for London and in her steadfast determination to find her. Even in her tears, she was the strongest person London had ever met.

She had no idea how much time had passed, but she was exhausted. Thankfully, Reid ran her fingertips over her eyelids and closed them for her. She let herself drift off. Reid would watch over her now. She was safe.

❖

Reid paced the hospital corridor outside London's private room. She felt her anger growing by the minute. Boyle was leaning against the wall, watching her. Garcia, Marino, O'Leary, and Boggs were in the waiting room. None of them were leaving London's side.

"It bothers you that he got away," Boyle said.

"You bet your ass it does," she spat.

"And you're pissed because as long as he's out there, Gold's not safe."

She nodded, unable to speak. She felt like she was about to explode. What she wouldn't give to get her hands on that bastard right now. All she needed was five minutes. Five minutes alone with him.

Boyle straightened from the wall and stepped in front of her, blocking her path. He took her by the shoulders and forced her to meet his gaze. "All of us feel exactly like you do. We'll stay with her, round the clock, until we find him. He won't have the chance to get his hands on her again."

Few people were allowed to touch Reid. Fewer still were granted permission to grab her and hold her in place like this. Boyle was lucky that she liked him. "And what if it takes us months to find him? The fucking FBI has been looking for this bastard for—"

"We're not the fucking FBI. We proved that today." Boyle released her but held her gaze with eyes that were just as intense as she knew her own to be. "I talked with the guys. Everyone's on board. We'll pair up, take shifts, and stay with London for however long it takes."

All she wanted in that moment was to take London far, far away from here—someplace where the killer would never find them. They could go underground until the killer was captured. But she knew London would never agree to that. Sitting back and letting someone else do the dirty work wasn't how either of them rolled.

London's doctor exited her room and made the mistake of addressing Boyle instead of Reid. She wasn't in the mood for a chauvinistic asshole. Boyle set his gaze on her and took a step back, obviously sensing that she was about to erupt.

Reid took a step closer to the doctor. "I know you're used to thinking that men are the superior sex, but I'm fully capable of kicking your ass if you don't treat me as an equal." She glanced back at Boyle. "Am I right?"

He nodded. "There's no one I'd rather have by my side in a bar fight."

The doctor frowned. "I was merely trying to explain that your friend—"

"Girlfriend," Reid corrected him. "Go on."

"I've reversed the effects of the paralytic she was given. There should be no long-term consequences."

She could only imagine how relieved London felt to be in control of her body once again. "When can she leave?"

"Your friend—" He cut himself off and started again. "Your girlfriend's vitals are stable. She's shown no adverse reactions to the medication we gave her to counteract the paralytic. She can go home tonight." He proceeded to make a wide circle around Reid before walking briskly down the corridor.

Reid watched him disappear around the corner, grateful to be able to take London back to the hotel tonight. She looked to Boyle. "Did you really mean that thing about the bar fight?" she asked, feeling herself get a little choked up.

"Like softball." He nodded. "You'd be my first pick."

Reid didn't know what to say. It was the nicest compliment anyone had ever given her.

"Go," he said, waving his hand dismissively. "Check on Gold. I'll stay put."

She stepped inside London's room as the nurse was taking her vitals. How had she gotten this far in life without getting into a barroom brawl? Maybe that's exactly what she needed—to blow off some steam in a mindless brawl with some fellow drunk patrons. Had Boyle ever been in one? She made a mental note to ask him about that later. If the answer was *yes*, her respect for him might just climb another few notches.

The nurse reported that London's vitals looked good, and she slipped out of the room, leaving the two of them alone. Reid sat on the edge of the bed and held London's hand between hers. She didn't trust herself to speak yet.

"We didn't get him, did we?" London asked, cutting right to the chase.

It didn't escape her attention that London used *we*. She was taking accountability for their failure as a team. It also didn't surprise her that London would want to know straight away. If they'd captured him, then there would've been a silver lining to her abduction. Reid answered honestly. No sugarcoating. "We didn't get him."

London studied their hands for long seconds in silence before she finally looked up. "He has three women right now."

"Alive?" she asked, panic bobbing to the surface like a four-day-old corpse. This panicked feeling was new to her. She'd never had so much to lose before. Every instinct she had said this killer was manipulative, calculating, and extremely dangerous—maybe the most dangerous person she'd ever come across in her twenty-year career.

London nodded. "He showed me a live video feed. They're hooked up to IV drips. He uses an app that dispenses the medication automatically."

Russo hadn't mentioned anything about the killer keeping a backup supply of victims. Something told her the FBI had no knowledge of that.

"The killer was comfortable at the airport, like he was in his element. My sense was that he either works there, spends a lot of time there, or..." London trailed off as she clearly struggled to put her finger on what her detective instincts were telling her.

Even in these circumstances, when most people would still be reeling at having narrowly escaped the clutches of a serial killer, London hadn't lost her touch. She was one helluva detective. Reid nodded in confirmation. "Looks like he's been using airports as his hunting ground for years. None of us put it together until today."

"Meaning, *you* put it together today."

She shrugged. "It was a team effort."

"Why do you feel like you need to hide it?"

Reid didn't have to ask what *it* was. She knew London was referring to her psychic abilities. "I'm scared," she said honestly.

"Of what?"

"Losing you, if things get too weird. Losing my people. Losing myself. I have no idea how far this thing goes, no idea where it'll take me. Nobody else I know can do what I can." She looked away, unable to meet London's gaze. "Makes me feel like a freak."

"You won't lose me, no matter how weird things get. And frankly I'm a little insulted that you think I'd jump ship so easily."

The tone in London's voice told Reid she was serious. And a little annoyed.

"I think I can safely speak for your people when I say they feel the same," London went on.

"You *don't* know that." She stood from the bed and started pacing. "You couldn't possibly—"

"I do know. The guys would follow you to hell and back without batting an eye. How can you *not* know that?"

"And I'd do the same for them." She set her hands on her hips. "But *this*…this is some weird shit, London. I can't expect them to just roll with the punches on this one."

"Do you really believe they don't already know?"

"Know what?" she asked, suddenly wondering if they were talking about the same thing.

"That you're psychic!" London shouted in exasperation. "They know, Reid. We all know."

She was momentarily confused. "Who's *they*?"

"Exactly who you think. Your people." London rolled her eyes. "The lieutenant, Marino, Garcia, O'Leary, Boggs. Even Cap's wife took me aside and asked me after dinner one night."

"Have you been talking about me behind my back?" The idea of being the topic of conversation when she wasn't around to participate had a ring of betrayal.

"No, of course not." London stood and stepped over to her. "We're detectives, Reid. You're not the only one who can read people. That's what we all do for a living, and I'd like to think we're pretty damn good at it."

London never cursed. "You just said *damn*."

"It was premeditated. I was trying to make a point." London reached for her hands. "Did it work?"

"Yeah." Reid nodded, impressed. She was still trying to wrap her mind around the possibility that her people already knew. Either they knew her better than she thought, or she was getting worse at pretending to be normal.

"So, that covers your fear of losing me and losing your people," London said matter-of-factly. "Which brings me to your fear of losing yourself."

Reid got the feeling that she was in the middle of a PowerPoint presentation, minus the projector.

"This gift you have, it's part of you. Even if it's a part of yourself that you don't readily accept, it's still there. Denying it doesn't make it go away or not exist. In fact, that's how I believe we lose ourselves—by not being honest with ourselves about who we really are. Not having the courage to embrace the parts that we're unsure of." London caressed the side of her cheek and kissed her sweetly on the lips. "Embracing your gift allows you to be who you were meant to be. *That's* the Reid I want. I want all of you, not just the parts you're comfortable showing me."

She studied London's face, looking for signs of dishonesty. London had never lied to her. Chances were good that she wouldn't start now. "What if things get weird—like, really weird? What if you start freaking out?"

"If chatting with you telepathically after I was abducted by a serial killer and locked inside a surfboard case didn't freak me out, I'm pretty sure it's safe to say I'm unfreak-out-able." London paused and bit her lower lip uncertainly. "Did that happen, or was I hallucinating?"

Reid nodded. "It happened. We were at La Franco's—"

"At a bistro table—"

"With an embroidered tablecloth and a candle," she confirmed.

"Wow." London stared at her. "Have you ever done that before?"

She shook her head. "I had no idea it was even possible."

"Can you do that with everyone?"

She shrugged. "I honestly don't know." But something deep inside told her that what happened between them was special. Her inner voice insisted that it took a very deep connection to be able to communicate so intimately with someone.

"I never lost faith in you, Reid Sylver. Not for one second." London's chin started to quiver. "I knew you would come."

She gathered London in her arms and held her as she cried.

"I need to tell you something," London whispered in her ear, "but you have to promise not to get mad."

She couldn't imagine anything that would make her feel angry with London, especially in this moment. "I promise."

"It'll sound bananas."

She raised an eyebrow. "Stranger than saving my girlfriend from a serial killer after she sent me telepathic paper airplanes?"

"Probably not, when you put it like that."

Reid guided her to the bed. They both sat on the edge. "Then lay it on me."

London looked away and chewed her lower lip.

Maybe this was going to be a doozy after all. "Babe, whatever it is, we can—"

"Your grandmother sat with me after you left," London blurted.

It took a beat for London's words to compute. "After I left you... at La Franco's?"

London nodded. "We talked."

CHAPTER NINETEEN

Reid fought the urge to get up and move around, but it was pointless. She stood from the bed and started pacing. Her mind raced. How was it even possible that London had talked to her grandmother?

"You've never told me her name," London went on. "Agatha. Aggie, for short. She said you used to call her Gran. Is that true?"

Reid was stunned into silence. La Franco's was *her* creation. *She* was the one who'd opened the door and stepped over the threshold. She'd obviously wanted to select a location that would put London at ease, and then she must've just plucked it right out of her mind. There was no intention behind it whatsoever. Everything had happened so quickly and effortlessly. It was all just…psychic instinct. But how could she have psychic instincts and not be aware of them?

Stepping outside that door in her mind was like stepping into her grandmother's territory, the place where spirits came from to seek her out. She hadn't realized at the time that it was a shared space. Had to be. It was the only thing that explained how her dead grandmother could communicate with her girlfriend, unless London had suddenly developed the ability to see and talk to dead people. Unlikely but not impossible, she supposed.

Her grandmother had found a damn loophole! Un-fucking-believable. She set her hands on her hips and met London's gaze. "What else did she tell you?"

"She told me not to be scared. She said you were coming to find me, that she was leading you to me and doing everything she could to help from the other side."

Perfect. How many people could say they had a dead, evil grandma who took credit from The Great Beyond for finding an abducted girlfriend?

"Did she, in fact, lead you to the van I was in?" London pressed.

She answered through clenched teeth. "It was a team effort." As much as it killed her to admit it, her grandmother had played a role in finding London. Saying she was a self-initiated member of the search-and-rescue team was a bit of a stretch but maybe not entirely inaccurate. Still, it didn't make up for everything her grandmother had put her through. Didn't even come close.

"She was holding a gift, Reid. It was the same gift you've described every time you see her."

"Who cares?" she said defensively. "That's irrelevant."

"It's very relevant. Don't you see?" London paused and kept her gaze on Reid's.

Reid stared back, waiting for London to go on. "Care to enlighten me? Or should we just stare at each other until I figure it out? I haven't mastered the art of mind reading yet." It sure would come in handy, though.

"The gift. It's wrapped in silver paper with gold ribbon." London rolled her eyes dramatically and pointed, first at Reid and then at herself. "Sylver and Gold." She shook her head. "And you call yourself a detective."

"*Retired* detective, thank you very much. And that probably means nothing. It's just a coincidence."

"She said she needs to give it to you directly. I offered to accept the gift on your behalf, but she's not allowed to give it to anyone else."

"It's a ruse, London. She's toying with me, trying to make me curious enough to invite her to talk." The gift was probably a demon from hell that her grandmother caught and stuffed inside a little box. All her grandmother cared about now was convincing her to open it so said demon could be unleashed and torture her forevermore.

"Come. Sit." London patted the bed.

She stepped over and reclaimed her place on the mattress.

"I trust you. Implicitly. With everything. You've earned it. And, just like the people who've known you longer than I have, I would follow you anywhere, Reid. Anywhere." London reached for her hand. "Do you trust me?"

"Of course I trust you," she answered, without reservation. There were very few people who made that list. London was at the top.

"Then talk to your grandmother. Invite her in. Hear what she has to say."

Her body betrayed her as she tried to stand and pace again, but

London kept a firm grip on her hand. "London, I can't. You don't know what you're asking."

"I *do* know what I'm asking. I've never asked for anything bigger. Please, Reid," she pleaded, pulling her back down to the bed. "Do it for me."

"Here? Now?" she asked, looking around the hospital room. This hardly seemed the place or the time.

London nodded with gentle eyes. "Here. Now."

She despised this idea from the depths of her soul, but she wasn't about to say no to London, not if it meant that much to her. "What if someone comes in and sees me talking to myself?"

London glanced at the door knowingly. "I'd bet anything Boyle's standing guard."

She sighed. "He is."

"Then go tell him what you're about to do. He'll keep everyone at bay and give you the privacy you need."

"Give *me* the privacy I need?" she asked, suddenly uneasy. "Where will you be?"

"Here. With you." London squeezed her hand reassuringly. "Where else would I be?"

Reid poked her head outside the door to meet Boyle's questioning gaze. "Can you make sure no one comes in for a little while?"

He frowned. "Can't you two wait until you get back to the hotel room for that?"

It took her a moment to figure out what he meant. She felt her face go hot. Knowing that Boyle was now thinking about her and London having sex made her want to plant a knee in his groin. "London wants me to have a chat with my grandmother. And she wants me to do it here, before we leave."

"Oh, well. Then I retract my previous comment," he said, taking a step back as he read her body language. "I'll divert unwanted guests on one condition." He crossed his arms to let her know he was serious.

She sighed, annoyed. "What?" she asked, crossing her arms back at him.

"You talk about this visit with your grandmother. With me," he added quickly. "Doesn't have to be today or tomorrow or next week. But you talk about it—all of it—when you're ready. Seeing her after all these years…" He shook his head and sighed. "I can't imagine what that'll feel like. Just want you to know I'm here. As your friend. Whether you like it or not."

Reid felt the damn waterworks starting. To hell with Boyle for making this a Hallmark moment. The difference between Boyle and her former captain was that Cap never pried. When it came to otherworldly stuff, as he'd put it, ignorance was bliss. And Cap was never sappy. He wouldn't be caught dead in a Hallmark moment.

She wiped at the corners of her eyes. It was times like these she wished she wore contacts, so she could have something to blame. "Fine. Whatever," she agreed on the heels of a sniffle. "Just run interference until this godforsaken visit with my grandmother is over with."

She returned to London and sat on the bed beside her. They put their feet up and leaned back against the pillows, shoulder to shoulder.

"Is she here yet?" London asked, weaving her fingers through Reid's.

"No. We'd need to start having sex for that to happen."

"Right." London frowned, apparently remembering the reason behind having to order a vibrator. "Her timing is awful. Maybe you should mention that while you have her ear."

Reid contemplated the idea of hearing her grandmother's snarly, gravelly voice—the same voice she'd been trying to wipe from her memory, unsuccessfully, since she was sixteen years old. She inhaled deeply to steady her nerves. "You sure about this?" she asked, half hoping London would change her mind. The thought of facing her grandmother again, after all these years, made her stomach somersault. There was also a part of her, however finite, that just wanted to get it over with.

London nodded solemnly and tightened her grip around Reid's hand. "I'll be here beside you the whole time."

On the heels of one final deep breath, Reid closed her eyes and imagined the door inside her mind. She opened it wide and stepped back. *Gran*, she called out.

Her grandmother appeared at the door in record time. In all her years of communicating with spirits, she'd never seen one show up so quickly. It usually took them a beat or two to heed her request. She'd gotten the distinct impression from Cap that spirits were required to seek permission before each visit. From who or what, though, she wasn't sure.

Her grandmother looked just the same as she remembered. At six feet, she was taller than most women of her generation. Her bronzed skin was leathery from too much time in the sun, and she had a surplus of wrinkles around her mouth from a lifetime of smoking. Reid looked more closely at her eyes. Gran's eyes were different. They weren't the hard, mean eyes she remembered at all. In fact, they had a lightness about them, a buoyancy that hadn't been there when she was alive.

Do you want to come in? she asked, knowing—and dreading—the answer.

Gran nodded and graciously stepped through the doorway, gift in hand. *Reid*, she said. *I'm not here to ask for anything from you.*

Good, she said, feeling her walls go up. *There's nothing I'd give you, including this damn visit. I came only because—*

London asked you to. I know. Gran's humble, solemn gaze was as startling as a sucker punch to the gut. It was like her grandmother was wearing someone else's face. The anger, criticism, and hatred that once resided there had been replaced with a gentleness and humility Reid had never seen on her, or anyone, before.

Everything I loathed in you, I loathed in myself first. Seeing you talk to your mom and dad after they passed, watching you get excited when they visited, it terrified me, Reid. I was raised to conform to very strict religious standards. My parents broke me at a very young age— younger than you, in fact. They conditioned me to repress that part of myself, no matter the cost. They were both scared—scared of what they didn't understand. Like any dutiful daughter, I honored their wishes, kept my head down, and pretended to be normal. I'd almost forgotten all about that part of my life, until you came along.

Reid felt like she needed to clean out her ears. Was her grandmother saying what she thought she was saying?

I did to you what was done to me. It was a legacy that I felt obliged to continue, but that doesn't excuse my behavior or my choice to hurt you. I'm sorry, Reid. All I can offer you now is an apology from the deepest part of my soul. You deserved better from me. Gran held out the silver and gold gift box. *I wish I'd had the courage to give this to you a long time ago.*

She studied her grandmother. This wasn't the same woman who raised her. Reid was suspicious by nature, but instinct told her that her grandmother's spirit had evolved and learned from her mistakes. She intuited that it was all part of a spirit's journey—one she wasn't privy to just yet.

What's inside the box? she asked suspiciously. Old habits died hard.

Permission, Gran answered, her gaze kind, forthright, and genuine.

Permission? she repeated, intrigued. *From who?*

Gran gestured to the great expanse beyond the door's threshold. *Permission from me, your loved ones, friends, colleagues, victims for whom you sought justice. We all stand behind you.* She set the gift box in Reid's hands.

Reid knew the answer before she asked, but she needed to make sure. *Permission for what?*

Gran smiled sadly. *Permission to use your gifts, honey.*

She stared down at the gift box, wondering what would happen if she opened it. Permission obviously couldn't be boxed, right? This had to be a symbolic gift.

There's also something for London inside, Gran prompted her.

The gift box had an ethereal quality. It was wrapped in shiny silver paper with a sparkling gold ribbon. Sylver and Gold. London was right. The gift was meant for both of them.

❖

London sat beside Reid on the hospital bed, their hands woven tightly together. Long minutes ticked by in silence. It was impossible to know how the visit with Reid's grandmother was going. Reid's eyes were closed. She was completely still and quiet. But there was no shouting. No tears. That had to be a good sign.

She thought back to her own visit with Reid's grandmother. The abusive woman Reid had described from her childhood and the woman she'd met at La Franco's were two very different people. Every instinct she had—as a woman *and* as a cop—told her that Aggie's intentions were honorable. Reid desperately needed closure with her grandmother, whether she would admit it or not. If this visit went the way she hoped, Reid might finally be able to leave the past in the past and give herself permission to move on with her life in the way she deserved.

Reid opened her eyes, released London's hand, and sat forward. She met London's gaze with an expression of complete and utter surprise.

"Well?" London asked. She could hardly stand the suspense. "Did you see her? Did you talk to her?"

Reid nodded, staring down at her hands.

"Why're you so quiet?" She frowned. "What's wrong with your hands?"

Reid looked up. "Nothing's wrong with my hands."

"You opened the gift, didn't you?" She couldn't contain her excitement. Why wasn't Reid giving her a play-by-play?

Reid stood and began pacing the hospital room.

London took a deep breath and dug a little deeper in search of her patience. She was usually really good at this part, giving Reid the space she needed until she felt ready to talk. Today, however, she was coming up short. She was just about to open her mouth to say something when Reid stopped pacing.

Reid said, "Gran has the same..." She set her hands on her hips and faced London with a look of bewilderment. "Gran *had* the same abilities as me."

"She could talk to spirits?"

Reid nodded and stared down at her hands again. "She knew things, too. Like I do sometimes. But her parents were devout Catholics. What she did scared them, so they beat her." She met London's gaze with tears in her eyes. "Until she said she couldn't see spirits anymore."

It saddened her to know that Aggie had suffered. Instead of breaking the cycle, she'd passed it on, like a virus, to her own granddaughter. London stood from the bed, stepped over to Reid, and hugged her.

"She said she was sorry for what she did to me," Reid said, her voice cracking with emotion. "And she meant it."

London squeezed her harder. She felt grateful to Aggie for sharing her story and giving Reid the closure she deserved.

CHAPTER TWENTY

Reid swiped the keycard and held the door open for London. They bid good night to Garcia and Boggs, both of whom were taking the first shift outside their hotel room door. They'd all agreed to meet in the morning over breakfast and devise a game plan for their next move. They were going to put their heads together and figure out a way to catch this bastard, so London could stop looking over her shoulder.

They set their bags on one of two queen-size beds and began unpacking the night's essentials. London showered first, and then Reid followed suit.

Reid was still coming to grips with everything her grandmother had shared during their visit. As she was shampooing her hair, she realized she felt lighter, prouder, free. Gran had essentially given her permission to embrace her psychic abilities. Part of her wanted to believe she didn't need permission, especially from the woman who made her childhood a living hell. But another, deeper part of her knew she did. It was the greatest gift Gran could have given her. For the first time ever, she wondered how her life could have been different if she'd had permission from the outset.

An even bigger question was, how many lives could she *and* Gran have changed if they'd been encouraged to embrace their gifts instead of deny them?

It had never occurred to her that her grandmother might have been mistreated as a child. She hadn't ever taken the time to contemplate how Gran had become the person she was when Reid met her. *Everyone has a story*, she reminded herself. It didn't excuse Gran's choices, but it did shed light on why she made them.

Gran's gift to London was definitely a surprise. She hadn't shared it with London yet, but she would. When the time was right.

She exited the bathroom and found London in bed. The covers were pulled down, and she was sitting in the middle, scantily clad in a spaghetti-strap tank top and a lacy black thong. The strap-on was positioned alongside her.

Reid couldn't help but laugh as she finished drying her hair with the towel. "You packed our toy?" She draped the towel over a nearby chair as she stood at the foot of the bed to admire London's incredible body. Her girlfriend was damn sexy.

"Is she here?" London asked uncertainly.

"No. She's gone." She didn't even have to check. Her grandmother wouldn't be returning. Ever. They'd said their good-byes and parted ways with a permanence that would last a lifetime.

"Gone," London repeated. "As in…gone for good?"

Reid nodded, already undressing. She pulled off her underwear and slipped the tank top over her head. Naked, she stepped around to the side of the bed and stood for a moment to let London gaze. She gave herself freely in this way because she knew London enjoyed gazing just as much as she did.

London sat up, shed her tank top and thong, and held out the toy. "Put it on."

Reid stepped into the harness and pulled it up over her thighs, cinching the straps until it fit snugly around her hips, thighs, and buttocks. They'd selected the equipment together but hadn't had the chance to give it a proper christening. The dildo looked and felt like the real deal. It was butter-soft and supple. Not too girthy. Not too long. And always erect.

Reid climbed onto the bed and set her body over the top of London's. They kissed, slowly at first. She followed London's lead. Their soft, gentle licks grew deeper, more frenzied and passionate. "Please," London begged, spreading her legs. She grabbed hold of Reid's fingers and guided them inside as she thrust her hips up to meet them.

London was soft, open, ready, and so wet. Reid pushed her fingers gently in and out, watching London's breasts bounce as she gyrated her hips to an unheard rhythm. Reid grabbed hold of a nipple between her teeth and pushed her fingers in a little deeper, harder, listening to the moans of pleasure she elicited from her lover.

Satisfying London's sexual needs pleased her on every possible level. London hadn't had an opportunity to climax in three long weeks. If Reid knew her—and she did, intimately—she knew London wouldn't last long. Fortunately for both of them, London had a secret weapon: multiple orgasms. She was the only woman Reid had ever been with who could achieve more than one orgasm in a single night. Three was their record, to date. But Reid planned on setting a new record tonight.

She withdrew her fingers and rose to her knees in front of London. She'd spent hours fantasizing about what she wanted to do to her with this toy. London wasn't shy in bed, and Reid was confident she'd be game for almost anything.

She nudged her to turn over onto her stomach. London complied but took it a step farther by getting on all fours, placing herself in the perfect position for Reid to thrust from behind. The sight of London's bare back, round ass, and wet pussy as she waited to be taken nearly sent Reid over the edge. She pried London's lips apart with one hand and guided the dildo inside with the other. She went in slowly and kept the thrusts shallow, giving her lover the time she needed to accommodate the dildo's length and girth. She reached around and began massaging London's clit with her right hand.

It didn't take long for London to adjust to the size of the toy. Reid drove the dildo in harder, deeper, watching it get swallowed up, again and again, as London bucked against it. The combined sounds of her lover's wetness and groans of pleasure were intoxicating. Fucking London like this aroused her beyond measure. It was carnal, raw. London wanted it hard, as hard as Reid could give it. London surrendered completely as the sound of skin slapping against skin filled the room.

Reid dripped down the inside of her own thighs. The base of the dildo was rubbing against her. With every thrust, she found herself inching toward an orgasm of her own. She caught a glimpse of London's breasts as they jiggled and swayed in rhythm with their bodies. When London's moans turned throaty, Reid knew her lover was on the edge.

They were both sweating now, totally in sync and consumed by a mutual need for release. She kept steady pressure on London's clit as she continued to fuck her as hard as she wanted to be fucked. The sound of skin slapping skin with London's throaty gasps, the sight of the dildo filling her up and her bare ass slamming against it, all of it shoved her over a cliff of sexual pleasure so intense and powerful that it made her wonder why the hell it took them so long to try this.

Reid couldn't stop her own groans of ecstasy as they climaxed in unison.

❖

Reid found herself longing to hold London's hand under the table as they ate, but that would force her to eat with her left hand. The intimacy they'd shared last night was still fresh in her mind.

"Fuck the FBI," Garcia said around a mouthful of chocolate-chip pancakes. He was obviously more than a little miffed. "Those fuckers are guilty of at least one of the following." He held up his thumb. "They fell for the killer's ploy, which just makes them idiots." He held up his index finger. "They used London as bait, which makes them enemy numero uno, and we squish them like the cockroaches they are. Or"— he lowered his thumb and index finger and held up his middle finger— "they just didn't give a rat's ass about London and abandoned us—*all* of us—to rot in a sinking ship."

O'Leary frowned. "Why did we rot and not drown?"

"Rot. Drown. Who the fuck cares?"

"I care. And so should you." O'Leary took a swig of his coffee. "I'd rather drown than rot, especially if the ship sank. If I didn't drown, that would mean I could breathe underwater long enough to rot, which, everyone here at the table knows, can take quite a while. Sounds way more painful than drowning."

Marino patiently waited for O'Leary to set his mug of coffee down on the table before reaching over to slap him on the back of his head. "The analogy doesn't matter because we escaped the drowning ship."

"Sinking ship," London corrected. She winked at O'Leary. "And I'm with you. I'd rather drown than rot, too." It was the first thing she'd said since they all sat down. "If we can breathe long enough underwater to rot, then I can't help but wonder if we're related to Aquaman."

Boggs nodded. "Distant cousins, maybe."

Marino and Garcia stared at Boggs. "You are *not* agreeing with them."

"You have to admit." Boggs shrugged. "They have a point."

The superhero debate that ensued was particularly heated. Reid decided to finish her omelet and let them battle it out.

The agenda for this morning's meeting was to discuss whether or not they should uphold their end of the deal and assist the FBI. The consensus seemed to be that the FBI hadn't just burned the bridge between them but had destroyed all evidence that it ever existed in the first place. There was a giant chasm between them now, and everyone at the table felt it.

Unfortunately, they were wedged between a rock and a hard place. There was no moving forward on this case—at least, not with the FBI—

and there was no going back to their nine-to-fives at the BPD. Not with a deranged serial killer on the loose who had London in his sights. What disturbed them most was that he'd traded Nicole for London. In his mind, it was a fair trade. Then, thanks to everyone at this table, he'd lost them both. They had no idea how he'd react. It could make him desperate and careless, or it could make him more resourceful, more determined, and more dangerous. They simply didn't have enough information to accurately predict his behavior.

Reid watched as a young woman approached their table. It was the concierge from the front desk. She was carrying a large white box with a big red bow. "Excuse me?" she said, glancing down at the gift box. "I have a parcel here for London Gold that requires hand delivery."

Everyone at the table except London pushed their chair abruptly from the table and stood. Unfortunately for the concierge, everyone at the table was armed. Their hands moved to the weapons in their holsters at exactly the same moment.

The woman's eyes grew wide with panic. "Sorry for interrupting your breakfast," she sputtered. "I can come back later."

Reid lowered her hand from her weapon. "Who's that from?"

"I don't know." The woman looked down and reread the label on the box. "It doesn't say."

"Where'd it come from?" Boyle asked.

"A bike courier delivered it a few minutes ago."

"What did he look like?" Boyle pressed.

"She," the concierge said. "It was a girl."

They all exchanged uneasy glances. Reid stepped forward. "I'll take it."

The woman gladly handed it over and hurried out of the restaurant. Theirs was the only occupied table in the establishment, which was probably why they'd been easy to spot. It could've been helpful to ask the woman how she knew where to find them. Was the killer keeping tabs on them? More to the point, was he keeping tabs on London?

"Maybe we should wait to open that," Boyle said, cautioning her.

O'Leary nodded. "Could be an explosive device inside."

Something told Reid they didn't have time to dick around. She set the box on an adjacent table and carefully lifted the lid to reveal a pair of slippers resting on top of a neatly folded nightgown. It was identical to what Nicole had been wearing when they'd found her in the bathroom stall.

"Is there a note?" Garcia asked.

She set the slippers aside and read the handwritten note that was stapled to the collar of the nightgown: *London, try this on. Get comfy. You'll be wearing this for me soon.*

She returned to her chair at the head of the table and passed the note to London. They obviously needed to figure out why the nightgown and slippers were significant. It'd shed some light on the killer's psychology.

Reid watched as her team passed the note around the table. The mood was somber. She cleared her throat. "I don't think anyone at this table has used their personal time, sick days, or vacation days in—"

"Three years, three months, and thirteen days," O'Leary finished. "We all took a day to attend Abuelita's funeral."

Garcia's grandmother—she became Abuelita to all of them many years ago—had passed away unexpectedly from a massive stroke. Reid still missed her infectious laugh, along with her green chili enchilada casserole.

Garcia lifted his chunky gold chain from inside his shirt and kissed the cross pendant. "May you rest in peace, Abuelita."

"We can work this case without the FBI," she went on. "We don't have the files anymore, but we know enough to give us a good head start. We'll fill in the blanks as we go."

O'Leary said, "Actually, we do have the files."

Boyle shook his head. "Russo took them back to headquarters."

O'Leary sat up straighter. "When all of you went home the other night, I stayed and copied everything. Digitally, of course."

"Everything?" Boyle's eyes grew wide. "All four boxes?"

O'Leary withdrew a flash drive from his shirt pocket and held it up. "Digital copies are not only more efficient, but they're better—"

"For the environment," they all finished, in stereo. O'Leary had a thing about trees and hated paper anything.

In place of the usual slap on the back of the head, Marino reached over and patted O'Leary's shoulder in approval. "Nice work, man."

Boggs looked across the table at Reid. "If we work this case on our own, we'll have to use the BPD's resources." He turned to Boyle. "Can you pull that off, Lieutenant?"

Reid already had an answer at the ready, but she deferred to Boyle.

Boyle leaned forward and whispered, "We know people who can get us whatever we need."

Garcia dropped his chain back inside his shirt and met Reid's gaze. "You proposing we hunt for this guy off-the-record?"

Reid had no doubt they all knew what off-the-record meant. If they managed to find the killer before the FBI, they could deliver their own version of justice so he'd never have the chance to hurt anyone, including London, ever again. She leaned back in her chair. "I'm suggesting we go underground. Work in secret."

"To what end?" Marino asked.

"Until we find him," she answered calmly. "Off-the-record."

Boyle was the first to cast his vote. "I'm in."

"Me, too," Boggs said.

Marino chugged the last of his coffee. "Yep."

"Goes without saying," O'Leary chimed in.

"Bastard's going down," Garcia said.

They all looked at London and waited. She had been quiet for so long that Reid worried she might not be a fan of working the case off-the-record. When it came to police work, London tended to color inside the lines.

"He has three women in captivity right now. Let's find him before he..." London trailed off as her eyes welled up with tears.

Reid reached out and squeezed London's left hand as O'Leary did the same with her right.

"We'll find him," Boyle said with a hard edge to his voice.

Reid nodded. "Damn right, we will."

CHAPTER TWENTY-ONE

London stared at the boxed nightgown in the center of the table as the team began to strategize. She couldn't shake the feeling that they were being watched. Maybe the killer was nearby. Maybe he was monitoring them on video. Security cameras were mounted in each corner of the restaurant. He could've hacked the hotel's security feed or planted cameras of his own. Maybe he'd planted a bug underneath their table and was listening to their conversation right now.

She felt her mind spinning out of control and inhaled deeply to quiet her thoughts. *Reel it in, Gold. Slow and steady.*

She was sitting with her back to the restaurant and fought the urge to look over her shoulder. If the killer was watching, she refused to give him the satisfaction of seeing that she was nervous. Besides, this team had her back. Hadn't they already proven that? They would do everything humanly possible to keep her safe.

It was the *everything humanly possible* part that set her on edge. After her encounter with the killer, she found herself believing that he was, in fact, something other than human. That predatory look in his eyes during their exchange in the airport bathroom had felt like ice-cold fingers against the back of her neck. There was nothing human about him. Compiling any kind of psychological profile with predictive behavioral markers seemed impossible. He was so far from human that they might as well profile a great white shark with a voracious appetite for human flesh.

She glanced around the table at her colleagues and felt grateful for their support. Part of her embraced their vow to keep her safe. And part of her admonished herself for needing it. She was a homicide detective with nine years under her belt as a Boston cop. She'd faced her share of dangerous encounters over the years but had always managed to keep herself safe. If push came to shove, her brothers and sisters in blue had her back. Just like she had theirs. But every cop was expected to function with a certain degree of autonomy. And she prided herself on her ability to handle most situations, including physical confrontations, on her own, without the need for anyone's assistance.

But *this*…this was different.

This wasn't about her needing to prove herself as a woman in law enforcement. She felt confident that everyone at this table knew she could hold her own. This was about her falling in the cross hairs of a sociopathic serial killer. Right now, it was all hands on deck.

"I know a guy," she said on the heels of a short pause in conversation.

Her colleagues turned their attention from Reid to her, their gazes sharp.

"This guy…he can keep us off the radar."

"Can he be trusted?" Boyle asked.

She nodded. "Yes."

"You hesitated," Reid observed, as perceptive as ever. "Why?"

She met Reid's gaze, all too aware that they had an audience. Now wasn't the time to hold back information. Tiptoeing around anything would only waste time. From this point forward—at least, until they caught the killer—her privacy was a thing of the past. Everything needed to be out in the open. "We sort of dated for a short time in college."

"Sort of," Reid repeated. "How do you sort of date someone?"

She was surprised Reid was asking. Either she was too curious to wait until they were alone, or she was asking for the full story to be shared publicly for the benefit of the group. Reid always exhibited more self-control when it came to airing personal information, so it had to be the latter. "I was assaulted the summer before I started my freshman year at Harvard. Mason helped me through it. He was always a gentleman. He showed me that men could be trusted."

"Assaulted." Garcia sat up straighter. "As in…*raped*?"

London swallowed hard. For a fleeting moment, she wondered if these men would see her forevermore as a victim. Being assaulted at eighteen and then selected as a serial killer's next target wasn't a great track record. But she knew who she was. She wasn't a victim. And she had faith that the men at this table already knew that. *Everything out in the open*, she reminded herself. *No secrets. No tiptoeing. No shame.*

"That's correct." She felt her face flush, despite her internal pep talk. "I was raped."

"Did they catch him?" Garcia asked, visibly pissed off as he set both fists on the table. "Did they put him away for what he did to you?"

She met Reid's gaze, and Reid nodded. "He met a fate worse than prison."

"No shit," Garcia said with a look of awe. He leaned back in his chair. "Did you take care of him yourself, off-the-record?"

London was momentarily stunned. Was he asking her what she thought he was asking—if she'd retaliated against her assailant by plotting and executing his murder?

"No," Reid answered, her gaze still on London's. "Everyone at this table knows you're by the book."

"Everyone except Garcia," O'Leary chided, happy to finally have something to tease someone else about. "Have you met Gold, man?"

"If it wasn't you who ended the prick, then…holy fuck." Garcia's eyes grew wide. "Your parents—?"

"My parents didn't have anything to do with it, either." There was no way around it. Time to reveal her secret to the group. "Bill Sullivan assaulted me." She didn't feel the need to share anything more. Just the name elicited gasps of surprise around the table.

"*Governor* Bill Sullivan?" Garcia prodded. "Holy fucking shit. That bastard!" He slammed his fists on the table. "I voted for him!"

Boggs set a hand on Garcia's shoulder. "He got what he deserved in the end, bro."

There was a moment of silence at the table. Governor Bill Sullivan had met his demise at the hands of a serial killer and had paid for his sins with an agonizing death. The governor's murder had landed in their laps, so everyone at the table was familiar with the case. Boyle was the only one in their unit who knew the sordid details of London's assault. He'd been first on the scene and stumbled upon Bill's confession in a journal. He'd disposed of the evidence to cover up her involvement as one of the governor's victims. She would be forever grateful to Boyle for that larger-than-life favor.

"That bastard certainly got one hell of a sendoff." Boyle raised his mug and winked at her knowingly. "Karma's a bitch."

"So, this Mason guy," Garcia went on. "He was good to you?"

She nodded and smiled reassuringly. "I wouldn't have become a cop if it wasn't for him."

All eyes turned to Reid, as if asking for her permission. "Can't say I'm thrilled with the idea of bunking with an ex-boyfriend." She shrugged. "But it's not like we have a shitload of options right now."

"Settles it, then." Boyle slapped the table. "Gold, reach out to Mason. Set it up forthwith."

"Nice use of our new word," Marino said.

"We've been over this," Reid warned, shooting Marino the stink eye. "It's *our* new word. Go find your own."

Boyle checked his watch. "We'll reconvene at nine hundred hours."

They paid their tab, took the elevator to the fifth floor, and walked to their rooms in silence. O'Leary and Boggs stood post outside Reid and London's hotel room door.

Reid turned to her as soon as they stepped inside. "I need you to promise me something."

Her fervent, bright green gaze made London momentarily lose focus. Those eyes. Those lips. She flashed back to a memory of Reid thrusting inside her the night before. Reid hadn't held anything back. Neither had she. She was sore today, but she had no regrets and would do it all again in a heartbeat. Judging from Reid's passionate moans of pleasure, London was pretty sure she felt the same.

They'd experienced a new level of intimacy, and it was amazing. There was no question about it. Receiving felt incredible. But she also found herself wanting to give. The idea of wearing the harness and taking Reid just as hard made her wet and achy all over again. It was only a matter of time before Reid granted her access.

"If you're cornered by this bastard, promise me you won't agree to go with him. Not even to save me."

"Reid, I can't make that—"

"You have to," Reid said, shaking her head. "I won't move another inch on this case if you don't give me your word right now."

"You're giving me an ultimatum?" She stepped back and crossed her arms. "Are you saying my life is more important than yours?"

Reid stepped closer, unfolded London's arms, and slipped her fingers between London's. "I'm not as strong as you are. If something happened to you, it'd wreck me." She shrugged. "I'd rather be the one to go. If it comes to that, you need to let me be the one."

London knew, down to the deepest fiber of her core, that Reid was telling the truth. If something happened to her while working this case—no matter the circumstance—Reid would feel responsible and blame herself. That's just the type of person she was. And she was right—it *would* wreck her. Reid would close down and shut everyone out of her life, without exception.

"Your word," Reid prompted. "Please, London."

She nodded. "My word." It was a promise she didn't make lightly. She was all too aware that what Reid proposed was possible. The killer was clever, resourceful, and downright dangerous. From this point forward, they had to be on their A game at all times. If one of them dropped the ball, the killer would sniff them out like injured prey. There could be no discernible weakness in their circle.

Instinct told London that the killer would home in on her. She was convinced that he believed he'd wounded her. He was following her blood trail until she succumbed to her injuries. She shared her thoughts aloud with Reid.

"So let him." Reid shrugged.

London frowned in confusion. "Let him what?"

"Let him believe you've been weakened by his attack. Let him believe you're unsure of yourself, that you're scared."

"But I *am*." She sat on one corner of the bed and looked up at Reid. "I'm all of those things."

"You should be scared. The killer's proven that he's a formidable opponent." Reid took a seat beside her and reached out to hold her hand. "But you're not unsure of yourself. And—correct me if I'm wrong here—you *haven't* been weakened by his attack."

She stared down at their hands as she considered Reid's words. Had she been weakened by her abduction? The terror she'd felt in those few hours was unlike anything she'd ever experienced in her life. In this case, fear was a healthy response to danger.

She suddenly saw her fear for what it was, a built-in defense mechanism. It had elevated her heart rate and blood pressure, causing her to be hyperalert. In fact, the sole purpose of fear was to increase her chances of survival. Right now, fear was her ally.

London realized that she didn't feel weak or unsure of herself. She had learned from her encounter with the killer. She saw her mistakes clearly now and knew, without a doubt, that she would never make them again. "You're right," she admitted, meeting Reid's knowing gaze. "Being abducted didn't weaken me. It made me—"

"Stronger, smarter, more intuitive," Reid finished. "Way I see it, you have an advantage over the rest of the team."

She thought for a moment. "Because I've seen him?"

Reid nodded. "In more ways than one."

She waited for Reid to go on, unsure of where she was going with this.

"You may not be psychic, but we both know you have incredible intuition. A cop's intuition. I suspect you now know more about the killer than you realize." Reid scooted closer. "What happened yesterday was traumatic. Just like with anyone in your shoes, you need time. Time to heal. Time to process. The more distance you get from what happened yesterday, the more you'll remember."

London was about to object because she remembered everything and had already shared the entirety of her experience with the team. But she suddenly understood, on a gut level, the point that Reid was trying to make. The predatory look in his eyes. The choices he made in the bathroom stall. The way he moved. His speech patterns. Each detail would inevitably fill in a piece of the puzzle.

Every puzzle she'd ever undertaken as a kid had a picture on the box. The picture, of course, served as a guide. Not only did her team not have the box, but they were also missing many of the puzzle pieces. It was like doing a five-thousand-piece puzzle with half the pieces and no picture to go on. A double whammy.

She decided to ask the question that had been on her mind all morning. "Can you communicate with the killer like you did with me at La Franco's?"

Reid didn't look at all surprised. Maybe she'd been wondering the same. "I honestly don't know," she answered with a shrug.

"Then maybe it's time to experiment." She couldn't help but feel excited. Testing the limits of Reid's psychic abilities intrigued her.

"How?" Reid frowned. "It sounds like you have something in mind."

"I do. But it'll have to wait until we get to Mason's." She stood from the bed and started packing.

"You've already reached out to him?"

She nodded. "I sent him a text."

"Did you hear back?" Reid asked.

"Not yet."

"Then how can you be sure he'll agree to..." Reid trailed off, obviously unsure of what Mason would be doing, exactly.

"He'll provide us with a safe space to work, off the radar," she explained. "Mason's also a total computer geek and a hacking aficionado. If we let him, he'll be an invaluable asset to the team."

Reid raised an eyebrow. "And you know he'll want to help because…"

London zipped her suitcase, lifted it from the bed, and set it on the floor. "He'll agree to help us because…" She bit her lip uncertainly, unsure just how forthcoming she should be in this moment.

"Go ahead," Reid said, rolling her eyes. "Out with it."

CHAPTER TWENTY-TWO

London second-guessed her willingness to be totally transparent. The timing couldn't be worse. But Reid deserved to know the truth. She'd been nothing but honest with Reid since the day they'd met. Hiding something now was akin to lying. "Mason will agree to help because he'd do anything for me."

Reid studied her, quiet, pensive.

London could imagine what was going through Reid's mind. She waited, giving Reid the time she needed to decide if she wanted to pursue this. They were going to have to talk about it sooner or later. In her mind, sooner was better. In fact, she should have thought to discuss this with Reid ages ago.

"How long did you date Mason?" Reid finally asked.

"A few months."

Reid tilted her head suspiciously. "Did you have sex with him?"

"God, no. I've never slept with a man."

"Did the two of you engage in other activities," Reid pressed, "to satisfy his sexual appetite?"

These were very personal questions, but she would hold nothing back from Reid. Total transparency was their deal. "No," she answered honestly.

Reid's expression was difficult to read. "Kissing?"

She nodded. "We kissed." If Reid needed to ask these questions, then London would do her best to answer them. Disclosing the details of a prior relationship to the love of her life made her feel a little sick to her stomach.

"Did you enjoy it?"

London stared at the floor as she thought. "It's complicated because—"

"You can't do that," Reid quipped. "In my book, it's a simple yes or no."

"But it's not your book," she reminded her gently. "It's mine."

Reid was quiet. She finally met London's gaze and sighed. "Explain it to me, then."

"Sit." London patted the mattress beside her. "Please."

Reid sat on the opposite bed, facing her. Her decision to place physical distance between them stung.

"I'd just come off the heels of being assaulted by my godfather—a man I'd known my entire life, a man who was supposed to be like a father to me. Even though I didn't remember a single detail about the incident—"

"The rape," Reid corrected her. "He raped you, London."

Another thing she loved about Reid was that she never let her get away with sugarcoating anything. Reid looked truth dead in the eye and faced it, head-on, no matter the cost.

It was still difficult to admit that Bill had raped her. In some ways, it felt surreal, like he'd done it to somebody else. She was drugged when it happened and, likely, unconscious. No matter how hard she tried, she had zero recollection of what took place in the guest room on that fateful summer night. She'd finally come to terms with her inability to recall the details and decided amnesia was a blessing. Still, a part of her knew it had happened. There was no denying it. She'd held on to her virginity for eighteen years, and he'd stolen that from her.

She'd never had any intention of sleeping with a man. Ever. She came out to her friends during her junior year of high school. They readily embraced and supported her. Being roofied and raped by a man she was raised with had turned her world upside down.

"When Mason pursued me, I gave him the cold shoulder. Literally, I shunned him at every turn for months. I wanted nothing to do with him."

Reid shrugged, clearly unimpressed. "Sounds like a normal guy to me. When they see a beautiful woman, the word *no* suddenly exits their vocabulary. At that age, everything—and I mean *everything*—boils down to servicing one thing: the p—"

"Penis," she finished, rolling her eyes. "I wasn't born yesterday, Reid."

"So? He wanted to get in your pants, and he was willing to work for it. How does that make him any different from every other man on the planet?"

"Mason was persistent, yes. But he was also gentle and patient and funny and as far from threatening as you can possibly get."

"So? He was clever. He figured out what it would take to get in your pants. Like I said, sounds like a normal guy."

"He listened," she went on, ignoring Reid's comments. "He asked questions. He wanted to know who'd hurt me, so I told him." She shrugged. "I didn't tell him *who* had hurt me, only that someone had."

"And?" Reid asked, looking as skeptical as ever.

"And, in that moment, I decided he was safe."

"You told him you were raped."

"I told him that someone roofied me and took advantage."

Reid frowned. "Did you also happen to mention that you were a lesbian?"

"Yes. I was upfront about that." London could see that all of this was like a punch to the gut for Reid, especially on the heels of learning that Mason was, presumably, going to be their host.

"Let me guess. He believed he could straighten you out," Reid said sarcastically.

She shook her head. "It wasn't like that."

"Is Mason still in your life?"

"Yes." She kept her voice even. "We're friends. *Just* friends."

"How could you not have mentioned this before?" Reid asked, her expression hurt.

She felt her face flush and wasn't sure if it was triggered by guilt or embarrassment. These questions were more intimate and difficult to answer than she'd anticipated. Why did it feel like she'd just cheated on Reid? Her relationship with Mason had ended years before they even met. "We only dated for a few months. I was never attracted to him, so we stopped dating and stayed friends."

"Is he still attracted to you?" Reid asked.

London wanted to ask why it even mattered because she and Mason had moved past this ages ago. But she knew why it mattered. Reid obviously felt threatened and probably betrayed, like she'd intentionally withheld this information. The truth was, she hadn't. The subject just hadn't come up. In the handful of times that she and Mason had communicated over the last year, bringing him up hadn't seemed relevant, necessary, or even appropriate. For the first time in her life,

London didn't know how to be honest about a choice she'd made in the past and explain it in a way that would make sense.

Everything that happened between her and Mason had made sense at the time. Somehow, deep down, it still did. He was an important part of her journey, and she liked to think that she was an important part of his. All that existed between them now was friendship. As far as she was concerned, all that had ever existed between them was friendship. It was simple and beautiful and honest. Nothing had ever felt complicated between her and Mason. There were no layers to sift through. He'd been there for her when she needed him, and she liked to think she had done the same for him.

"I never saw this coming." Reid shot up from the bed and started pacing. "I can't believe I agreed to be under the same roof as Mason."

"Stop," London said firmly. She stood from the bed and stepped in front of Reid, blocking her path. "Look at me." Reid was falling down a rabbit hole. London had to retrieve her before she went too deep. "I need you to trust me right now." She reached out to take Reid's hand.

Reid took a step back before she made contact. "*Don't*," she spat, shooting her a look of warning. "Do you have feelings for him?"

"Of course not," she said, surprised by the question. "I'm in love with *you*."

"Does he have feelings for you?"

"I can't imagine that he—"

"Is he married?"

"No." She shook her head, confused. Reid's questions were coming faster now. There was an edge to her voice. It was the same cutthroat, no-nonsense tone she used when interrogating a suspect.

"Does he have a girlfriend?"

"I…I don't know if he has a girlfriend or not. We don't usually—"

"How do you communicate with Mason?"

"We text." She shrugged. "We talk on the phone occasionally."

"How occasionally?"

"Once or twice a month." Was Reid really going here? Did Reid believe she had feelings for Mason? Did she believe they were having an emotional affair? The thought of cheating on Reid made her want to vomit.

Reid persisted. "How often do you text?"

"A few times a week, give or take. You can go through my phone and read them, if you want," she offered. She had nothing to hide. The thought that Reid was questioning her loyalty set her on edge.

"Have you told him about me?"

She hesitated, unsure if Reid was referring to her psychic ability or the fact that they were in a relationship. "If you're asking whether or not I've shared that you can communicate with spirits—"

"Have you informed him that you have a girlfriend?"

And there it was. Reid had cornered her. She should've seen this coming and headed it off at the pass. "No. I haven't told him about our relationship. And I don't appreciate being interrogated like a suspect."

"Actions, London. They speak louder than words. The fact that you haven't told him about me speaks volumes."

Reid's words stung. London hadn't shared the news of their relationship with Mason because she didn't want to mistakenly reveal Reid's secret. It was difficult to talk about Reid and *not* mention how amazing she was. Reid's ability to communicate with spirits was such a big part of their everyday lives. It'd be too easy to let something slip.

In some ways, Mason knew her better than anyone. His intuition, emotional intelligence, and book smarts were a lethal combination. He didn't let her get away with much. In fact, now that she thought about it, she was surprised he hadn't recognized the signs that she was in a relationship: fewer texts, shorter calls. In the past, Mason would never have shied away from bringing that to her attention. Why hadn't he called her out yet? Maybe he didn't want to pry. He'd always respected her boundaries. He was probably waiting for her to decide when she was ready to share.

Her watch alerted her to an incoming text. "It's Mason," she said, reading it aloud. *"Bring the troops. Mi casa es su casa. Whatever you need."*

"Well, you're about to meet each other." London grabbed her phone and texted him that they were on their way. She met Reid's gaze with a smile. "And I'd like to introduce you as my girlfriend."

"Don't bother," Reid shot back. She zipped up her suitcase, set it on the floor, and grabbed her coat on the way to the door.

"Wait. What does that mean?" she asked, confused.

Reid didn't even give London the courtesy of turning to look at her. "It means you're free to do whatever you want with Mason." She swung the door open and stepped into the hallway before London had a chance to respond.

❖

Reid wheeled her suitcase into the hallway and let the door close behind her as Boyle was exiting his hotel room across the hall. "You good?" he asked, obviously picking up on her mood.

"Nothing a few beers won't cure," she admitted as they walked to the elevator. O'Leary and Boggs were still stationed outside the hotel room door, waiting to escort London. She needed some space from London right now and trusted the duo to keep her safe.

Boyle called back over his shoulder. "Meet us in the lobby."

"Copy that," the duo replied in unison.

She and Boyle stepped inside the elevator. He pressed the *L* button and turned to her. "So, what's the deal with this Mason guy?"

She shrugged. Boyle had a sixth sense of his own, which made him a quadruple pain in the ass. He knew her too well, he cared, he was disarming, and he was too damn good at ferreting out the truth. "Hard to say," she answered honestly.

"Might interest you to know that I ran a background check on Mason," he admitted. "Came back clean."

She slid her hands in her pockets and nodded. "That's a start."

"We don't *have* to avail ourselves of this guy's services."

"You have another idea?"

Boyle shrugged. "Not sure how I'd feel if me and my wife had to stay with my wife's ex-boyfriend." He frowned. "Actually, I know exactly how I'd feel about it. I'd be fucking pissed off." He turned to look at her. "Especially if I didn't know about him, and then I found out they were still friends."

"Fuck, Boyle. Were you listening at our door?" she asked, more than a little irritated.

He looked utterly offended and pleased with himself all at the same time. "No way, Sylver. I'm just that good."

Reid didn't argue because she knew he was telling the truth. Boyle respected their friendship too damn much to pull something like that. "Mason's a tough pill to swallow," she admitted as they both stepped off the elevator.

"There are other options."

She dropped her keycard into the hotel's return box. "Like what?"

"We can find someplace off the grid."

"It'd take time to set that up." She shook her head. "Time is a luxury we can't afford right now. The faster we get this bastard, the sooner all this will end." She and Boyle leaned up against the lobby pillar, surveying guests as they checked out at the counter. "Gold says he'll be an invaluable asset to the team."

"Last I checked, you're not a big fan of outsiders."

"He's not an outsider—at least, not to Gold. That should count for something."

"You're a bigger man than me, Sylver." He nodded at the shop adjacent to the lobby. "They carry zuPOO. I'll go grab some before we head out."

"What for?" she asked, intrigued.

"It's better than a laxative. Totally cleans you out. Just give me the signal, and I'll add it to Mason's coffee." He winked. "I've got your six, Sylver."

She shook her head and laughed as she watched him cross the lobby.

CHAPTER TWENTY-THREE

R eid and Boyle stood shoulder to shoulder as they waited for the rest of their team in the hotel lobby. Garcia, Marino, Boggs, O'Leary, and Gold stepped off the elevator, dropped their keycards into the designated slot, and joined them with suitcases and duffel bags in tow.

"What now?" Garcia asked, looking back and forth between her and Boyle.

"Depends," Boyle said, nodding at London. "Heard back from your guy yet?"

Reid watched as London visibly cringed at *your guy*. "He sent his driver to pick us up." She checked her watch. "Should be here in about five minutes."

"His driver?" Garcia frowned. "He has a driver?"

"Tony Stark has a driver in *Iron Man*." O'Leary grinned. "Is Mason a superhero?"

Marino slapped O'Leary on the back of the head. "Focus, man."

"Where's this driver taking us?" Garcia pressed.

London shrugged. "He wouldn't say."

They all glanced around at one another uneasily. Reid wasn't thrilled with the idea of climbing inside a stranger's vehicle and being driven to a secret location by someone she hadn't vetted.

"You sure about this guy?" Boggs asked.

London nodded. "This is the guy we need right now. Trust me, he won't disappoint."

Garcia set his duffel bag on the floor. "You said you knew him in college. When's the last time you actually laid eyes on him?"

She watched as London hesitated. "June," she said finally. "He flew into Boston on business."

Reid crossed her arms. London saw Mason just five months ago—

something she'd neglected to mention. She and London had already been in a relationship for seven months by then. She'd had ample opportunity to share her history with Mason, as well as the nature of their relationship. The burning question of the hour was, why hadn't she?

Trust had never been an issue between them. As must as she hated to admit it, it was now. She wanted to trust London. Desperately. Suddenly having to question the reason behind London's secrecy felt like a kick to the balls. As far as she knew, London had never lied to her. But an omission of this magnitude was impossible to ignore.

Her watch vibrated, alerting her to an incoming call. She flicked her wrist. "Russo," she announced to the group.

"Nice of her to check in," Marino said, his tone rich with sarcasm.

She accepted the call. "Sylver."

"Where are you?" Russo asked impatiently.

"Just checked out of our hotel."

There was a brief pause. "You're not staying?"

"She's kidding, right?" Marino said as he made an obscene hand gesture.

"Why would I be kidding?" Russo shot back. "We still need your assistance with this case. I thought I made that clear."

Boggs stepped forward and spoke directly into Reid's watch. "Because you left us to rot in a sinking ship, which, as O'Leary pointed out, is way worse than drowning. Turns out, we can breathe underwater because we're related to Aquaman."

There was a moment of silence, followed by a round of high fives and fist bumps from everyone in their circle. Reid couldn't have said it better herself. She looked to Boyle, who nodded.

"May I?" he asked, pointing at her watch.

"Of course," she said, holding her wrist aloft as he tapped the red icon to end the call.

O'Leary smiled broadly. "That was fun."

"And weirdly satisfying," Garcia admitted, shaking his head.

London nodded at the entrance as a black Hummer limousine pulled up to the curb. "Ride's here."

Marino turned and made a catcall whistle.

"What the...?" Boggs blinked repeatedly, as if trying to clear his vision.

"Hard not to like this guy already." Garcia locked gazes with Reid and shrugged apologetically.

O'Leary leaned in. "My affections cannot be bought," he whispered.

She caught Boyle salivating and elbowed him hard in the ribs. "ZuPOO," she reminded him.

"ZuPOO," he whispered back.

The driver exited the limo, walked around to the passenger's side, and greeted them with a curt bow.

"Are you related to Happy Hogan?" O'Leary asked with boyish enthusiasm, referring, of course, to Tony Stark's driver in *Iron Man*.

"My uncle," the driver replied, his expression dour. He loaded their luggage in the back as they all climbed inside.

They'd been driving for over an hour when the driver made a hasty exit and parked in the service area of an abandoned used-car dealership. Reid gazed out the tinted window. She'd been keeping close tabs on their direction of travel. There was nothing around for miles.

"We've stopped," O'Leary announced as he craned his neck to look out the windshield.

Marino rolled his eyes. "Thanks, Captain Obvious."

The driver slid the glass partition aside. "Mason wants you to power down your phones and watches and put them in here." He handed London a New Balance shoebox.

"Right." Marino laughed coldly. "Over my maggot-riddled, rotting carcass."

"Fuck, no." Garcia sat up straighter and clenched both his hands into fists.

"Sure," Boggs said, flipping the driver off, "and I'll bend over for you when we shower together."

"Not on your nelly," O'Leary said with his meanest scowl.

They all turned to stare at him. "Really, man?" Marino said. "You couldn't come up with anything better?"

O'Leary shrugged. "You guys took all the good ones."

"Relax," the driver assured them as soon as they'd all simmered down. "You'll get everything back by the end of the day. Mason needs to make sure no one's tracking you." He turned in his seat and fixed a steely-eyed gaze on London. "You came to him for a reason, right?"

London dropped her phone and watch into the box.

"We're still armed," Boyle observed, dropping his in, too. "Besides, how do we know the killer *isn't* tracking us?"

They all followed suit and watched as the driver threw his door open, stepped over to the abandoned building, and let himself inside.

"Are we supposed to get out?" Boggs asked.

Marino tried opening the limo door, to no avail. "Doors are locked."

"But he left the car running and the heater on," London said in a chipper tone.

O'Leary leaned forward, his forehead creased with worry. "I have to pee."

Marino sighed and shook his head. "Boston cops say *take a piss*, O'Leary. How many times do we need to go over this?"

The driver exited the building empty-handed. He climbed back inside the limo and put the car in gear.

"Hey!" Garcia banged on the glass partition. "Where's our stuff?"

The driver slid the partition aside. "Safe. I told you—you'll get everything back later today." He drove around the building until he arrived at a metal gate on the other side. Reid watched as he pressed a button on the console. The gate opened, allowing them entry onto a hidden dirt road.

Clever. They must be close to Mason's.

She was mildly uneasy with the thought of giving up her phone and watch, even if it was on a temporary basis. Those devices were a lifeline to her team. If she and her team were separated, she had no way of contacting them.

She glanced at London and locked gazes with her, out of habit. The pull she felt toward London was so strong that it took her a moment to catch her breath and look away. Every instinct in her mind and body had encouraged her to trust London from the get-go. Even now, it was difficult to remember that she didn't. But London's blatant omissions were inexcusable. Reid needed to retreat and regroup.

She also needed time to observe Mason and London interact with one another. Would there be palpable chemistry between them? Maybe. Maybe not. Either way, she needed to make sure she was mentally prepped for the answer. But how did one go about preparing for something like that? Shutting down and keeping London outside her walls was out of the question. Too late for that because she'd already invited London in, cleared some space for her, and tossed all her old furniture—figuratively speaking, of course. She already loved London, to an extent she'd never believed was possible. How could she be expected to turn that off if things swayed in Mason's favor?

She couldn't. And *that* was the problem.

If her worst fears were realized and London hit it off with Mason, it was going to hurt like hell. Something told her there was no way to prepare for something like that. No amount of foresight or reasoning or talking aloud would save her from the unbearable pain of losing the love of her life.

For the first time since they'd started dating, Reid wished she didn't know what it was like to love London and be loved by her. Whoever said ignorance was bliss hit the nail square on the head. She was at London's mercy, and there was nothing she could do to stop it.

❖

London considered greeting Mason with a handshake upon seeing him, but that would just be weird. They always hugged when they visited. Shaking hands would be solely for Reid's benefit. If she started behaving differently now, it would just make Reid more suspicious. The truth was, she had nothing whatsoever to hide. Reid was obviously taking a step back in response to the news of her relationship with Mason. She was keenly aware that Reid would be watching her with Mason, looking for signs of emotional or physical chemistry. But there were none. They were friends. Nothing more, but nothing less. Sooner or later, Reid would realize she was telling the truth.

London had no one but herself to blame for the position she found herself in now. Without meaning to, she'd dug a very deep hole. Not disclosing her relationship with Mason had hurt Reid deeply. She could see that now. Why hadn't she shared him with Reid sooner?

Nine years had passed since she and Mason had made the decision to stop dating. They'd both moved on to date women and had never— not once—spoken of their history. No one in college knew. She hadn't shared with any of her friends, and neither had he. In fact, she'd gone to great lengths to keep it under wraps and had made him promise to do the same. Even at that time, in the midst of her involvement with Mason, she knew she was a lesbian. She didn't want to give anyone in her life reason to question that.

It hit her then why she'd been reluctant to share her story with Reid. She didn't want Reid—or anyone—to question her sexuality. Coming out of the closet as a junior in high school was nerve-racking, but her friends readily supported her. Coming out to her parents, on the other hand, was a much different experience. They'd disowned her on the heels of learning that she was gay. Rescinding her sexuality bombshell by revealing that she'd dated a man would confuse her parents or, worse, mislead them. The very thought if it terrified her.

Not that there was anything wrong with being heterosexual or bisexual. It just didn't match up with who she was. She knew who she was, and no one would ever convince her otherwise.

She trusted Reid in a way she'd never trusted anyone before. And before today, she was pretty sure Reid felt the same. Trust didn't come easily or naturally to Reid—it had to be earned. Had London irreparably damaged that trust?

They made a series of turns and walked for several minutes through underground tunnels until they arrived at a formidable-looking metal door. London looked on as the driver typed a four-digit code on the door's keypad: the last four digits of her student ID number at Harvard. Mason had been using that as his password for the last decade. She shook her head and smiled. Some things never changed.

The door unlocked with an audible *click* as the driver led their group inside.

CHAPTER TWENTY-FOUR

Reid watched as Mason stood from a nearby armchair. He checked all the boxes of the type of man she imagined most women would fall for—tall, dark, handsome, well-built. She rolled her eyes. He'd be the perfect candidate for a hunky bachelor role in any Hallmark Christmas movie.

Mason ushered them inside with a smile and a slight bow. "Welcome," he said humbly.

They went around the room and made brief introductions. Reid looked away as London and Mason hugged. It felt like a slap in the face. London obviously wasn't going with the hands-off approach when it came to the three of them being in the same room.

Reid's knee-jerk reaction to the hug surprised her. She felt territorial, angry, and irrationally jealous in one fell swoop. Had she expected that they wouldn't hug? Maybe. Had she hoped that London would alter her behavior to limit physical contact in her presence? Definitely. Physical contact felt inappropriate and disrespectful, especially on the heels of the bomb London had just dropped.

"Bedrooms are that way." Mason pointed behind him. "Take your pick, and make yourselves at home."

Her team dispersed, their luggage in tow. Reid stayed put. Part of her wanted to follow them. The other, more primitive part of her refused to leave London alone with Mason. Henceforth, she was the self-designated hug monitor.

From what Reid could tell, the entire house was underground—a bunker of sorts. And it was massive. The walls and high ceilings were composed of jagged rockface. Each interior wall had colored climbing holds that flanked the length of the wall all the way up to the ceiling.

Looked like climbing the walls wasn't just a figure of speech here. Mason was obviously a rock climber, evidenced by his broad shoulders and muscular arms.

Furniture had been pulled away from the walls, positioned in the center of the room, and grouped into different work and hangout stations. There was a plethora of comfy-looking chairs from which to choose—chaise lounges, papasans, armchairs, sofas, beanbags. She had to admit, the dragon's lair was kind of cool. "You live here?"

"Mostly," Mason answered. "In my line of work, anonymity is paramount."

"What do you do, exactly?" Reid asked, taking the bull by the horns.

"I'm a gray hat."

"I've heard of a white hat and a black hat." She frowned. "What the hell is a gray hat?"

"A professional computer hacker. White hats work for the good guys. Black hats don't." Mason shrugged. "I'm somewhere in the middle." He closed the gap between them and extended his hand, meeting her gaze with large dark brown eyes. "Mason McCormick," he said with a genuine smile. "It's a pleasure to finally meet you."

Reid could hear London holding her breath as Mason stood before her, waiting patiently for her to return the handshake. He didn't attempt to hide or sugarcoat what he did for a living, even though he knew she was a retired cop. She appreciated that. "Reid Sylver," she said, extending her own hand as they sealed a formal introduction.

His eyes lit up. "Sylver and Gold," he said, looking back and forth between them. "Neither of you should change your name."

"Wasn't planning on it." She pulled her hand away from his when he extended the handshake beyond the standard three seconds. Either he was using a prolonged handshake to be warm, or he was trying to dominate her. She wasn't sure which. Another possibility occurred to her. Was he using the handshake to get a feel for her…to read her?

"What I meant to say," he explained, "is that the two of you should keep your names the same when you get married."

She stared at him, confused. London said she hadn't shared the news of their relationship with Mason. Had she texted him about it from the limo on the way here?

"Sorry. Did I get this wrong?" he asked, looking to London for help.

"No." London came up alongside her and slid her fingers between Reid's. "You got it right."

"Excellent." Mason grinned broadly. "The air between you two sizzles."

"What gave us away?" London asked.

He glanced at their clasped hands before meeting Reid's gaze. "You looked away when we hugged and then stayed behind to keep tabs on us."

Direct. Honest. No beating around the bush. She was finding it hard not to like him.

"You told her about our dating history in college," he said, his gaze still on hers.

London gave Reid's hand a reassuring squeeze. "I did."

"Okay. Well…" Mason set his hands on his hips, lowered his head, and sighed. "If I want to stay in your lives, then I guess this means I have a lot to prove." He looked up, zeroing in on Reid with eyes that cut through layers of bullshit as quickly as a hot knife sliced through butter. "I should get started then."

There was a long and uncomfortable silence as Mason continued to study her. "On what?" Did he intend to get started on proving himself or helping them with their case?

"Finding the bad guy. London hasn't filled me in yet, but I'm guessing you'd prefer to work this case on the down-low so you can deliver your own form of justice. Otherwise, you wouldn't be here."

Reid withdrew her hand from London's and met her gaze. "Have you done this with him before?"

"No." London shook her head. "Never."

"And you haven't told him about our guy?" she asked, referring to the serial killer they were hunting.

"Not a thing."

"Then how the hell—"

"It's okay," Mason said, cutting her off. "I get this all the time."

She stared at him. What the hell was going on here?

"Computer geeks aren't usually people smart. Before I started hacking, I made a decent living as a mentalist."

No way. "Are you saying you can read minds?"

"I'm just good at reading *people*—body language, facial expressions, tone of voice, clothing, accessories, fingernails, the way they respond to a longer-than-normal handshake," he admitted with a wink. "Even someone's hairstyle reveals a lot about them. So it *appears* that I can read minds. But as we all know, appearances can be deceiving. Take you, for example. Tough cop exterior. Confident. Suspicious. Forthright. Thorny. No offense," he added quickly.

"Thorny's a compliment," she said, waiting for him to go on.

"People look at you and assume that what they see is what they get. That's obviously not the case. Not by a long shot."

What could he possibly have learned about her in the time it took to have this exchange? She glared at London.

"Don't look at *me*," London said, taking a step back. "I told him nothing. Mason didn't even know you existed until a few minutes ago."

She met Mason's gaze, quiet for a moment as she observed him observing her. She couldn't help but be intrigued. "Fine. I'll bite. What about me is so deceiving?"

"You have a gift."

"A gift," she repeated.

He nodded. "You do everything you can to hide the existence of this gift behind the thorny persona you've built."

"I play a mean cello," she admitted, trying to throw him off track.

"Wow." He shook his head. "You're the real deal, aren't you? I've never met a real psychic before."

She said nothing. Either London had already told him about her gift, or he'd hacked into the BPD's database and found something about her there. The bottom line was, somebody somewhere had told him something.

"Nope. No one told me anything. Mentalism is *my* gift." He crossed his arms as he studied her some more. "There's something else, though—something else you can do."

Maintaining her poker face was getting more and more difficult. Were he and London playing with her? Whatever the hell was happening, it was making her uncomfortable.

"Spirits," he said, stepping so close that he was now inside her personal bubble. "Can you *really* communicate with the dead?"

She was still unconvinced. But if Mason had figured this out about her in the span of a few minutes, he was a damn good mentalist. If *he* was the real deal, then he might as well be psychic.

"Thank you," he said. "Coming from you, that's quite a compliment."

Reid was sure she hadn't voiced her thoughts aloud. Had he just read her mind?

London set a hand over Mason's arm. "I think she's had enough."

"Right. Sorry." He visibly snapped out of whatever mental space he was in and took a step back, freeing up her personal bubble once more. "Sometimes I go too far." He looked to London. "Did I go too far?"

London ignored the question and turned to her. "I should've given you fair warning. I was foolishly hoping that he would behave."

"You should know me better by now," he said.

Reid sighed, surprised at their juvenile antics. Did they really expect her to believe that they hadn't set this whole thing up? "You expect me to believe—"

"That we didn't set this up ahead of time?" Mason finished. "I assure you, we didn't. Here." He dug his phone out of his pocket, unlocked it, and handed it to her. "Read our text thread."

She did. Their last exchange was, *Bring the troops. Mi casa es su casa. Whatever you need.*

"Doesn't prove a thing," Reid said, unconvinced. "She could've called you when I left the hotel room."

"Then look at my call log," he replied coolly, making no motion to retrieve his phone.

She scrolled through his list of recent calls. There was no record of London's number. "Still doesn't prove anything. You could've deleted your texts and call history. Or she could've used the hotel room phone."

"A nonbeliever," Mason said, grinning. "This should be fun."

"I don't have time for games. We came here to catch a killer. If you're as good as you say you are, then maybe you can help us find him."

"*Maybe* isn't even in my vocabulary." He locked gazes with London. "You never told her about me before today."

London shook her head.

"You deceived yourself into believing our friendship was no big deal. But subconsciously you were afraid Reid would see me as a threat. Which is ironic because that's exactly what ended up happening." He turned his focus to Reid. "When you perceive a threat, you dig your heels in hard. You're unforgiving, slow to open your mind to new possibilities." He shook his head. "That's very interesting, considering your gifts are all about keeping an open mind."

Mason had summed up the issue at hand in less than five minutes. Was he really that skilled? For the moment, Reid was stumped. But she couldn't give any more of her time or energy to this right now. There was a killer on the loose—a killer who had London in his sights. They needed to get to work. If Mason was all he cracked himself up to be, the hunt for this killer could be on the verge of drawing to a close.

"Got it. You're the boss." Mason switched gears as if reading her thoughts once again. "I have a room set up with everything we need. Follow me." He led them down the same tunnel where her team had disappeared in search of their bedrooms. They were now MIA.

Mason called back over his shoulder. "We'll scoop them up on the way."

"Who?" she asked as London kept pace beside her.

"Your team."

This was getting downright creepy. Reid was beginning to wonder if she was in the company of a fellow psychic. She vowed to herself then that she would never do what Mason was doing now, no matter how good she was at reading someone's thoughts. Thoughts were private. Unless someone's life was at stake, they should remain private. Boundaries. Before she embraced anything, she'd need to set certain rules for herself.

"Does your team know?" Mason asked, still walking ahead of them. "About what you can do?"

She chose not to answer. She refused to confirm or deny the existence of anything.

"That's fine. I'll be able to tell for myself when I watch them interact with you." He slowed his pace just a bit and glanced back at her. "I can help, you know."

"In case you haven't noticed, that's why we're here," she said sarcastically.

"Not just with finding this guy you're after. That's the easy part."

She was about to ask what the hell he was talking about when Boyle and the others stepped out from nearby bedrooms to join them. They followed Mason to an office at the end of a long hallway. The walls were made of stone, so it felt less like a hallway and more like an underground tunnel. From what she could tell, the entire dwelling was windowless, but each room was well-lit.

The office was spacious and uncluttered. Mason had chosen comfort over formality. There were eight giant beanbag chairs—enough to accommodate everyone. Each beanbag had an armrest with a built-in table that held sparkling water, a Butterfinger, and a bag of chips.

Mason stepped inside the room and gestured to their snacks. "Sweet and salty. That's how I work best, so I figured I'd extend the same courtesy." He kicked off his sneakers, took a seat on the beanbag at the front of the room, and waited for each of them to do the same.

The beanbag chairs were low to the ground but solid and much more comfortable than Reid had imagined. Maybe she needed one of these for her house. Boggs tore open his bag of chips and started crunching noisily beside her.

"Tell me about your case," Mason said, taking a sip of water. "In a hundred words or less."

"Why a hundred words or less?" Boggs asked around a mouthful of chips.

"My answer to that question has always been the same—time is money. In this case, though, time could literally cost lives."

Everyone, including Mason, looked to her.

A hundred words was more than she needed. "Our guy has abducted twenty-nine women over three years. Released eleven unharmed. Tortured and murdered eighteen. FBI can't find their own asses if someone screwed their heads on backward. Enter us. We fly into Reagan National to assist them. Killer abducts London from under our noses. We found her, no thanks to the FBI. Now he wants her back." There was obviously more to the story, but everything else was extraneous.

"Fifty-nine words," Mason said, nodding. "Not bad." He stood, stepped to the door, and pressed a button near the light switch. A soft mechanical hum filled the silence as the wall at the front of the room lifted and slowly disappeared into the rock ceiling. Eight huge wall-mounted flat-screen TVs stared back at them. "Reagan National, you said?"

Reid nodded.

He set his gaze on London and gave her a once-over. "He didn't hurt you."

"No," she replied, shifting in her seat a little self-consciously. "I'm fine."

"I'm glad you're okay," he said sincerely. "When did this happen?"

"Yesterday," London answered.

"Let me take a stab here." Mason thought for a moment. "He ambushed you in the terminal bathroom?"

London nodded.

"Near which gate?" Mason grabbed his laptop from a nearby shelf, flipped it open, and began typing.

"C30."

"What time?" he pressed, casting a glance at Reid.

"Eighteen hundred hours."

"That him?" Mason set his laptop aside and studied the wall of TV screens. Each screen was divided into eight squares. Sixty-four images of the killer's face and body appeared before them. Mason typed something on his laptop to bring up video of the killer pushing an industrial-sized laundry cart from the women's restroom. "Sonofabitch. He knocked you out and put you inside that thing?"

London nodded.

Mason rewound the video and studied the screen as the killer pushed the laundry cart into the restroom, prior to London's abduction. "He has someone else in there. Another body." He turned to pierce London with a narrowed gaze. "He tried to negotiate with you—wanted you to trade your life for whoever was in that cart."

London nodded again. Her voice quivered as she spoke. "And he's holding three women captive right now."

Reid reached for London's hand as Mason turned back to the wall of screens. He walked from one screen to the next, scrutinizing the images with an intensity she'd seldom seen. He was reading the killer, drawing a picture in his mind. She was sure of it.

CHAPTER TWENTY-FIVE

R eid looked around the room at Boyle, Garcia, Marino, O'Leary, and Boggs. It appeared everyone was just as fascinated with Mason's exceptional focus as she was. The only one who seemed less than impressed was London. She'd probably been down this road with Mason too many times to count.

"What stands out to me right off the bat is this guy's height. He's five foot four—*maybe* five five, but that's probably pushing it. So he's definitely short, at least by our standards. His height is a source of frustration for him because he's gone above and beyond to perfect his physical image in every other way—handsome, full head of hair, great body." Mason zoomed in on his fingernails. "He even gets regular manicures. A man doesn't go to this much trouble just to compensate for his height."

Reid watched Mason closely. How could he get all that simply by studying the killer's image?

"He's smart, resourceful, willing to put in the time to create the ultimate version of himself," Mason went on. "He's also well educated—probably attended an Ivy League school. He chose a career that gives him power, prestige, money, and a sense of importance. He worked hard to get where he is. His entire world revolves around one thing—finding a woman to love him. But he doesn't want just any woman. He wants a trophy woman. He *deserves* a trophy woman and won't settle for anything less." Mason turned away from the TV screens and locked gazes with Reid. "Does he sexually assault his victims?"

She nodded but offered nothing more.

"But no semen has been found. Is that right?"

"That's right," she confirmed.

"His penis is damaged, disfigured, mutilated, or a combination of all three, either due to an accident or prolonged physical abuse as a child. My guess is the latter, which would explain his psychopathy to a great extent. Someone obviously did a number on him early in life."

He paused and gazed around the room. "I can give you more, but there are some things I need to know first."

O'Leary withdrew a flash drive from his pocket and held it up. "Everything's on here." He tossed it to Mason.

Mason caught the flash drive in one hand. "The whole case?" he asked.

"Everything the FBI gave us," Reid clarified.

Without another word, Mason plugged the flash drive into his laptop and began reviewing the documents that O'Leary had downloaded prior to their departure. He studied the screen for long minutes in silence. With a heavy sigh, he slapped his laptop shut and turned to Reid. "I need to speak with you," he said, his gaze darting over the rest of their group, "alone." He stood, stepped to the door, and held it open for her.

She returned his gaze from her chair but didn't move to join him. "You can speak freely. There's nothing my team can't hear."

"If you want what I have in my brain right now—and trust me, you do—then you'll take a walk with me. I don't bite. London will vouch for me."

Instead of looking to London for confirmation, she kept her gaze steady on his. Was this a case of two alphas squaring up, or was one alpha getting ready to concede to the other? Maybe it was something else entirely. She wasn't sure. The one thing she did know for sure was that she'd do anything—she'd give *anything*—to catch this killer and keep London safe.

With that in mind, she stood, joined Mason at the door, and stepped out into the hallway. He set his hands behind his back and stared at the floor as they walked through the tunnels of his underground lair. Reid said nothing. She gave him all the elbow room he needed with his thoughts.

It was clear that Mason had no experience in law enforcement, and it was, therefore, safe to assume he'd never seen crime scene photos before today. The images on the flash drive were startling, to say the least. She'd seen some pretty awful things on the job over the years, but everything else paled in comparison to this case. If seeing the crime scene photos had left *her* shaken, she could only imagine what he was going through right now. Chances were, he was trying to wrap his brain around it as best he could. She was happy to give him the time and space he needed to do that.

She glanced over at Mason and realized he was crying. For the first time since they'd met, Reid saw him for who he was and not as London's ex. She should've given him fair warning about the photos.

Mason led her to the kitchen, opened the refrigerator, and grabbed two beers. He popped the top off his and slid the other across the granite countertop to her. "Cheers," he said, raising his bottle in a toast before taking a long swallow. They drank and finished their beers in a comfortable silence. Mason rinsed the empty bottles, tossed them in a recycle bin, and grabbed two more from the fridge. "Thank you," he said, meeting her gaze with dry eyes.

"For what?"

"Saving London from that monstrosity of an excuse for a human being."

"It wasn't just me. My team—"

"I realize your team helped, but you and I both know that you're the MVP."

She shook her head. "I don't agree with that."

He nodded, studying her. "They're important to you."

"They're everything to me," she admitted a little too honestly. She was halfway through her second beer with no food in her stomach. "They're—"

"The wind beneath your wings?" he asked with a smirk.

"More than that. I wouldn't be where I am today without them."

"Doesn't mean you can't be, though. There's a difference."

She studied him as she drank. He was inching closer to making a point. "Quit tiptoeing. Whatever it is you're trying to say—"

"With your team by your side, you've accepted mediocrity," he said, his gaze steadfast and strong. "They're holding you back."

"Fuck off." She was instantly insulted. "You don't know what the hell you're talking about."

"They're holding you back because you believe that living up to your potential means you'll have to leave them behind."

"We're done here." She stood.

"You're misunderstanding my point. It's *you* who's holding you back. You're afraid to outshine them."

She glared at him.

"But the thing is, they're not riding your coattails. If they're anywhere near as capable as London, they can more than hold their own."

"Damn right they can," she spat, suddenly unsure what he was driving at.

"All I'm saying is"—he stepped around the island and took a seat on the stool beside her—"alter your mindset. Accept your gifts. Using those gifts won't jeopardize your relationship with your team or undermine their contributions. Have faith in their value and abilities, just like they have faith in yours. Trust that they'll adjust accordingly and keep pace alongside you. From what I can tell, it's a symbiotic relationship. One can't survive without the other."

She stared at him. "Why are you telling me this?"

"Because you're the real deal. You have a real shot at making a difference. But it's not with the Boston Police Department. You need to start thinking outside the box. Bring your team with you. You can all have one hell of an adventure together."

She studied Mason. "What's your angle?" He was obviously trying to work her. She just didn't have a clue what he wanted.

"No angle," he said, holding his palms up defensively.

Then it hit her. Mason wanted in. He wanted to be part of her team. Money obviously wasn't the driving force because it looked like he had plenty. Was it London? Was he looking to win London back? A chance to rekindle what they once shared?

"You want to be part of my team," she said, crossing her arms. "Nope. No way." The thought of having to look at Mason's handsome, chiseled face every day made her want to dive headfirst off the Tobin Bridge.

"You don't get it, do you?" he asked, shaking his head. "She doesn't feel about me the way she feels about you. Never did. Never could. London's gay. I knew that back then, and I know that now. The only thing that's changed is she met her person. You're it for her, Sylver. I saw that thirty seconds after meeting you. London will never stray. She wouldn't even be tempted. Ever. For the sake of your relationship, you should consider making peace with that now."

London's ex was giving her relationship advice. Was this really happening?

"Don't get me wrong," he went on, undeterred by her pissed-off cop face. "London loves me, and I love her. I love her because she's my family, just like your team is *your* family. There's nothing I wouldn't do for her. If I'm not mistaken, there's nothing you wouldn't do for your team and nothing they wouldn't do for you. It's the same. You and I are cut from the same cloth, Sylver."

Mason's sincerity was palpable. Something told her that no one in his life was ever left wondering what he really thought because, like her, he held nothing back. She respected that. Admired it, even. Shit. Maybe they *were* cut from the same cloth.

"Good," he said, sighing with obvious relief. "Now that we have that out of the way, we can move on to my proposal."

But she wasn't ready to move on to anything, except the case. There was a dangerous killer on the loose. Every minute she wasted chatting was a minute the killer could use to his advantage. She chugged the last of her beer and stood from the barstool. "I need to get back to my team. We have a case to solve, with or without you."

"My point exactly. I read the files, saw the crime scene photos. I know the kind of threat he poses—not just to London, but to society in general. Doesn't take a rocket scientist to figure out what you're planning to do with that piece of shit once you get your hands on him. Before we go any farther, you should know that I fully support you. Whatever goes down, I'll take it to my grave."

She stared at him but said nothing, neither confirming nor denying her team's intentions.

"I've already told you that I'm a gray hat. Every business transaction I make walks the line between ethical and unlawful. There are things I've done that were lucrative—things that would be frowned upon by those who uphold the law."

"People like me," she said, raising an eyebrow. Was he attempting to make a trade? He wouldn't tell on her or her team as long as they didn't rat him out?

"You've heard of the dark web?" he asked.

Reid nodded. She didn't claim to know much about the dark web, only that what occurred within it was hidden from plain view and, more than likely, against the law.

"Most of my business is conducted there. When I'm in the market for work, there's a fifty-fifty split. Half the jobs available would let me sleep at night. Half wouldn't. Working together to ferret out lowlifes from the second half—lowlifes not unlike your serial killer—would make the world a better place." He shrugged. "I'd like to put that offer *under* the table for you and your team to consider. It would be very different from the line of work you're in now, but it would also be much more satisfying."

She'd be lying if she said the offer didn't pique her interest, but she wasn't about to admit anything of the sort.

"Will you at least think about it?" he pressed.

"No." She turned and started walking in the direction of her team.

He jogged over to accompany her back to the office. "What if I sweeten the deal?"

"Not interested," she replied, walking faster.

"You'll consider my offer if—and *only* if—I can identify your killer and give you his exact location in under five minutes."

Reid halted in her tracks and turned to glare at him. Was he pulling her leg? This was feeling more and more like a game. She didn't have time for games. Not now. Not ever. More to the point, she didn't give her time to the people who played them. She had no problem calling his bluff. "I'll consider your offer if you identify him, give us his exact location, *and* we're able to apprehend him. Today," she added, keenly aware of her unreasonable terms.

Mason wrinkled his nose. "That last part is entirely dependent on how well you and your team work together. It's literally the only part I have no control over."

She rolled her eyes and resumed her walk through the tunnel.

He jogged to catch up. "However, you'll be happy to know that I have faith in your team's abilities."

"I don't care if you have faith in my team. You don't know them," she said candidly. "Hell, you don't even know me."

"True. But I've learned more about you in our time together than you realize."

She sighed. "Because you're a mentalist."

"*Was* a mentalist," he corrected her. "But alas, once a mentalist, always a mentalist. It's a difficult habit to break." They arrived at the door where she'd left her compadres. Mason reached for the doorknob and paused. "You have a deal."

How the hell could he accomplish in five minutes what the FBI couldn't do in three years? "Identify the killer and provide us with his exact location so we can apprehend him today."

Mason nodded with enthusiasm. "That's the deal, banana peel."

CHAPTER TWENTY-SIX

Reid pressed the crown on the side of her watch and turned it until the stopwatch icon appeared. She positioned her index finger above the icon and glanced up to meet Mason's gaze across the room. "Three...two...one. Go."

She looked on from the comfort of her beanbag chair as Mason began typing furiously on his laptop. He didn't even bother to look down at the keyboard. He kept his gaze steady on the eight giant screens before him.

O'Leary cleared his throat. "Are we having a quiet contest?"

"Mason claims he can identify the killer and give us his exact location in five minutes or less."

"Sweet," Boggs said.

Garcia narrowed his eyes. "What's in it for him?"

"Maybe a place on our team," she said honestly.

"So this is, like, tryouts?" O'Leary's eyes were glued to Mason's laptop. "I bombed every tryout I ever tried out for," he admitted gloomily.

Marino rolled his eyes. "I think I speak for everyone here when I say I find that shocking."

O'Leary looked back over his shoulder at London. "He's making fun of me again, right?"

London winked. "You aced tryouts with me, O'Leary."

Images flashed across all eight screens in rapid succession—the killer walking on a sidewalk, driving through a toll behind the wheel of an SUV, paying for a croissant at a small café. "Your killer has layers upon layers of aliases—Derek Wilson, James Mitchell, Luke Bennett, Andrew Hughes. I have no idea what his real name is. It'll take some time to sift through all these." Mason started scrolling through pages of computer code against a black backdrop. A property deed popped up on the screen to the far left. Phone records appeared on the screen beside it. His attention leaped from one screen to the next as he continued to type faster than Reid could think.

"Almost there," Mason said, turning his focus to the screen on the far right. He brought up the website of a water well company. "Your killer lives off the grid. There's no history of utility, gas, or electric bills. He paid a contractor to dig a water well on his property six years ago." He zoomed in on the address listed on the bill. "Lives in a cabin in Maryland, but it's off the beaten path. No GPS will recognize this address. Hang on a sec," he said, typing furiously once again.

O'Leary stood and stepped toward the centermost screen. "Are you hacking into a satellite?"

"Not just any satellite," Mason answered, beaming. "ISS."

"The International Space Station?" O'Leary said, clearly awestruck.

Mason's fingers danced across the keyboard. "That's his cabin. And his car. This is real time." He turned to Reid. "He's home."

She stopped the timer on her watch: two minutes, thirty-four seconds. Brotherfucker. Now she had no choice but to uphold her end of the bargain. As long as they apprehended the killer—and they would, she was sure of it—she'd have to consider Mason's offer.

"Welcome to the team, bro," Boggs said cheerfully.

Boyle, Garcia, Marino, and Boggs joined O'Leary and stood, shoulder to shoulder, gazing back and forth from one screen to the next.

"That's our guy," Boyle said, sounding just as shocked as Reid felt.

Marino nodded at the satellite image of the killer's cabin. "How far is that from here?"

"Two hours, by car." Mason replaced the image of the contractor's bill with a map of the drive from his bunker to the killer's residence.

"Is the cabin the only structure on the property?"

Mason zoomed out. "It is," he confirmed.

"Looks awfully small to house a backup supply of victims," Marino observed.

London stood and joined them. "The women he showed me on his phone were in separate rooms. Each room had a bed and a hospital monitor, so the rooms were small. But I don't think the cabin I'm seeing here would accommodate that. It's too small."

Mason brought up the cabin's blueprints on one of the screens.

"The living space is only six hundred square feet. There's no way he's keeping his victims inside or doing his work there. Too messy. He's keeping his work and personal lives separate."

"Does he own another property?" Boyle asked.

Mason shook his head. "None that I can find. Doesn't mean it doesn't exist. Chances are, though, if it did, I'd have found it by now."

"What about an underground bunker, like this one?" London asked, wide-eyed. "There were no windows in the rooms where he was keeping those women."

"It's possible." Mason scratched his chin thoughtfully. "And it would make sense from a logistical standpoint. I just don't see any permits for digging or construction of any kind in his property records. A project like that is a huge undertaking. I obviously speak from experience. It's unlikely he'd be able to complete that kind of project by himself."

"Unless it was preexisting," Reid said. "When was the cabin built?"

Mason zoomed in on the property records. "Nineteen forty-six. After World War II. Bomb shelters were all the rage in the fifties and sixties." He shrugged. "It's possible one of the previous owners built an underground fallout shelter and kept its existence a secret."

"It *has* to be there." Reid could feel it in her bones. "He wouldn't want his victims far from him. He'd want them readily accessible."

O'Leary nodded in agreement. "He'd require access to them twenty-four seven—work, eat, sleep, repeat. He wouldn't settle for anything else. This guy's obsessive. His work is his life."

Boggs gestured to the screen. "The immediate area surrounding the cabin has been cleared. A stealthy approach is totally off the table."

Garcia nodded. "We should wait until nightfall."

"Night-vision goggles weren't on my packing list." Marino looked around at the group. "Anyone think to bring some?"

They all shook their heads.

"I have some," Mason volunteered. "From a previous job," he added when they all looked at him suspiciously. "I'm happy to share my toys. Just promise you won't arrest me."

Garcia raised an eyebrow. "What kind of toys are we talking about?"

Mason shut his laptop. "Easier if I just show you." He withdrew a remote from his desk drawer and aimed it at the back of the room. The rear wall slid aside, revealing a formidable-looking metal door.

"It's a candy shop for cops." He typed in a code on the keypad, stepped back, and looked over his shoulder to gauge their reactions as the door unlocked. "You're welcome."

Curiosity got the best of Reid as she led the way inside. Assault rifles, sniper rifles, stun grenades, smoke, tactical vests, body armor, ballistic shields, military-grade helmets and headsets, night-vision goggles, and thermal-imaging cameras lined the walls and shelves.

Boggs started to drool. "This is like that scene in *Kingsman*—"

"Where Harry takes Eggsy to that secret arsenal and lets him choose his weapon?" O'Leary asked excitedly.

"Yeah." Garcia stepped inside. "Except this is better because—"

"It's us," Marino finished, giving Garcia a high five.

Mason slipped his hands in his pockets and leaned against the doorframe. "None of those weapons are registered. They won't be able to trace the killer's murder back to any of you."

"I thought gray hats worked behind the scenes, with computers." Boyle crossed his arms and narrowed his gaze. "Computer nerds don't usually have a secret arsenal."

Mason didn't skip a beat. "I've been collecting this in anticipation of finding a team like yours. As you can see, it's all brand new. None of what's in here has ever been used. Don't get me wrong—I know my way around a weapon, but I don't care much for them. Computers are more my speed, and I'm good at what I do. There isn't a soul on earth who's better at hacking than me."

Boyle frowned. "Something tells me you're more than just a hacker."

"I might have some other skills." Mason made a point of meeting Reid's gaze directly. "Skills that could make me a valuable member of the team."

"Humility obviously isn't one of them," London said, rolling her eyes. "But I have to admit, Mason walks the talk. That's the only reason he's been in my life for as long as he has."

Mason pretended to look shocked. "I thought it was for Guillaume Brahimi's salted caramel and chocolate ganache tart."

"That, too," London admitted. "You probably shouldn't have mentioned that."

"Yeah. Now we want some." Garcia selected a pair of NVGs from a nearby shelf.

"You had me at salted caramel," Marino said.

They gathered their supplies, locked up the arsenal, and

reconvened in the office to discuss their plan. Mason would stay behind and maintain visual and audio contact with each member of the team from the safety of his bunker. They were separating into three teams, driving in three separate vehicles, and approaching from three different directions.

"Gold and O'Leary, you're with me," Reid said. "Boggs, you're with Marino, which leaves Boyle and Garcia bringing up the rear." Each team selected a destination on the map. They'd park their vehicles and travel the rest of the way to the cabin on foot. The hunt for the killer would begin at nightfall.

"Gear up." She checked her watch: 1:22 p.m. "We'll head out at fourteen hundred hours."

"That puts your arrival at four p.m., which is sixteen hundred hours in stick-up-your-ass military time," Mason mocked. "The sun sets in Maryland at 5:06 p.m. Gives you an hour and six minutes to make it to the cabin on foot before nightfall."

Without another word, they parted ways and headed off to their respective bedrooms to prepare for the hunt.

❖

London watched as Reid slipped into her bulletproof vest. "You like him."

"Who?" Reid asked absently.

"Mason," she answered, adjusting the tactical headset to fit around her ponytail. "You don't want to like him, but you do."

"*Like* is a big stretch, London. I don't even know the guy."

"Admit it." She turned away from the mirror to meet Reid's gaze. "You don't hate him."

"Fine. I don't hate him. But if that salted-caramel-something tart isn't everything he promised, that could definitely change things."

"I'm sorry," she said sincerely. "I should've told you about Mason before today."

Reid thought for a moment. "If today hadn't happened, you could've kept him a secret indefinitely. That scares me."

"I get it. I do. And I'm sorry." She slid the headset off, stepped over to Reid, and pulled her close. "The thought of you not being able to trust me terrifies me."

"I need to be able to trust you, London."

She hesitated, unsure if she had the courage to ask. "I realize I've damaged the trust between us. Can it be repaired?" Reid had always lived her life in very black-and-white terms. London wasn't sure how she'd answer.

"Is there anyone else still in your life today that you were intimate with in the past?"

"No." London shook her head, adamant. "No one." With the exception of Mason, all of her relationships had been with women. Each relationship had ended amicably. She'd ultimately decided to sever ties with all of her exes because maintaining a friendship after intimacy was tricky. None of the women she'd dated could handle it.

"Okay," Reid said, nodding.

London could tell there was more on her mind. "Ask me anything. Ask me all the questions you want."

Reid tried to put some distance between them by taking a step back, but London moved with her. They were practically nose to nose. "Go ahead. Ask." She wanted Reid to be close enough to see her pupils. Reid knew just as well as she did that pupils dilated when someone was telling a lie.

"Have you ever been attracted to Mason?"

"Never," she answered, unblinking. "Not even when we dated."

Reid thought for a long moment, her gaze raw, vulnerable, unwavering.

She smiled reassuringly. "Ask me if I've ever wanted anyone as much as I've wanted you."

"Have you?"

"No." She brushed her lips against Reid's. "Ask me if I see myself marrying you, loving you, and being faithful to you until my dying breath."

Reid ran her tongue over the surface of London's lips and set her on fire. "Will you marry me, be faithful, and love me until your dying breath?"

"Yes." She opened her mouth and invited Reid inside as their tongues danced seductively.

Reid pulled back. "For the record, that was *not* a marriage proposal. When I do propose, it'll be much more romantic." She arched an eyebrow. "And it definitely will *not* be in your ex-boyfriend's underground lair." Reid shoved her onto the bed, pulled her shoes off, and began unbuttoning London's jeans.

"Wait. I don't think we have time for this," she said, laughing.

"We have time," was all Reid said as she expertly slipped London's thong off and settled between her thighs.

The feel of Reid's tongue was exquisite. She felt herself instantly swell within and ache with the need for Reid's fingers. But she didn't have to beg. Reid slid her fingers inside ever so gently, as if sensing that she was still sore from last night's toy.

London writhed and moaned as Reid licked her clit in all the right ways. She pushed her fingers in and out, keeping pace with London's hips until she came, long and hard.

CHAPTER TWENTY-SEVEN

Reid pulled off the dirt road at their designated spot. She cut the engine and glanced at London in the passenger's seat. The second Mason had unveiled his collection of off-road vehicles, she and London had argued over who would get to drive the Land Rover Defender. With less than fifty miles on the engine, Mason hadn't even broken it in yet. They'd ultimately battled it out in a fierce game of rock-paper-scissors, which Reid had won, fair and square. But London was convinced she'd used her psychic gifts to her advantage.

Two hours had passed, and London was still pouting. Enough was enough. They needed to find a way to put this behind them. "You get to drive on the return trip," she said, setting a hand on London's knee.

"Doesn't count." London continued to stare out the window. "You went first. Second isn't any fun."

They were about to trek through the forest at night to capture a psychopath and put an end to his killing spree, once and for all. Things had to be right between them before they set out on such a dangerous mission. With so much at stake, it was time for Reid to pull out all the stops for London. Go big or go home. "What would cheer you up right now?"

London crossed her arms. "Nothing."

"We can't go find this guy. Not now. Not with you feeling like this."

"Maybe you should've thought of that before you cheated."

"I didn't cheat." Reid sighed. "But I love you, so I'll be the bigger person and offer you something that I know will cheer you up."

"Nothing could cheer me up right now," London said, fitting the tactical headset over her black skullcap.

Reid both loved and hated the fact that her girlfriend was so competitive. She could only imagine what London would be like when she and the rest of her softball team got their asses handed to them in this year's tournament. The Toe Tags got lucky last year, but Reid's team was stronger than they'd ever been before. Packin' Heat would be back on top in no time. Whether she liked it or not, London would have to find a way to deal with defeat. "I'll let you use the toy on me," she said, savoring the look of surprise on London's face. "Tonight."

O'Leary piped up from the back seat. "What toy?"

"No way," London said, ignoring O'Leary.

"Way."

"What toy?" O'Leary repeated.

"Wait." London narrowed her eyes. "What's the catch?"

"No catch."

"Are you setting a time limit?"

She shook her head.

O'Leary stuck his head through the gap in the middle of the seats and looked back and forth between them. "What toy?" he asked again.

"You don't want to know," Reid replied, winking at London.

"I do want to know. If I didn't, I wouldn't have asked."

"You don't."

"But I really do," he pleaded.

She took a deep breath and met his inquisitive gaze. "We're talking about a harness with a dildo, O'Leary."

"Oh God." His face went pale. "I really didn't want to know that."

"Told you." She set a hand on his shoulder. "Maybe next time, you'll listen."

"Is now a bad time to mention that I feel like I might pass out?" He sat all the way back in his seat. "Do we have a bucket? I think I might throw up."

"I second that." Garcia's voice sounded over their headsets. "Searching for a bucket as we speak."

Shit. If Garcia heard their private conversation, then that meant the headsets were on and—

"*Not* the pep talk I was hoping for," Marino said.

"I can't feel my dick anymore, guys," Boggs jumped in. "It'll never get hard again. Like, ever."

"I think it's safe to say we're all permanently scarred," Boyle admitted with a heavy sigh. "But we need to figure out how to move past this and keep our heads in the game."

"*You* did this." London met Reid's gaze, red-faced. "The lesson here is that cheating is never the answer."

"For the love of God, I didn't cheat."

"I just hopped on," Mason said. "What'd I miss? Did Reid cheat on London?"

Perfect. Now London's ex was involved. At least he hadn't heard about the dildo.

"Do tell," Mason insisted. "Inquiring minds."

"Reid pulled a fast one with the Land Rover," O'Leary said angrily.

"I suspected as much. Never trust a psychic in a game of rock-paper-scissors."

"And she's trying to make up for it by letting London use a toy on her," Boggs explained.

"By *toy*, you mean…?"

"A strap-on," Marino said matter-of-factly.

"Oh," was all Mason said. Might be the first time in Mason's life that he was rendered speechless. Served him right.

There was a long moment of silence. Reid glared at London from the driver's seat. She was as angry with herself as she was with London.

"God help us," Garcia said, breaking the silence.

"I need a stiff drink."

"I need a support group."

"Maybe the killer can hook us up with some meds to help us forget what just happened."

"I'm just glad I'm not the only one," O'Leary admitted.

"No worries," Boggs said gently. "We're here for you, bro."

The surrounding pine trees cast long shadows over the car and the dirt road behind them. It was finally starting to get dark. Reid checked her watch: 5:06 p.m. The sun was setting. It was time to begin their trek through the woods. She prayed their impending hunt for the killer would be enough to redirect the topic of conversation.

"Is his vehicle still on the property?" Boyle asked, coming to her rescue.

"Sure is," Mason confirmed. "Hasn't moved all day. I'm looking at live satellite images of his property as we speak."

"Everyone geared up?" Boyle asked.

She was ready to get the show on the road. "Team one is good to go."

"Team two's a go," Marino confirmed.

"Team three's a go, as well," Boyle said.

She, London, and O'Leary exited the Land Rover and began their trek over unfamiliar terrain. The tree canopy above was thick, shielding them from whatever leftover rays the sun had to offer. Before she knew it, total darkness had enveloped them. They switched on their NVGs and hiked, single file. Reid took point while O'Leary brought up the rear.

Reid moved slowly, carefully. Her senses were heightened. She forced every thought from her mind to ensure that she was fully present. Her natural ability to focus on the task at hand, to the exclusion of all else, came in handy at times like these. They'd all committed themselves to the same mission—capture the killer and wipe him out of existence. Whatever it took was what they were all prepared to give. There was a lot on the line tonight. Everyone that mattered to her was here.

An ambush was unlikely but not impossible. They were approaching the cabin from three directions. Since the killer worked alone—there was no evidence to suggest he had a partner—their numbers were to their advantage. As far as she knew, they also had the element of surprise on their side. Even so, she refused to go into this hunt overly confident. The killer was clever. London's abduction had taught all of them that the situation could take a dangerous turn in the blink of an eye. Things could get ugly fast. She couldn't let her guard down. Not until he was dead and buried and gone for good. Then, and only then, would she be able to breathe freely once again. She knew London felt the same. Hell, she had no doubt the entire team felt the same.

All for one, and one for all. That was how they rolled. Every last one of them needed to come out of this unscathed. And if one of them had to go down, she'd do everything in her power to make sure it was her. Whatever it took. She was all-in.

Mason's voice sounded in her ear. "Team one, you're closing in on the target."

As team one, her team was first to arrive. "How far?" she whispered.

"About five hundred yards, due east."

Team two was approaching from the north. They'd stacked their arrival times four minutes apart. Four minutes was the sweet spot for an operation like this—enough time to convince the killer that no one else was coming but not enough time for him to get away without running into team two. "What's your ETA, team two?"

"Four minutes, max," came Marino's whispered reply. "Sooner, if you need it."

So far, so good. If things went sideways, Marino's team would intercede. "Team three?"

"Eight minutes," Boyle whispered. "On schedule for targeted arrival behind team two."

Reid moved closer to the edge of the tree line. The cabin sat in the middle of an open field. Every tree and bush had been cleared from the property to provide an unobstructed view of the surrounding terrain. There was nothing to hide behind or mask their approach. To make matters worse, motion sensor lights had been mounted on each corner of the cabin.

A generator hummed in the distance—the killer's source of power. If they disconnected the generator, the lights would cut out, and he'd be momentarily in the dark. But she and her team had night-vision goggles.

"Be advised, there are motion sensor lights on all four corners. There's also a generator on the northwest side of the cabin." She met London's gaze in the darkness. "Gold, can you take out the motion sensors on the northwest and southwest corners?" London was the best sharpshooter on their team. With any luck, London could fire the sniper rifle from the tree line without having to set foot on the open field.

London studied the cabin and nodded confidently. "Two shots. Three max."

They wouldn't have much time after London took out the exterior lights. The killer would likely hear the commotion and know they were there. "I'll make a run for the cabin and enter from the south side while O'Leary's disconnecting the generator. When the power goes out, London and O'Leary will meet in front of the generator and enter the cabin from the northwest side. Team two will enter the cabin from the northeast side, and team three will enter from the southeast." Assuming the killer was inside, he wouldn't stand a chance because they were launching an attack from all sides, like a pack of wolves.

O'Leary cautioned her. "Give me a few to disconnect the generator before you enter the cabin."

But there was no way she'd let O'Leary take that risk. He'd be a sitting duck. Her part was to act as the decoy and distract the killer.

"Stick to the plan, O'Leary." She turned to London. She loathed the idea of leaving London's side. She, London, and O'Leary would be parting ways for just a few minutes. Knowing that London would be alone, even for that short period of time, made her uncomfortable.

She had a moment of self-doubt and fought the urge to devise an alternate plan. They were running out of time. Presumably, the killer was here, now. His SUV was parked outside, and he likely wasn't expecting them. This was their chance—maybe their only chance. She couldn't baby London. She needed to have faith in London's abilities, now more than ever before. Her plan would work. It had to. There was no room for self-doubt. Not tonight.

First things first. The lights. She turned to London. "Gold, you're up."

London lined up her sniper rifle, took a breath, and pulled the trigger without hesitation. The left motion sensor light exploded. Shards of glass were still falling when London aimed and fired a second time. Bingo! Two lights. Two shots. Just like London had promised.

"Lights on the northwest and southwest corners are down," she announced, not bothering to keep her voice down. The killer had likely heard the sound of exploding glass. She turned to O'Leary. "On my mark. Three...two...one. Go." They both bolted from the tree line and out into the open. O'Leary went left. She went right.

She'd just reached the entrance on the south side of the cabin when O'Leary's voice sounded in her ear. "Made it to the generator," he said, out of breath. "Disconnecting now."

She climbed the porch steps. The cabin was eerily quiet. She reached the door but decided against using it. Too predictable. There were three windows facing the porch. "I'm going in now." She walked quickly past each one, shattering all of them with the butt of her gun. If the killer was armed, he wouldn't know which window to aim for.

The lights inside the cabin went out. "Power's down," O'Leary reported.

Reid climbed inside the window farthest from the door and stayed low to make herself less of a target. There was an empty armchair facing a small TV in one corner with a twin-size bed in the other. A kitchenette lay on her right with what looked to be a small bathroom off that. Unless the killer was hiding under the bed, the cabin appeared to be empty. As far as she could see, there wasn't anywhere for someone to hide.

Something wasn't right. For a moment, she wondered if Mason

had gotten it wrong. Maybe this wasn't the killer's home. But the paper trail that Mason had found online pointed here. If the killer wasn't here, but his SUV was still parked outside, then where the hell was he?

He was in his lair. With his victims. His workspace had to be hidden underground, like they'd hypothesized back at Mason's bunker. "He's not here," she said, standing.

"Where the hell did he go?" Boyle asked angrily.

"Did he climb out a window?" Garcia asked.

"He couldn't have. I've been monitoring the cabin since this morning." Mason must have kicked or thrown something because there was a loud crash on the other end of the line. "He has to be inside."

"Gold, where are you?" O'Leary's panicked voice came over the headset. "Gold, what's your twenty?"

Reid held her breath and waited for London to respond.

CHAPTER TWENTY-EIGHT

"What's your twenty, Gold?" O'Leary repeated shakily. "I'm returning to our last point of contact," he panted.

Reid felt certain he was sprinting toward the tree line. Her heart picked up speed as she exited the cabin to follow suit. It felt like ice water was running through her veins. *Not again. This can't be happening again.* "London," she barked, "where the hell are you?" She shouldn't have let London out of her sight. What the hell had she been thinking?

"Gold's gear…It's all here…" O'Leary was out of breath. "No sign of Gold. There's an empty syringe on the ground."

"Shit," came Boyle's response. "Everyone, fan out. His vehicle is still parked. He can't have gotten far with Gold."

Reid arrived at the tree line and met O'Leary's haunted gaze. He was holding Gold's headset in one hand and her NVGs in the other. "I'm sorry," he said. "I should've come back for her. I shouldn't have left her alone."

"You did exactly what I asked you to do." She set a hand on his shoulder. "But we need to find her. Now." She studied the ground. London's watch and phone had been left behind, obviously intentionally so. An empty syringe had been carelessly discarded about three feet away. There was no evidence of a scuffle, suggesting that the killer had probably injected London with the paralytic before she even knew he was there. At Reid's direction, London had been monitoring O'Leary's progress with the generator, waiting for him to finish so she could join him. How could Reid have been so shortsighted? Why in the world had she believed it was okay to leave London alone and unprotected, even for one second?

Because you didn't want to treat her like a victim.

Reid spun around to find the spirit of her deceased captain. Cap was standing beside her with a look of concern, his hands in the pockets of his khaki trousers. *You were giving her the respect of treating her like the capable woman she is. Don't waste time doubting yourself, kid. Trust your instincts. While you're at it, trust hers, too.* And then, like smoke, he was gone.

Cap popped in and out of her days at his leisure. Never before had he made an appearance to tell her what to do and then vanish without waiting for a response. The moment was significant.

Trust your instincts, he'd said. *While you're at it, trust hers, too.*

She looked down at where Cap had been standing. Wagon wheel tracks. "Do you see those?" she asked, pointing.

O'Leary knelt in the dirt. "Sure do. That's how he moved her." He set his hand over the scattered pine needles and peered up. "Put her in a wagon."

Thanks, Cap. "Teams two and three, stop moving. Do *not* disturb the ground."

"Copy that," Boyle replied.

"Copy," Marino echoed.

"He has an underground shelter somewhere on this property. Take out your flashlights, and start searching the ground for any signs of disturbed earth." She checked her watch. No more than a few minutes had passed since London was abducted. This guy worked fast.

"I'm doing some calculations," Mason's voice sounded in her ear. "Based on the last verbal exchange you had with London, the killer had exactly three minutes and twenty-nine seconds to abduct her. I'm subtracting a conservative thirty seconds for injecting her with a syringe and placing her body inside a wagon, which leaves us with a window of two minutes and fifty-nine seconds in which to flee. The average walking pace for a healthy adult is two-point-five to four miles per hour. He'll hurry to evade capture, so I'm putting him at three miles per hour because he's also pulling a wagon with an adult woman inside who weighs approximately a buck twenty. At three miles per hour, he can cover a distance of approximately two hundred and sixty-four yards in three minutes. That's seven hundred and ninety-two feet, which is roughly equivalent to the length of two football fields, with seventy-two feet remaining."

"Two football fields," Boyle said. "Christ. That's a lot of ground to cover with a fine-tooth comb."

"I'm sending detailed schematics of the areas you should search, based on the surrounding terrain." Mason was typing furiously as he talked. "My map is color-coded—red for hot and blue for cold. Red areas are more hospitable to an underground shelter. It's possible that the shelter is located in the blue, but it's far less likely."

No one made a peep as they awaited direction.

"There," Mason said. "Sent."

Reid's watch vibrated. She pulled out her phone and clicked on his text. If she wasn't in the middle of a crisis, she might've been impressed by Mason's attention to detail.

O'Leary was already tracking the trail that the wagon's wheels had left in the dirt. She jogged to catch up and walked alongside him, careful not to step on the disturbed earth. They followed the trail for a hundred yards or more before they lost it.

"It has to be around here somewhere," O'Leary said, clearly distressed. "It's not like he up and vanished."

But maybe that's exactly what he did. What if the entrance to the killer's underground shelter was, quite literally, at their feet? "Look for a trapdoor, an entrance to a bunker," she said excitedly, feeling her heart race at the possibility of imminent rescue.

They dropped to their hands and knees in the dirt and started feeling their way along the ground.

"Found something?" Boyle asked. "We can make our way to you—"

"Hold your positions." Chances were probably slim that the killer was still wheeling London around in a wagon. They had a better chance of spotting him if they were fanned out along the property rather than congregating in one spot.

Reid was still running her hands through the dirt when she suddenly *knew*. She was close to London. Very close. Goose bumps broke out all over her body.

Cap's words returned to her. *Trust your instincts, kid.*

"Teams two and three, get your asses here. Stat."

O'Leary looked over at her. "You found it?"

She was about to admit that she hadn't when her hand brushed against something metal. "Got it." She yanked upward and watched as the earth expelled a moss-covered trapdoor.

"Wait for backup, Sylver." Boyle's accelerated breathing told her that he was on his way and moving fast. "Do *not* go down there alone. I repeat, do not—"

"I'm going in," she said, cutting him off. "O'Leary, wait here until—"

"No." O'Leary stood and stepped toward her. "Not a chance in hell I'm letting you go in alone."

Reid was momentarily conflicted. She had no idea what she'd be walking into down below. She was willing to put her own life on the line, but she refused to risk anyone else's. Defying an order was out of character for O'Leary. He and London shared a bond that he didn't share with anyone else on their team. She couldn't—shouldn't—begrudge him this chance to save London. "I'll take point," she said, already stepping into the stairwell, her gun drawn. "You got my six?"

"Bet your ass I do," came his whispered reply over the headset.

There was another door at the bottom of the stairwell. She tried the doorknob—unlocked. This fallout shelter had likely been built in the fifties. Securing the entrance obviously wasn't a concern back then. Since the killer was confident that no one would ever find this place, he hadn't bothered to update the entrance with reliable security. Or he was setting her up to open the door and get her head blown off. She wasn't willing to take the time to ensure her own safety. London's life was on the line. Every second counted right now. "Door's unlocked at the bottom of the stairwell," she announced to the group. "I'm going in. Stand back."

Rather than heeding her warning, O'Leary closed in behind her and held out his weapon. "You go right. I'll go left."

"Stay low," she whispered. She pulled the door open, and they both stepped inside. A cold waft of air with a faint stench of decay washed over her. There was a short hallway with four closed doors on the right and a large open room on the left. No sign of the killer. A hairline crack of light along the bottom of the last door suggested that the killer was inside.

Was he truly unaware that they'd found his underground shelter? No locks. No video cameras. No motion sensor lights down here that she could see. He clearly never expected a security breach.

She and O'Leary moved stealthily through the small space, careful not to disturb anything. The three female victims that London had mentioned flashed through her mind. She put two and two together. Four doors. Four victims. One of them was London.

There was no discernible light source in any of the first three rooms, and each door was closed. Assuming he hadn't murdered any of his victims in the last twenty-four hours, the women were probably still attached to IVs to keep them sedated.

Her gaze returned to the strip of light under the last door. That had to be London's room. She was the newest addition to his collection.

The killer had made London an offer in the airport bathroom—her life for the life of the three women he was holding captive. He'd shown her that he could control their medication through an app on his phone. Reid couldn't let the killer use that as a bargaining chip this time.

She whispered into her headset. "Last room on the right—I think he's in there with Gold. I'm betting the three female vics are in the first three rooms. We need to take out their IVs before he knows we're here."

"Teams two and three are here," Boyle whispered back. "Approaching the stairwell now."

Reid watched as Boyle, Garcia, Marino, and Boggs rounded the corner, weapons drawn. They stood nearby, awaiting her instruction.

"Marino, Boggs, Garcia—remove IVs from the vics in the first three rooms. No lights," she reminded them. "Boyle, O'Leary, and I will cover your six." She thought it was unlikely that the killer would be armed with a gun—syringes seemed more his style—but she wasn't going to take any risks. "On my count. Three…two…one. Go."

They all moved together like choreographed dancers. Boggs and Marino stepped to the first room. Garcia and Boyle went to the second. She and O'Leary took the third. If there was ever a time when she hoped none of them were squeamish, now would be it. Blood from a dead vic was one thing. Blood from a live one was another. She prayed her guys would hold up.

She heard O'Leary's whispered instructions to his comrades: "Once you remove the IV, apply pressure for thirty seconds to stanch the flow of blood."

They were all silent as they waited. Reid's heart raced as she thought of London in the next room. Thirty seconds felt like an eternity. But it gave her thirty seconds to plan her attack. "Status?"

"Vic one is alive but sedated. IVs out," Boggs reported.

"Same with vic two," Garcia said.

"Vic three is stable." O'Leary gave her a thumbs-up and joined her at the door's threshold.

They closed the doors to the rooms and reconvened. Everyone looked on edge.

"Plan?" Boyle asked impatiently.

"I'm storming the room," she said firmly. "Alone."

Boyle scowled. "Like hell you are. Two of us go in."

She shook her head, adamant. "He'll feel threatened by a man. Needs to be me." Reid trusted her team. All of them. Equally. There was no one she'd rather have by her side in a life-or-death situation. But London's life was already hanging in the balance. She refused to do anything that might push the killer into a final act of retaliation. She removed her headset and NVGs and handed them to Boyle. "Stay close," she whispered. "You'll know if I need you."

Marino and Boggs hugged the wall to the left of the door as Boyle, Garcia, and O'Leary hugged the right.

Reid set her hand over the doorknob and held her gun in front of her as she pushed the last door open with the toe of her sneaker. The look of surprise on the killer's face confirmed her suspicion that he wasn't expecting them to find him. He set a finger over a button on the IV monitor. "She'll be dead before you can pull the trigger."

Her gaze darted to the metal autopsy table in the center of the room. London was dressed in the same old-fashioned nightgown that the killer had sent to their hotel. London's eyes were taped shut, but she was still breathing. No visible wounds.

"Put your gun on the floor, and kick it over to me."

Reid lowered her weapon, set it on the floor, and kicked it out into the hallway. There was no way she'd take part in arming a dangerous killer. Having a shootout in a small room made entirely of concrete wouldn't end well for anyone.

"Are you trying to piss me off?" he asked.

"I'm trying to save your life," she lied.

He narrowed his eyes.

"This room is made of concrete. Every bullet you fire will ricochet." She nodded at the IV monitor. "We'll all be dead before you can press that button."

"Then maybe I should just press the button." He withdrew his phone from his pocket, tapped the screen with his free hand, and held it up with a sneer. Live video of the women in the adjacent rooms appeared on the screen. "I have three others. Go rescue *them*. Give me some time with this one."

Over my dead body. Reid kept her tone in check. "You're the one in control." She needed him to think he had all the power.

He studied her. "Where's the rest of your team?"

"Still looking for you." She glanced at the ceiling. "Aboveground."

"I don't believe you."

"You think I'd be in here alone if they were with me? We would've stormed this room together. There's safety in numbers. That's how cops work when it comes to apprehending the bad guy."

"You think *I'm* the bad guy?" he asked, clearly offended. "You've got it all wrong. I'm obviously the good guy here. These women"—he gestured to London—"any one of them would be lucky to have me. I'm giving them the chance of a lifetime, but they've all refused to take it."

She'd struck a chord. "But they haven't been able to love you through the pain."

"Not a single one," he said, shaking his head. "Love and pain are so closely interwoven. It's like splitting hairs to differentiate between the two. Only the most evolved woman would be able to comprehend that. I just haven't found her yet." He gazed down at London and hungrily licked his lips. "Something tells me she could be the one."

Every instinct in Reid's body insisted that she needed to keep him engaged and focused on her. *Love and pain.* Two things she understood all too well. There was a time when she'd loved her grandmother, the same woman who'd brutally abused her. But it was eons ago—so long ago that she struggled to recall having any warm feelings toward the woman.

Once again, Reid was about to share more than she cared to, which was ironic because this was exactly what happened with the last serial killer she'd cornered. Her team had heard more about her childhood than she'd ever imagined sharing with anyone. And she was about to do it all over again.

CHAPTER TWENTY-NINE

R eid met the killer's shrewd gaze. "You chose the wrong member of our team. You should've picked me."

He stole another glance at London before shifting his focus to her. "Why?" he asked suspiciously.

"Because I've already loved someone who hurt me. My grandmother. She beat me, burned me, withheld food and water, locked me in a dog crate in the basement—"

"You're trying to empathize with me in an attempt to build a bridge of trust between us. Nice try, Detective. But I'm a psychiatrist. I know all the tricks."

O'Leary had hit the nail on the head. He'd guessed the killer's profession. She could almost feel O'Leary beaming with pride on the other side of the wall. "That's why I'm choosing to share my own story." She lifted her shirt to show him the extensive scarring on her stomach where her skin resembled melted candle wax. There was no mistaking the root cause of her disfigurement. "She used cigarettes, lighters, hot glue guns, blowtorches—pretty much whatever was handy. Prolonged torture and abuse were kind of her thing."

He studied her, his gaze cold, calculating.

"For a long time, I was afraid of my grandmother. Afraid of the abuse, afraid of the pain. Until I wasn't. At some point—I don't know when—I embraced the pain and even started to crave it because I realized it was her way of loving me. And I loved her. I loved her every step of the way. She was my grandmother." The words felt disgusting in her mouth, but she tried not to think of the lies she was telling. She was simply saying what a killer needed to hear. She'd say anything—*do* anything—to save London. "So I get it. I really do. But you picked the wrong woman." She threw a glance at London. "You should've picked me. I'm the woman you've been looking for. I'm the one who can love you through the pain—probably the *only* one," she lied.

"Are you proposing a trade?"

"I am," she said with a decisive nod. "Truth is, until you came along, no one has ever truly understood me. I'm guessing no one's ever understood you, either. Now we understand each other. How can we fight that? You and I were meant to be in this moment together. We're made for each other. That's all that matters." His body language had relaxed some. He was taking the bait. Time to make her move. All she had to do was convince him to remove London's IV.

"Reverse the effects of the drugs in her body," she went on. "If you wake her up, she can put the IV in my arm. As soon as I'm under your control, you'll let her go. But I'll need proof that she's alive, free, and safe before I agree to love you. If you pull a fast one or refuse to provide proof, the deal's off. It's me for her. You can do whatever you want to me. And I promise to love you, through all of it."

There was a long moment of silence as he studied her. "Answer one question," he said finally, moving his thumb closer to the button on the IV monitor. "What was the reason your grandmother gave for hurting you?"

"You first," she said, aware that playing hard to get would be irresistible to him. "Who hurt you?"

"My mother," he said, all but bursting at the seams to share his story. Every serial killer she'd ever heard of had extreme narcissistic tendencies. Giving them the stage to talk about themselves was usually met with enthusiasm. "She was fourteen when she had me. Young. Smart. Beautiful. Determined. She was fiery and passionate to the core," he said wistfully. "She loved me. Fiercely. *And* she felt resentful of being saddled with me. She never held anything back. I was all too aware of what she was feeling in any given moment because she wasn't afraid to show me. There's beauty in that kind of unabashed honesty."

"And the nightgown?" Reid knew she was testing the boundaries of their newfound rapport, but she couldn't help it. She needed to know how the lacy Victorian-style nightgown fit into the puzzle.

"The nightgown was a gift to my mother from her father. My mother raised me in my grandfather's house. He loved her the same way she loved me. You see, that's how I was made." A phantom smile touched his lips but never reached his eyes. "I was literally created out of love and pain."

The full picture of the killer's life swam into focus. Not only was he the product of incest, but the abuse he'd endured at the hands of his own mother was likely reinforced by his grandfather. God only knew how many generations of innocent children had been poisoned in that family.

"Your turn," he said with a sneer. "Why did your grandmother hurt you?"

Reid didn't hesitate. Something told her he would know if she deviated from the truth. She'd already pushed her luck with stretching it. There was one thing she'd learned from interrogating suspects over the years—the most convincing lies were always peppered with truth. "She thought I was possessed by the devil."

"And?" He arched one eyebrow. "Were you?"

"I can talk to the dead, so I guess that's up for debate."

"Interesting," he said, nodding as he gave her a once-over. "Prove it."

Reid breathed deeply. She imagined the door inside her mind and willed someone from the killer's life to pay him a visit. What came through, instead, surprised her—a paper airplane. Was this a message from London? Her arms and legs broke out in goose bumps as she unfolded it and read, *He can't kill me by pushing the button. He hasn't put the IV in my arm yet.*

Reid looked up. The autopsy table was in the middle of the room in a horizontal position. She didn't have a clear view of the right side of London's body. She'd just assumed the IV was in London's right arm. Was the killer bluffing?

She had a moment of indecision. What if she had simply imagined the paper airplane? The stakes were high. If she was wrong about this, it could cost London her life.

At that moment, Cap appeared beside her. He gazed across the room at the killer. *No one's coming to visit him*, he said sadly. *It's above my pay grade. Damien's beyond our help.* Cap turned to her. *As for you, you were always thickheaded. What did I just tell you, kid?*

She met Cap's all-knowing gaze. *You told me to trust my instincts.*

Then trust your damn instincts, he said, and he vanished on the heels of a frustrated sigh.

The killer regarded her curiously. "Have you been able to conjure up the spirit of my mother?"

Damien. That was the name of the killer standing before her—the name of the man who'd brutalized eighteen women without mercy or regret. Once again, she decided to give him the truth. "No one's allowed to visit you, Damien. You're beyond anyone's help. Fortunately, your journey ends here. Take him out," she hollered over her shoulder. "Now."

She stepped aside as her team filed in and riddled him with bullets before he had a chance to respond.

❖

London stepped out of the shower, grabbed her towel from the heated rack, and wrapped it around her body. She cleared the fog from the bathroom mirror and caught sight of the small bruise on her neck where the killer had injected her with a paralytic drug. She was lucky to be alive and forever grateful to her team for their timely rescue.

She, Reid, and the rest of their team had returned to Boston several nights ago. They'd all gone back to their jobs at the precinct like nothing had happened. They'd closed the case for the FBI and rescued three women in the process—four, if London counted herself. With a dangerous serial killer out of the way, London knew they were all sleeping better at night.

Boyle, O'Leary, Garcia, and Marino had passed their twenty-year mark with the department. She was the only one in their group who still had a way to go before retirement was even an option. Even so, she couldn't stop thinking about Mason's proposal. Reid had shared Mason's desire to be part of their team—a redefined team that would work on the outskirts of the law. Starting something on the side and working cases in an unofficial capacity was intriguing. They had all agreed to meet up and discuss the possibility after the holidays.

London rubbed the Bath & Body Works lotion into her skin. This was Reid's favorite scent on her—warm vanilla sugar. She didn't bother with pajamas. She and Reid slept naked every night, and Reid was already in bed. They hadn't been intimate since their return. London had needed a few nights to regroup. Ever so patient, Reid had given her exactly what she needed to feel safe again—time, gentle words, and unconditional love. The spooning didn't hurt, either. Reid was a master at spooning her each night, never letting go until she was sure London had drifted off into a deep slumber.

She stepped out of the bathroom and made her way over to Reid, her towel the only barrier between them. She glanced down at Reid's phone as she was scrolling through a long list of houses for sale. "Thinking of buying?" she asked, surprised.

"Selling, actually." Reid set her phone on the bed and turned to face her. "I was thinking of putting my house on the market."

London was rendered momentarily speechless. One year ago, when they'd first met, Reid had told her that she planned to live out the rest of her life here. "But you *love* this house. You've put your blood, sweat, and tears into this house to make it exactly the way you want it. Why would you ever want to sell it?"

Reid smiled sadly. "Because I've put my blood, sweat, and tears into this house to make it exactly the way *I* want it."

She shook her head, confused. "I don't understand."

"We spend every night in this house." Reid reached for her hand. "You still have your houseboat, but your clothes are here."

London nodded. Reid had graciously given her half of the main bedroom closet. She'd moved her entire wardrobe in, bit by bit, over the last twelve months. She hardly spent any time on the houseboat anymore. After Mug's surgery, it was just too hard for him to get around in the confined space. Besides, London got the feeling that he was more comfortable recovering in the house he grew up in.

"I was thinking," Reid went on, "that maybe I can sell this place, and we could look for a house together. A house that feels like both of us, not just me."

She'd been feeling like she was in limbo with the houseboat but was never sure what to do with it. Even though they worked together and spent their weekends together, she never grew tired of being with Reid and couldn't imagine spending a night without her. "You think I should sell the houseboat?" she asked, still processing Reid's proposition.

"Not if you don't want to. I just...I thought...maybe we could..." Reid sighed and shook her head. "It was dumb. Forget everything I just said."

Reid's sudden lack of self-confidence made London love her more fiercely. "You thought you could sell this house, I could sell the houseboat, and we could buy a home together? Then we could live together, officially. Under one roof. All of us," she said, motioning to Mug on his dog bed in the corner.

"Something like that." Reid ran a hand over her face and sighed. "But, shit, London. We don't have to do any of it, not if you don't want to."

"I want to." She leaned in and brushed her lips against Reid's.

"Didn't mean to put you on the spot. You don't have to sell your houseboat."

"I want to," she repeated. London had no reservations whatsoever. Her place was with Reid. It would be nice to buy a house and furnish it together. For the first time in their relationship, she imagined what it might be like to start a family with Reid. They hadn't even talked about it yet, but she had a feeling Reid would be open to the idea. Something to consider for the future, perhaps.

She opened the nightstand drawer, withdrew the dildo, and held it up with a mischievous grin.

Reid laughed. "Feels like you're hoping to collect on my promise to give you a turn," she said, more casually than London had expected.

"I am," she admitted. She couldn't wait to make Reid hers. "But first things first. We need to get you wet."

Reid raised an eyebrow and pierced her with a sexy, green-eyed gaze. "That shouldn't be too hard."

London unfastened her towel, let it drop to the floor, and scooted back onto the bed, dildo in hand. "Will you dim the lights?"

She watched as Reid climbed out of bed, naked. Reid had the most enticing body of anyone she'd ever dated. Toned. Athletic. Curvy in all the places that mattered. Reid wasn't even aware of how stunning she was, which somehow accentuated her beauty. London felt herself grow wet and achy at the thought of penetrating Reid. She'd never felt this type of fiery passion for anyone else. Just Reid. Only Reid. Always.

She'd also never done for anyone else what she was about to do for Reid. "There's only one rule," she said as soon as Reid returned. "Look, but don't touch." London lay across the bed and spread her legs.

Reid took a seat on the bed beside her. "I get to watch?" she asked with a look of astonishment.

"Look, but don't touch," she repeated. London dipped her fingers inside to gather her own wetness. As she massaged her clit with one hand, she reached for the dildo with the other. She heard the telltale sounds of her own wetness as she slid the dildo in and out, riding waves of pleasure so intense that her moans of ecstasy surprised even her. She opened her eyes to gaze at Reid's face as she leaped off the cliff in an orgasmic free fall.

Reid pressed her body against London's and kissed her, long and hard. She was begging for release.

This was it. This was the moment London had been waiting for. Would Reid let her in? Would Reid enjoy being penetrated as much as she had?

She reached between Reid's legs. She was wet. Wet and ready.

London slipped into the harness. She attached the dildo and started to climb over the top of Reid's body.

Reid set a firm hand against her chest to stop her. "I'll let you do this, but we do it my way," she said, her tone commanding. She pushed London onto her back and straddled her, effortlessly guiding the dildo in with one hand.

Wordless groans escaped Reid's lips as she rode London, slowly and deliberately at first. It didn't take long for Reid to lose herself as she picked up the pace with enthusiasm. The sounds of Reid's wetness consumed her. London was thankful they'd left the lights on. She watched the dildo as Reid ground against it, her needs carnal, uncensored. In and out. In and out. Sweat dripped from Reid's body. Her full, round breasts dipped teasingly close to London's mouth as they bounced and swayed in rhythm with her grinding hips.

The harness was striking London's clit in just the right way as Reid devoured every inch of the dildo. She felt a second orgasm building within her as Reid approached the edge. They locked gazes and climaxed in unison, sweating, panting, breathless.

EPILOGUE

Reid was up at bat. It was the championship game, and the Toe Tags were up by three. There was no way in hell Packin' Heat was walking off the field without a trophy. Not again.

It was the last inning. Two outs. Two strikes. Bases loaded. London was pitching, and she was damn good. Reid regretted the day she'd unloaded London on Frank the medical examiner, who also served as the Toe Tags' team captain. The Toe Tags had been coming in last place for years until London started pitching for them. She should've scooped London up when she had the chance.

The next pitch was make or break. London wound up and let it go. Reid swung hard and felt the satisfying *thwack* of the ball against the bat as it reverberated up her arm. She watched the ball climb high and far—too far for the outfield to do anything but watch as it sailed clear past the fence. A home run. Cheers and whistles from her teammates accompanied her all the way to home plate. They'd won the game by the skin of their teeth. One measly point. But a win was a win. She'd take it.

Boyle was sitting on the bleachers with Mug at his side. Mug was still recovering from surgery, but he was finally able to walk without assistance. She nodded to Boyle as he handed the tennis ball to Mug.

She glanced over her shoulder. London was still on the pitcher's mound, talking with her team captain, as planned. Reid and Fred, the ME, went way back. He was more than happy to help out with the surprise. She called to Mug and watched as he limped to her side. They walked together slowly to join London at the pitcher's mound.

"Good game," London said sincerely, ever the epitome of good sportsmanship as she reached out to shake hands.

Instead of reaching back, Reid dropped down on one knee. Mug sat beside her and spit the tennis ball into her outstretched palm, just like they'd practiced. The engagement ring was wedged into a small hole that she'd carved out the night before. Thank God Mug hadn't swallowed it.

She held the tennis ball aloft. "London Gold, will you marry me?"

"Of course," London answered, her cheeks already wet with tears.

Reid smiled and stood and tried hard not to cry in front of her teammates. She pulled the ring from the tennis ball, wiped Mug's drool on the sleeve of her jersey, and slid it over London's finger.

About the Author

Michelle Larkin is an award-winning author of lesbian romantic thrillers, a long-distance runner with no sense of direction, and a nunchuck-wielding sidekick to a pair of superhero sons.

Books Available From Bold Strokes Books

Curse of the Gorgon by Tanai Walker. Cass will do anything to ensure Elle's safety, but is she willing to embrace the curse of the Gorgon? (978-1-63679-395-5)

Dance with Me by Georgia Beers. Scottie Templeton mixes it up on and off the dance floor with sexy salsa instructor Marisa Reyes. But can Scottie get past Marisa's connection to her ex? (978-1-63679-359-7)

Gin and Bear It by Joy Argento. Opposites really can attract, and as Kelly and Logan work together to create a loving home for rescue cat Bear, they just might find one for themselves as well. (978-1-63679-351-1)

Harvest Dreams by Jacqueline Fein-Zachary. Planting the vineyard of their dreams, Kate Bauer and Sydney Barrett must resist their attraction while battling nature and their families, who oppose both the venture and their relationship. (978-1-63679-380-1)

The No Kiss Contract by Nan Campbell. Workaholic Davy believes she can get the top spot at her firm if the senior partners think she's settling down and about to start a family, but she needs the delightful yet dubious Anna to help by pretending to be her fiancée. (978-1-63679-372-6)

Outside the Lines by Melissa Sky. If you had the chance to live forever, would you take it? Amara Rodriguez did, and it sets her on a journey to find her missing mother and unravel the mystery of her own heart. (978-1-63679-403-7)

The Value of Sylver and Gold by Michelle Larkin. When word gets out that former Boston homicide detective Reid Sylver can talk to the dead, the FBI solicits her help on a serial murder case, prompting Reid to assemble forces once again with Detective London Gold. (978-1-63679-093-0)

When It Feels Right by Tagan Shepard. Freshly out of the closet Marlene hasn't been lucky in love, but when it comes to her quirky new roommate Abby, everything just feels right. (978-1-63679-367-2)

Lucky in Lace by Melissa Brayden. Straitlaced stationery store owner Juliette Jennings's predictable life unravels when a sexy lingerie shop and its alluring owner move in next door. (978-1-63679-434-1)

Made for Her by Carsen Taite. Neal Walsh is a newly made member of the Mancuso crime family, but will her undeniable attraction to Anastasia Petrov, the wife of her boss's sworn enemy, be the ultimate test of her loyalty? (978-1-63679-265-1)

Off the Menu by Alaina Erdell. Reality TV sensation Restaurant Redo and its gorgeous host Erin Rasmussen will arrive to film in chef Taylor Mobley's kitchen. As the cameras roll, will they make the jump from enemies to lovers? (978-1-63679-295-8)

Pack of Her Own by Elena Abbott. When things heat up in a small town, steamy secrets are revealed between Alpha werewolf Wren Carne and her human mate, Natalie Donovan. (978-1-63679-370-2)

Return to McCall by Patricia Evans. Lily isn't looking for romance—not until she meets Alex, the gorgeous Cuban dance instructor at La Haven, a newly opened lesbian retreat. (978-1-63679-386-3)

So It Went Like This by C. Spencer. A candid and deeply personal exploration of fate, chosen family, and the vulnerability intrinsic in life's uncertainties. (978-1-63555-971-2)

Stolen Kiss by Spencer Greene. Anna and Louise share a stolen kiss, only to discover that Louise is dating Anna's brother. Surely, one kiss can't change everything…Can it? (978-1-63679-364-1)

The Fall Line by Kelly Wacker. When Jordan Burroughs arrives in the Deep South to paint a local endangered aquatic flower, she doesn't expect to become friends with a mischievous gin-drinking ghost who complicates her budding romance and leads her to an awful discovery and danger. (978-1-63679-205-7)

To Meet Again by Kadyan. When the stark reality of WW II separates cabaret singer Evelyn and Australian doctor Joan in Singapore, they must overcome all odds to find one another again. (978-1-63679-398-6)